THE BREAKING POINT

DIGNITY

D1519629

This is a work of fiction. Names, characters, places, and incidents are products of the author's imagination or are used fictitiously and are not to be construed as real. Any resemblance to actual events, locales, organizations, or persons, living or dead, is entirely coincidental.

DIGNITY Copyright © 2017 by Jennifer M. Voorhees. All rights reserved. Printed in the United States of America. No part of this book may be used or reproduced in any manner whatsoever without written permission except in the case of brief quotations embodied in critical articles and reviews. For copyright information address: Jay Crownover LLC 1670 E. Cheyenne Mnt. Blvd. Box# 152, Colorado Springs, Colorado 80906.
Congress Cataloging—in—Publication Data has been applied for.

ISBN-13:978-1977870445
ISBN-10:1977870449

These are the talented folks who helped bring my book to life:

Cover design by: Hang Le / www.byhangle.com
Copyrights for cover images: Stockphoto Source: Getty Images Credit: quavondo Creative #: 492630396 "Handsome Guy with Tattoos Wearing Tank Top" www.gettyimages.ca/detail/photo/handsome-guy-with-tattoos-wearing-tank-top-royalty-free-image/492630396
Source: Shutterstock Credit: MILA Zed Creative #: 485161804
"Beautiful sexy asian woman model posing in desert"
www.gettyimages.ca/detail/photo/handsome-guy-with-tattoos-wearing-tank-top-royalty-free-image/492630396

Interior Design & Formatting by: Christine Borgford, Type A Formatting
www.typeAformatting.com

Editing by: Elaine York, Allusion Graphics, LLC/Publishing & Book Formatting
www.allusiongraphics.com

Proofreading & Copyediting by: Beth Salminen. / basalminen@gmail.com

BY JAY CROWNOVER

Getaway Series
Shelter (coming this December)
Retreat

The Saints of Denver Series
Salvaged
Riveted
Charged
Built
Leveled (novella)

The Breaking Point Series
Dignity
Avenged (crossover novella)
Honor

The Welcome to the Point Series
Better When He's Brave
Better When He's Bold
Better When He's Bad

The Marked Men Series
Asa
Rowdy
Nash
Rome
Jet
Rule

Dedicated to those of us who think a big brain is just as sexy as a big, thick, fat . . . wallet. :D

Also, dedicated to my fellow four-eyes out there. Glasses are hot. I know I look damn cute in mine, and I'm sure you look adorable in yours. Here's to finding the right person to fog them up. ♥

INTRODUCTION

I ALWAYS SAY YOU can learn a lot about what's going on in the world and pop culture at the time I'm writing each specific book. Whatever I'm currently focused on or obsessing over always seems to find its way between the pages.

I wrote *Dignity* over February, March, and April of this year . . . so, right after the election. Everything felt like it was in turmoil and unsettled. There was a lot of anger and uncertainty everywhere I turned. It was impossible to escape, no matter what side of the political fence you fall.

When it was time to head back to the Point for Stark's book, a lot of that unrest came with me. The idea that so many people were questioning the government, the choices being made, the shift in our world paradigm, again, applies to both sides. There was no shaking the idea that maybe, just maybe, the people we trust to have our best interests in mind, the ones we put in charge of speaking for us, might not be representing us in the way we want them to. In the Point, the bad guys have always done good things when it suited them, so it only made sense that the good guys do bad when it benefits them. I wanted the good guys to be the worst bad guys the Point has ever seen. It makes sense in its own twisted way.

This is my disclaimer. I DO NOT think all politicians are corrupt.

I DO NOT think that all—or even very many—police officers are dirty. (Though, here in the Springs, we recently had a sheriff who was filthy as hell! He was legit run out of town.) I DO NOT believe, at all, that our military forces and the people in charge of them have any other agenda than keeping our country safe! I appreciate their service. This is fiction . . . and I mean FICTION! This isn't even a real place I'm writing about. I take liberties and make things as bad as they can be . . . so I can turn around and make them better. It's supposed to be an escape, a story that is larger than life, nothing more, nothing less! Also, digital hitmen are a real thing and a death certificate really can screw your entire life up. It's a new form of identity theft that I found super interesting when I was researching hackers and what happens down in the deepest, darkest parts of the interwebs.

During this time, I also ended up on a superhero kick. I mean, don't we all want someone larger than life who has perfect timing and can swoop in and save the day? That means, unbeknownst to me, I somehow turned Snowden Stark into a cross between Elliot from *Mr. Robot* and Luke Cage . . . lol. An incredibly broken genius . . . someone who seems bulletproof and stronger than anyone can imagine. He comes with a tragic history, befitting of the Point and the men he calls his friends. He's the quiet guy, the thinker, and fitting him into this savage, cruel world was tricky. There had to be a reason he fit in with the likes of Nassir and Booker, I just wasn't sure what it was, until he decided to tell his story. It's a little outlandish, exaggerated, and unbelievable . . . but hey . . . all superheroes start off that way. Even the superheroes who have a hard time being heroic: Jessica Jones, Tony Stark, Wolverine, and Deadpool. I like the idea that they have something that makes them special, something that sets them apart, but it is ultimately up to them to choose to use those powers for good or evil and to decide if what makes them special is a blessing or a curse. My Stark was absolutely influenced by Iron Man and I have zero regrets about it.

A funny little side note: Huck from *Scandal* is apparently also an accurate character inspiration. I've never seen *Scandal* . . . I don't watch any of the Shondaland-produced shows, but when I was telling Cora Carmack about this crazy plotline and my idea for a tortured computer genius with ties to a shady government agency, she told me I was writing Huck. After watching a few episodes of *Scandal* (she made me when I told her I had no clue what she was talking about), I have to agree that I see the similarities, but it was totally unintentional . . . lol. Still not a fan of the show, but I did love Huck's character. So, if you see some of him in Stark, you aren't wrong. :D

Not gonna lie: writing not just one, but two characters who are way smarter than you is challenging, but at the end of the day, it's always about what we have in common, not what makes us different. These two struggle with their choices and their pasts, just like I do . . . and I would bet, just like you do. And for being smart as hell, it sure takes them a long-ass time to figure their shit out!

Welcome back to the Point, my friends. I sure hope you love Boy Genius. Smart is so sexy!

xoxo

Love and Ink,

Jay

THE BREAKING POINT

DIGNITY

JAY
CROWNOVER
NEW YORK TIMES BESTSELLING AUTHOR

If the world seems cold to you, kindle fires to warm it.

~ Lucy Larcom

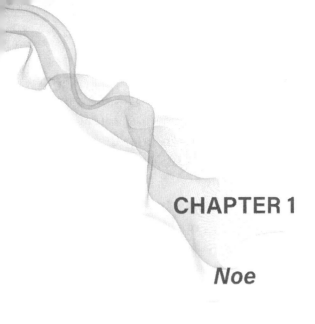

CHAPTER 1

Noe

I WAS GOING TO do something I swore to myself I would never, ever do again in my life . . . ask for help.

I'd learned early in life that the only person I could rely on, the only person who would never let me down or disappoint me, was me. No one else had my best interests or wellbeing in mind. I was the only one who cared if I made it through each day and into the next. I didn't need anyone. I'd been doing all right on my own while surviving some pretty shitty circumstances for a long time. I watched my own back and called all my own shots. That was the way I liked it, the way I needed it to be. But right now, I was scared. Terrified really. I was also smart enough to know that I was in way over my head.

I needed help and there was only one person I felt comfortable enough asking to yank me out of the murky, dangerous mess I'd waded into.

It didn't make sense because we'd only met once. Oddly enough, in that brief encounter, he had called me a thief and a bitch. He wasn't going to be happy to see me. In fact, there was no guarantee that he was going to agree to get me out of the bind that had me so wound up that I couldn't even move, but I had to ask. I needed someone on my side, someone else needed to know what was going on. In this moment, my mind was telling me that someone was him.

I was afraid to show my face. Afraid to come out of hiding. Afraid of every dark corner and every shadow that lurked in the back alleys I called home. I was afraid that I'd finally gone too far, something I never really thought was possible before now. People were looking for me, and while I was notoriously hard to find, they seemed to have eyes everywhere and enough money to pay people to look in the places I normally hid. I was no longer invisible. No longer overlooked and dismissed like most homeless and displaced people were. The streets were never safe, but now, day in and day out, I was actively being hunted. There was a price on my head and everyone in the Point was looking for a payday.

The last time I'd been at this fancy townhouse complex on the outskirts of the Point, I'd been using a lock picking set to jimmy the front door open so I could rob a guy blind. He had come looking for me, and I didn't like it when people I didn't know tried to find me. Especially guys like him. I really didn't like it when people had money, drove nice cars, had obvious free time to blow at the gym, and were as good with computers and tech as me. Everything about him rubbed me the wrong way, and when I heard he was trying to find me, I wanted to make sure he never made that mistake again. I didn't want to be anywhere on his radar even though he was a huge, gigantic blip on mine. He pinged and beeped alerts all over the place long before he dragged me down to the Lock and Key to meet with his enigmatic boss.

I'd never had the opportunity to meet Snowden Stark before he came looking for me, but I knew all about him. Everyone in the digital underground did, and not because he was tied into some shady business dealings with Race Hartman and Nassir Gates, the undisputed golden king and dark knight of the Point. The two of them ruled this broken kingdom and it was no secret that Stark was their tech wizard. He was the one who made magic happen. Even before he sold his soul to the highest bidder, he'd been into some questionable practices behind his keyboard. It was rumored that he was the one who had hacked the state's police database and sent the names, addresses, and mug shots of each and every possible sex offender to all the parents in the Point. Not the registered, supposedly rehabilitated pedophiles, but the ones who had gotten away with their crimes. The ones who hadn't managed to get caught yet.

The watch list was long and terrifying. The list made its ways through schools and was talked about for weeks on the news. People were torn between fury at the invasion of privacy, since the names on the list belonged to people never convicted, and relief that the bad guys had names and faces before they could offend, or offend again. It was always trial by fire in the Point and nobody was really innocent until proven guilty. They were always guilty, and most of the time, they didn't get caught. There was little the police could do without solid proof and witnesses. Stark didn't operate that way. No one seemed too concerned when the people on that list started dropping like flies. Vigilante justice was nothing new in the Point. In fact, it was often the only kind of justice this place saw. Sure, some of the people with their name on Stark's hit list left town and disappeared on their own, but it was common knowledge that most of them were run out of town by Nassir, and those who didn't want to go disappeared another way. A more permanent and bloody way that involved shallow graves dug under the moonlight.

My favorite Stark story floating around was the one where he'd grounded an entire fleet of aircraft when his airline lost his luggage and proved less than helpful when it came to locating it. He jacked their entire system for two days, only relenting when his bags showed up in pristine condition. Of course, no one could ever prove it was him, but Twitter and the dark corner of the web—the figurative watercooler for hackers—were flooded with speculation. Everyone was impressed by him, and a little scared. Even the guys who made the Darknet . . . well . . . dark.

When he was a teenager, he supposedly hacked the un-hackable Department of Defense, just to prove he could. I heard he ended up in a federal prison for a year or so for that little act of defiance, but no one could actually verify it because he'd disappeared and any records that might have proved it ceased to exist. Years later, when he came back to the Point, the rumors about his time away and illegal acts were less outrageous, but no less persistent.

He hacked his college's sexual assault complaint database and released the names of all the attackers who were never brought to justice. Everyone who had been named over the years, but had been excused or had their stories swept under the rug by both the school and law enforcement, was put on blast. Their faces were plastered on digital billboards and scrolled across the bottom of the news ticker bar. Their crimes spelled out in excruciating detail for the entire Point to see. It was another digital hit list, and once again, the eyes of Lady Justice remained blindfolded when the people behind the names started disappearing and turning up in the county morgues.

It was clear Stark didn't like it when justice was overlooked and he didn't mind a challenge. He had contacts on the Darknet, and some were digital versions of the men who ran the Point. Through cyberspace, they sold humans, sex, drugs, guns, murder . . . anything illegal and unsavory. Stark didn't approve of some of the more chilling reasons people trolled the dark recesses of the Internet so he went out of his way to shut them down. Chat rooms dedicated to child pornography and pedophilia were annihilated and sites dedicated to human trafficking were mercilessly shut down. He was a one man wrecking ball and no one tried to stop him.

I was hoping both of those things would work in my favor as I prepared to beg and plead with him to pull my ass out of the proverbial fire.

I knocked on his door this time . . . like a normal person.

I shifted uneasily in my well-worn combat boots and ran my sweaty palms down the front of my freshly washed cargo pants. I made an effort to clean up before coming to see him. I didn't want to show up unwashed and filthy, like I normally was. I needed him to take me seriously, and I figured if he were distracted by my smell and ratty hair, it would be counterintuitive to my endgame. Since I slept on the streets and in shelters most of the time, it paid off to be gross and unapproachable, but Stark didn't live wild like I did. In fact, aside from his dealings with Race and Nassir, he didn't have much to do with the Point. His only connection to this place was his longstanding friendship with Race. They went to high school together before Stark was taken away by men in dark suits with serious expressions. He seemed insulated from the violence and vitriol that came out of the place I called home. From what I knew, he kept his heavily tattooed hands clean of actual blood, just dabbling in digital carnage and warfare. I had no idea if he really knew what it was like out there in the real world, but I needed him to get a clue real quick. I needed him to understand that messing with someone's life online had very real consequences. I still had no idea how my identity had been leaked to the guys looking for me, but they knew exactly who I was, and I knew what they could do with that knowledge. That's why I was scared, standing on his doorstep, shaking, and willing to do whatever it took to guarantee his help.

I was lifting my hand to knock again when the door was suddenly flung open. Of course he knew I was there. When I broke in weeks ago, I'd had to bypass a security system that rivaled the NSA's. He had cameras everywhere. He saw everything and everyone that was trying to get close. It wasn't a simple case of breaking and entering; I'd had to work my way inside the labyrinth and was lucky I made it out in one piece.

I let out a yelp as my momentum pitched me forward, hands landing against rock-hard muscle as I braced myself against his chest. It was easy to forget how big he was. Massive all around. Tall, strong, and covered from his neck down in colorful, bold tattoos. His dark hair was cut short, showing off the multiple silver and diamond studs that dotted his ears and the tiny scar that curved across his temple, which left a startling straight line of white on his scalp. He had what looked like a barcode of some kind inked behind his ear and I wanted to ask him what it meant.

He didn't look like any kind of geek—computer or otherwise. He looked like a brawler, a leg breaker, a leviathan. He looked like a beast, except for those dark, thick-framed glasses that sat over his slate-colored eyes. They were undoubtedly out of place with his fierce expression and intimidating appearance. They didn't belong with the nearly shaved head and the tattoos. His eyes were narrowed at me under lowered brows. His mouth was in a hard, flat line as he grabbed my upper arms and purposely set me away from him. His hands were rough, calloused, and abrasive, but his hold was gentle. He crossed those massive arms over his broad chest once

I had my balance, muscles popping and flexing with the smallest movement. It was annoying that he was so impressive to look at. I already had a semi-crush on him for his magnificent brain and the lure of his rumored sense of honor. I liked that he wanted to right wrongs, that he looked out for those who were constantly overlooked. It wasn't fair that he was ridiculously hot on top of being the smartest guy I had ever encountered, willingly or not. I didn't want to like him, and I really, really didn't want to need him.

"What are you doing here, Noe Lee?" I couldn't stop the little shiver of delight that worked down my spine when he remembered my name and said it right. Not that N-O was all that hard to remember. I liked the way he strung my first and last name together so that it sounded like Noley. When we first met, he thought I was a boy. It was a ruse I often used to keep unwanted attention off myself. He was obviously annoyed that I'd been able to fool him. He was supposed to be too smart to be tricked by a street rat. There was no way he could make that mistake today. My black and red hair hung in a shiny sheet, arrow straight where it brushed my jaw. My bangs were long enough that they touched my eyebrows and also hung pin-straight across my forehead. I even scrounged up some lip gloss for this little charade and put on a v-neck shirt that showed a hint of cleavage. I hated it. I usually went out of my way to make sure no one knew I had boobs. I was way outside of my comfort zone, but I would do what I had to do in order to survive.

"You already took everything that wasn't nailed down the first time you paid me a visit. Don't have anything left for you to steal." His voice was a deep rumble that matched his fearsome appearance. No high-pitched, nerdy whine for Snowden Stark. Again, he was annoyed. This time because I'd managed to breach his supposedly secure fortress. I guessed he wasn't the type to forgive and forget.

I cleared my throat and twisted my hands together in front of me. I hated being intimidated, but he effortlessly towered over me so there was no getting away from it. I was on the short side as it was, so even regular-sized men tended to come across as looming and overbearing. Stark was anything but regular, so I was feeling slightly unsettled and anxious even though he wasn't doing anything.

I figured that even though he was still pissed I'd ripped him off, he wasn't missing any of his gadgets and toys. I knew for a fact that the guy was a tech-junkie. There was no way in hell he hadn't gone out and replaced his stash the second he knew it was gone. He couldn't survive being unplugged. He was all man, but very much dependent on machines. They were almost an extension of who he was. It was obvious in the cold, calculating way he dealt with people. There were no unnecessary or needless pleasantries. There was no warmth and compassion. Stark was not a guy who oozed sympathy or even basic human understanding. He wasn't a guy who had patience or any kind of practiced civility about him. Humans were flawed and defective. Computers weren't. They did what you told them to do and reacted in predictable, expected ways. Computers didn't break into your house and steal all your stuff. Computers didn't irritate you and disrupt your precise and orderly life. Computers didn't expect anything from you. I got the feeling that was exactly why this man surrounded himself with them instead of a bevy of beautiful women and throngs of impressed hangers-on. He could easily be ruler of the intellectually elite, but instead, he lived like a hermit and rubbed elbows with crime lords. It might be off-putting to anyone else, but since I tended to lean toward cold and calculating myself, I appreciated his lack of normal social graces. It meant I didn't have to force myself to play nice with him.

He was all legend and myth. No one knew what the real Snowden Stark was like or what he was about, but I'd gotten a glimpse when he dragged me to meet the Devil. He was furious that I'd disrupted his routine and touched his stuff. He was livid, even, but he never hurt me. He never used force or threats. His anger simply popped and snapped like an electrical current between us. Cold fury. Like being in the middle of a blizzard with no protection and nowhere to hide.

No one and nothing in the Point operated that way.

We all put ourselves first. We all focused on what was best for us and what would ensure that we stayed breathing a few more days before we considered anything or anyone else. It's how you had to think and react if you wanted to keep your head above water in this place.

Not Stark.

He got exactly what he wanted, obtained what his terrifying employer needed, and he did it all without hurting or threatening me in the slightest. He didn't push. He didn't shove. He didn't use the fact he was bigger than me as a threat. My first impression stuck. He was impressive . . . I was impressed . . . and it had nothing to do with his muscles or his harshly hewn face with its unreadable, blue-gray eyes.

I took a breath and told myself to get it over with. The worst he could do was tell me no, and if he did, well, then I would be back to trying to figure it all out on my own, which was nothing new.

"I'm in trouble and I need your help." My voice shook and I loathed the little tremor of sound that betrayed just how scared and desperate I was.

One of his dark brows arched over the top of his Buddy Holly-style glasses. The line of his mouth grew harder and turned down so that he was frowning at me instead of scowling. He uncrossed his beefy arms and lifted one above his head to lean against the door jamb. That was a lot of muscle and tattooed skin stretched out in front of me. I would have appreciated the view if it weren't a clear signal that he was not inviting me into his space anytime soon. I'd worn out my welcome when I stole from him, and as much as I wanted to be irritated by his reluctance to let me in, I couldn't be. I'd been betrayed more than once, which is why I set out to live my life on my own terms, and I never forgave or forgot those who had wronged me. I could hold a grudge like a mother . . . and it appeared Stark was the same way.

"What kind of trouble? Did you get caught stealing from someone bigger and meaner than me?" No concern. No curiosity. He asked like he would ask about the weather or the time.

I unlocked my fingers from their death grip and slid my hands into the front pockets of my cargo pants so he wouldn't notice my fingers digging into my palms. "No, I helped someone disappear."

That was what I did.

If you could find me, if you knew what rocks to turn over and which alleyways to slink through in order to ask for my help, I could turn you into a brand-new person. If you wanted to be older or younger, I could help you out with that. If you wanted to be someone who had a clean criminal history so you could get a job, I could fix that for you. If you were on the run from someone with heavy fists and a nasty temper, I made sure you were impossible to find.

And, if you were a scared teenager knocked up with your stepdaddy's baby because the man was a predator and a pervert, well, then I would do my best to make sure no one knew who or where you were until you decided what to do about your situation. I would make sure you were safe, even when your stepdad was the mayor of the City: the place where both the Point and the Hill were located. It had never been a secret that the man was as immoral and unethical as the shot callers who ran all the illegal activities that happened in the dark under his less-than-watchful eye. As it turned out, no one really knew what kind of monster he was behind the closed doors of his home.

When Julia Grace found me, I wanted to turn her away. I liked money and she had a lot of it, but I knew helping her would come with more risk than I typically like to take on. But there was no way I could send the poor girl back to that man once she told me the things he made her do, the things he did to her, that made my stomach crawl. No one should have to suffer like that and no one should be forced to bring a child into a situation like that. She didn't know if she was keeping the baby or if she was going to carry it to term and give it up for adoption. She was nothing more than a confused little girl trying to work her way through problems that were too big and too life-changing for someone her age to face. I helped her, made her disappear, hid her away where no one would ever think to look . . . and now I was paying the price for it.

Her powerful and paranoid stepfather wanted her back and his dirty secrets buried. He would stop at nothing until he achieved both.

Stark lifted his other eyebrow and raised a finger to push at his glasses as the motion made them slip down the bridge of his nose. "You're good at making valuable things vanish, so I'm unsure why you are standing at my front door."

Shit. There was detachment and ice wrapped around every syllable. I swallowed and looked down at the ground. It was time to appeal to that rumored streak of righteousness I'd heard so much about. "Stark, the Mayor has been molesting his underage stepdaughter. For years. She found me. I don't know how, but she did. She begged me to get her out of the city and as far away from the Hill as she could go. She cried and told me all the things that monster did to her. He knocked her up. She's just a baby, herself. There was so much wrong with all of it, I had to do what I could to make it right." I lifted my head and stabbed my fingernails even deeper into my palms so I wouldn't cry. I refused to show that kind of weakness in front of him. In front of anyone. "He's been looking for me. He has resources and reach that I can't outrun. I'm out of places to hide."

He cocked his head to the side and silently considered me for an annoyingly long moment. When he spoke, his voice still lacked any kind of real emotion or investment. "Why haven't you done for yourself what you do for everyone else? You could be in the wind, gone, and no one would be able to track you down, not even Jonathan Goddard." It was a shock to hear him call the bastard Mayor by his given name. I'd taken to thinking of his title as more of a supervillain name, like the Joker, or the Riddler . . . he was *the Mayor.*

Frustrated, I blew out a breath and tugged on my multi-colored hair. I was used to having it tucked under a beanie or hidden under a ball cap, so the loose strands bugged me. I had to remember how to be a girl half the time. "You're right. I can go. I could have a new identity, a new name, and place to call home in under five minutes. But why should he be allowed to get away with what he did to Julia? Why should he have the opportunity to do that to any other girl who's too young and too scared to fight back? Someone needs to stop him. I need to stop him . . . but I can't do it on my own." I really couldn't. The man had too many people on his payroll, too many dirty cops who wouldn't hesitate to hurt me. I'd spent so many years telling myself I wasn't scared anymore, that I was the one in control. I hated that it was all slipping away, and once again, I felt trapped. It would have been so easy to send an email blast to the media with the accusations, but with Julia in hiding, there was no proof. I wanted to protect her almost as much as I wanted to stop the Mayor in his tracks. "I need you to help me."

He was shaking his dark head before I even finished speaking. The tattoos on the sides of his neck flexed as he clenched his jaw, sending a muscle in his cheek twitching. "I learned a long time ago not to pick fights I can't win."

I snorted and then slapped a hand over my face to muffle the sound. He watched me as I cleared my throat. I couldn't stop an eye roll when I muttered drily, "I'm having a hard time picturing any fight you can't win, Stark." He was too big, too smart, too shrewd, and too controlled not to come out on top time and time again. He didn't strike me as a guy who ever lost at anything.

He shook his head again and pushed off the frame, one hand reaching out to grab the edge of the door like he was ready to close it in my face. "I don't mess with people who have their hands in politics, Noe. It's a bad idea. They have too much to lose and know how to keep their secrets buried deep. They play by a different set of rules and they don't share the playbook. They have an army of very rich, very entitled people at their disposal who have too much to lose when they fail. They leave graves all over the place, and they might be just as good as you are at making people disappear. I was dumped in one of their holes when I was stupider and younger. There was no climbing out of it no matter how hard I tried. I barely made it out with my sanity intact, and I have no intention of ever going back. You might as well pack a bag and hit the road before he really gets desperate to find you."

I knew he had things in his past that built up the enigma of who he was, but I had no idea that they still scared him. He didn't seem like the type of man who was afraid of anything.

"I can't let this go. I'm so sick of guys like Goddard thinking they can do whatever they want with no repercussions. Everyone should be held accountable for the bad things they do."

"When you have money and influence, there's no need for accountability." He sounded like he knew that from first-hand experience. I gasped as he fell back a step and started to close the door.

"Wait!" I shoved my battered boot into the swinging door and slapped a hand on the surface as it inched closer to shutting out my last hope and lingering resolve. "That's it? You're really going to ignore everything I just told you? You're going to throw me to the wolves and let a guy like Goddard get away with doing despicable things?" I couldn't believe it. That's not who he was rumored to be. He was supposed to fight for the little guy. He was supposed to believe in justice and fairness.

He was a lie.

He frowned at me and looked pointedly at my hand on the door and my foot bracing it open. "I don't have a dog in this fight, Noe, and I know you're smart enough to know exactly what you were getting into when you helped that girl ghost out of town. You knew the risk and you took it anyway. You're a smart girl who made a very dumb choice."

Of course I did. I was a fucking human being and not a machine like he apparently was. I had a heart. It was a used one, one that didn't run right half the time, one I had to wind up every single day if I wanted to feel any damn thing, but it was there. Tiny but beating furiously. His seemed to have been replaced by circuit boards and wires somewhere along the way.

I fell back a step and threw my hands up in aggravation. "You're unbelievable, and not in the way I was hoping you were." I was no longer impressed . . . I was devastated.

He nodded in agreement, mouth dipped low in a fierce frown. "It's good not to have expectations. When you do, you're bound to be disappointed. Keep your head down, Noe. Buy a bus ticket and put the Point in your rearview. You can start over somewhere else. You can get off the streets and do something useful with that big, sexy brain of yours."

I wanted to tell him to take his advice and stick it so far up his ass he choked on it. I came here for help, not for a lecture on all the ways I'd gone wrong in my life. I was very aware of just how badly I had screwed up, but before I could say anything else, the door was unceremoniously shut in my face. It was a definitive 'go-away' and I couldn't have been more disappointed if I tried. I felt like he sucked all the optimism and confidence out of me, leaving me deflated and empty.

Swearing, I kicked the closed door, taking immense satisfaction in the greasy, black streaks that my boot left on the white surface. I thumped a balled-up fist on the hardwood as well and swallowed hard so the threat of tears wouldn't spill over. I hated feeling defeated. I was a survivor. I was a fighter and a master at making any situation work for me. Over the years, I'd had no choice. In this moment, his closed door mocking me, I hated that not only did I no longer have the upper hand, but that I was barely holding on as things were spiraling quickly out of control around me.

Sucking in a breath, I pushed my bangs back from my face and gave myself a mental shake. So, I'd struck out with Stark. I knew there was no guarantee he was going to help me out, but that didn't mean I was willing to walk away from this fatal game of hide and seek I'd started. The Mayor didn't get to sit in his mansion and chase little girls while his corrupt city burned. Someone had to hold him accountable, and even though this situation sucked and was scary as hell, that someone was going to be me.

I quickly walked back down the front steps of the townhouse, pulling my beanie out of my pocket and slapping it back on my head as I went. I tucked all my hair up in the cap and stopped at the line of decorative hedges that dotted the front of the property so I could pick up my backpack from where I stashed it. Everything I owned was in that camo knapsack, and I felt naked without it. I also paused long enough to pull on a hoodie that was two sizes too big and covered me almost to my knees. No more minimal cleavage on display and no more pretending that my limited feminine wiles would get me anywhere with the moody, distant, computer genius. His heart was missing, and in its place was a processor that did nothing more than calculate and compute.

Sighing and lost in thought, I wasn't being as careful as I should have been as I walked across manicured lawns and cut across driveways full of expensive cars. I wasn't blending in or sticking to the shadows like normal because I was in such a hurry to leave Stark, and my disappointment in him, behind.

I was almost out of the subdivision, almost back to the main road that led into the Point, when I heard sirens and realized the blue and red flashing lights were for me. I was so close to the road— near plenty of gullies and ditches to slither through. The road that was relatively safe. I was so close to getting away. I'd never been a fan of law and order, but now that there was a price on my head, I'd done my best to avoid any kind of law enforcement or people in uniform. Too many were in the Mayor's back pocket. I'd let desperation cloud my judgment. I should have known the police would be present in a nice neighborhood like this. It was their job to keep out people like me.

I contemplated dropping my backpack and making a run for it, but the cop car was too close and I didn't, for one second, doubt that whomever was driving would put a bullet in me to slow me down.

Swearing, I slowed and lifted my hands to face the burly, mean-looking cop. He climbed out of the car, one hand on the grip of his gun, the other on his phone. I had a sinking suspicion every cop in the city had my picture and a basic description of me. They were all looking, and like a dumb ass, I put myself right in their line of sight.

"Can I help you, Officer?" I tried to keep my voice calm, but there was a thread of fear in it that I couldn't hide.

"Got a complaint about a trespasser." He was lying. I hadn't been here long enough for anyone to complain, and even if Stark wasn't my biggest fan, there was no way he would turn me in. I wasn't sure how I knew when everything else I thought I knew about him turned out to be so wrong, but I knew it all the way to my bones.

"Well, I was just visiting a friend. I'm on my way back to the Point right now. I'm sure it was just a misunderstanding."

He grunted and looked from his phone toward me and back. I knew he was checking my image against one on that little screen, and I also knew if I went anywhere with him, no one would ever see me alive again.

Throwing my backpack to the ground, I turned and started to run.

I had no idea where I was going. I had no idea what I was doing.

All I knew was that I couldn't let that cop get his hands on me.

I made it across one more yard before I felt a lightning bolt blast through my body. It was like being tackled by a charging rhinoceros.

I screamed and screamed and screamed, but the sounds of the traffic coming from the road, from freedom, drowned out my sounds of agony as the cop hit me with another charge from his Taser. I laid on the ground twitching, spasming out of control, watching in dread as his black boots got closer.

The last thought I had before everything faded away was . . . *help* . . . but like always, no one was there to offer it.

I was alone.

Every man has his secret sorrows which the world knows not;
and often times we call a man cold when he is only sad.
~ Henry Wadsworth Longfellow

CHAPTER 2

Stark

Fourteen fucking days later . . .

I COULDN'T STOP STARING at that battered, torn, duct-taped backpack. It had been sitting on my coffee table for two weeks. Fourteen days. Each one of them seemingly longer than the one before. Each one dragging, endless, as I waited for information. I spent hour after hour calling myself every kind of asshole and was pretty sure I had given myself an ulcer and gray hair from the guilt that was tearing my insides apart. That backpack and the person it belonged to were forcing me to feel . . . more than I'd allowed myself to feel in years.

She needed help and I turned her away.

I told her no, shut the door on her pretty, hopeful face like it was nothing, because I wanted to convince myself I felt nothing. I was a void, a wasteland, a dry and arid desert. But I told her no, and now that empty, open space was flooded with the worst kind of emotion. Guilt. Raw, unrelenting guilt.

No one would have known that I had pulled the door open a few minutes later and tried to chase her down and tell her I was sorry for being a dick, but I was too late. Noe was gone. Vanished. Disappeared. The only sign that she'd really been on my doorstep, dark eyes wide with fear, was the backpack I found in the yard a few houses down from mine. It was the same one she'd clutched like a lifeline when I dragged her to meet Nassir. She wouldn't leave it behind. Not when it was all she had.

Someone took her and it was all my fault.

Once again, I let someone down who thought they could rely on me. The girl before Noe had kept the fact she needed my help, needed me, hidden. I thought I knew her better than I knew myself, but I was wrong, and that mistake cost me everything that mattered. And yet, Noe had been right in my face with her desperation and fear, and I'd still walked away.

I failed to protect someone who was smaller, softer, and far more defenseless than I was . . . again. I didn't need the reminder that if something didn't have a motherboard and a Wi-Fi connection, I had no clue what to do with it.

I swore and kicked the leg of the expensive table that sat in front of my equally expensive couch. Half empty beer bottles toppled over, one spilling onto the keyboard of my open laptop. Typically, the sight of one of my babies getting destroyed would make my head explode, but not today. Not until I found out where Noe was. Not until I had her back and knew she was safe. That was the only thing that mattered at the moment. Not the couple of grand I just annihilated with the remnants of a stale beer that I couldn't even bother to clean up, and not the fact that I now owed the Devil more than a simple favor or two. Selling your soul for a shot at redemption didn't come cheap.

I was in so deep, I couldn't even see the sunshine anymore. It didn't matter, because he promised me he would do whatever he could to get her back. I tried not to cringe when I remembered the hard warning look in Nassir Gates's amber eyes as he told me it might be her body we got back and nothing else.

I couldn't think about that. I was good at shutting away whatever I was feeling, locking it down, and pretending like I was immune to basic feelings and reactions. I'd lost the other half of myself, the one thing that kept me human and functioning, so it was easy to pull anything that threatened my tenuous hold on sanity away from the tender places that remained inside of me. I was made of things that were hard, cold, industrial, and it allowed me to feel nothing. Steel, iron, wires, and gears. There wasn't anything empathetic or gentle left. All of that had died when my twin sister did.

All those rigid things that made me who I was were churning and grinding under my skin at the thought of what Noe might be going through. The pipes had run dry for a long time and now there was a river of fury and regret blazing through them. I slammed the door in her face because she was the one person who made me feel something I couldn't ignore. Even when I thought she was a boy, I was curious and confused. Lured in by her sharp wit and outright rebellion. She seemed fearless and it called to me. Her defiance echoed loud in the cavernous depths that were left behind when my soul was ripped away from me. I couldn't get away from the feelings that she energized within me, and I couldn't shake them off fast enough.

She needed me and I couldn't handle it. I relinquished the desire to be *needed* by anyone, and I willingly accepted that I didn't *want* to need anyone. I couldn't stand with the weight of others' expectations on my shoulders because I was weak, because I was scared and scarred from things that had nothing to do with her. I disappointed her and put her in danger. Whatever happened to her was on me, and I was fully prepared to accept any and all responsibility. If she was dead, well, then the hard fact of the matter was that I didn't deserve to draw another breath. Her life had been in my hands and I let it slip through my fingers without even attempting to hold onto it. I'd lost another fight my mind couldn't afford to lose.

From the start, Nassir had use for me in his criminal empire. He considered me a valuable commodity, and more than that, his business partner long considered me a friend. Neither would let me go without a fight, but if Noe didn't make it out of this, I wouldn't either. The emotions I'd ignored for so long would take over, and I would be helpless to stop them. I wasn't strong enough to survive looking at the still, silent face of another innocent woman taken because life wasn't fair. I was a failure and eventually both men who ruled the Point would realize I was more of a liability than an asset. Over the years, I had perfected the art of faking being useful and invaluable. The expiration date on my usefulness was fast approaching, I just knew it.

I kicked the table again, this time sending the liquid-laden laptop and Noe's backpack crashing to the floor. When it hit the hardwood, the broken zipper split open and her few meager belongings spilled onto my cork floors. All she had were a couple of old t-shirts, a pair of sneakers that also had duct tape on them, a water bottle, a paper-thin blanket, and a laptop that I knew cost as much as the one I just ruined. After all, it was one she'd jacked from me when she robbed my place. I wasn't surprised to see it when I went through the bag trying to find any kind of clue as to where she might be.

She had good taste in computers. She snatched one of my more tricked out toys. I was also suitably impressed that she got past all my security firewalls in order to use the damn thing. I told her that her brain was sexy, and I wasn't lying. It was the first thing I noticed about her. Intelligence was the only thing that ever really caught my attention and held it. I was impressed that she had alluded me for so long when Nassir sent me after her for information. I was intrigued by the way she showed no fear when she faced me down. That day, my anger had been hot and heavy, uncontrollable from lack of use. It raged between us in my empty, unplugged apartment. I wasn't sure where it was going to land or how to handle it, but she hadn't even flinched. I was curious about her defiance in the face of a well-known threat when she went toe to toe with Nassir. I was very aware of her on every single level and I hadn't even known she was a *her,* at the time. That anger and fascination with her from the start was a lot to process for a man who had been mostly numb and entirely emotionless for far too long.

Now that I knew she was, in fact, all female, and a particularly cute one at that, I let myself like more than her mind. I liked her dark, untrusting eyes. I liked the sassy arch of her midnight-colored eyebrows and the little beauty mark that rested high on the sharp curve of her cheekbone. I liked her full lips and the way they looked like they were painted a rosy pink even though I knew she didn't wear any kind of lipstick. There was no makeup in that tattered backpack. She didn't need it sleeping on the streets. I was secretly obsessed with her streaked hair. The red looked like fire, and the black was so dark and shiny it didn't look real. She wore it short in the back and longer in the front so she could pull off her androgynous look if she wore a hat, but it suited her. It was no-fuss and striking at the same time. I hadn't liked anything about anyone long before my mind had been broken and my heart had been shattered, but even with everything inside of me misfiring, I could tell I was attracted to Noe Lee. It was another reason I had to turn her away. I didn't want to work through new feelings when I could barely contain the old ones.

I was man enough to admit that I wanted all parts of her back, and there was no pushing down the bitter regret at the fact that I was the reason she was gone in the first place.

I pushed off the couch and lowered my big frame toward the floor so I could carefully put Noe's stuff back where it belonged. She didn't have much, and that pissed me off. There was that wild, uncontrollable anger again. It loved being off the leash and was happy to snap and pop all around me. She had the brains and the looks to get whatever she wanted, but she wasn't a user like that. She wasn't part of the problem. She was the solution to everything that was wrong in the corrupted parts of the city.

There was a sharp knock on my front door, and before I could fully turn my head or climb to my feet, it swung open, and a dark-haired man in a sharply tailored suit strolled in like he owned the place. On his heels was a large African American man, also in an expensive suit, and another man I had never met but had heard plenty about. He was in a suit, as well, but unlike the other two men, his was flashy, pin-striped, and accented with a patterned silk tie, gold pocket watch, and bling on his fingers that looked like it cost more than the down payment on my townhouse.

The first two men may have been mistaken for well-off businessmen if you weren't paying attention, but there was no way the third guy could ever pass for anything but what he was . . . even with the beard that covered his jaw. He was a hustler. A player. A dealmaker and a game changer. This guy was a criminal and proud of it. He wore that fact with pride and aplomb. He earned the money to buy that suit and those rings by doing bad shit—and he didn't care who knew it. He was the opposite side of the spectrum of what the streets could do to a person in the Point. Crime and corruption moved this man to the top tiers of power and respect, and he thrived in the chaos. He was the enemy, and he liked it that way. He was great at being bad.

I pulled off my glasses and made a big production of wiping them on the bottom of my t-shirt. I blinked several times and sneered at the unwelcome visitor. "I thought you were dead. Heard you got shanked in prison when you refused to cooperate with the feds."

Benny Truman used to be the man who made other men cower in fear. He was the right hand to the old crime boss who ruled the Point with a heavy hand and a thirst for blood. There wasn't anything Benny wouldn't do as long as money was the primary motivator. That blind loyalty made him just as ruthless, cruel, and callous as the man who used to be in charge. When the old crime boss was taken out of play, his entire crew went down with him. Everyone knew Benny wouldn't sell out anyone, even if it meant a lifetime spent locked up, but word on the street was that someone on the inside wanted to make absolutely sure he didn't open his big, fat mouth. No one grieved his loss when he was declared dead, and the two men standing with him in my living room didn't seem at all surprised by his miraculous return from the grave.

"I'm hard to kill." Benny grinned at me and tilted his head slightly so I could see the long, thin scar that ran across the entire width of his neck. It looked like someone had tried to take his cocky head clear off.

Two minutes in his company and I could see why. There was something about him that made me very uneasy. That was also a new emotion. I was big enough and intimidating enough that it was usually the other way around. I was the one who made people uncomfortable, and I typically didn't give a shit about it.

I rubbed a hand over my short, dark hair and sighed. "I wouldn't tell Bax that. He'll see it as a challenge."

Nassir Gates, my de facto boss, the man who now called the shots in the Point, lifted his hand and gave his dark head a little shake. His voice had the faint trace of an accent. The more time I spent around him and the more I listened to him, I was confident that his original home was somewhere in Israel. I was good with dialects. Hell, I was good with a lot of useless shit that would put a price on my head at a very early age. Nassir never mentioned where he was from, and I never asked, but he slipped into Arabic when he was frustrated or annoyed, which somehow made his quiet, intense anger even more intimidating when it was directed at you.

"Bax doesn't need to know about this little visit. Neither does Race. That won't end well . . . for any of us."

Chuck, Nassir's head of security and quite possibly his only friend, chuckled from where he had sprawled on my sofa. "Personally, I'd like to see just how creative our boy would get if we let him loose on you, Ben."

Bax was our boy. All of ours, even though he was only tied directly to Race. Nassir tolerated him since he was Race's best friend, Chuck considered him one of his flock, and I hesitantly considered the guy a friend. We'd gotten tight when the deep muck of the Point sucked me in, and Bax was the only one who bothered to warn me that struggling only made guys our size sink faster. He was full of good advice when it came to dealing with the shit the Point could throw, and sometimes he seemed just as emotionless and detached as I was. He cared about his girl, his car, his city, and not much else. He was slowly softening toward his older brother and the cop's growing family, but even that was hit or miss.

Benny flipped Chuck off and watched me warily as I climbed to my feet. Chuck was big; I was bigger. None of the guys filling up my tastefully decorated space were exactly petite, but I had at least a couple of inches and fifty pounds on all of them. Nassir had asked me more than once to bust heads in his underground fight ring. I always told him no, but with Noe missing and nowhere to put the new rage and loathing I was feeling, I was starting to reconsider bloodshed as an outlet. My recently awakened anger was a powerful thing and I had no idea what to do with it.

"You don't look like a ghost, even if that's what you are. People are going to notice you and word will get back to Bax and Race." Logic. I couldn't escape it even when I wanted to. It was coiled around my brain like a squeezing fist. Race and Nassir might be the shot callers in the Point, but Shane Baxter—Bax, to those in the know—*was* the Point. All the others might make things happen, but those things didn't happen unless Bax let them. The Point was all he knew, and the worst part of the city ran through his blood. If he didn't want Benny back, then Benny wouldn't be back, and whatever plan Nassir had would go up in a puff of smoke, even if it meant that Noe died.

"Race and Bax are with their women in Colorado for a long weekend. Something happened between the giant and the teenager . . . something . . . not good, I would guess." The teenager was Race's fiancée's little sister, Karsen. The giant was Noah Booker, another bruiser on Nassir's payroll. There had been something tenuous and unnamed going on for years between the ex-con and the quiet, shy teenager. Race hated it; everyone else was waiting cautiously to see what would happen when the girl hit legal age.

But something went sideways right after her graduation, and

Karsen Carter decided to go out-of-state for college after months of declaring that she would never leave the Point. She'd been gone for a couple months and now it was her first winter break. I wasn't surprised her family was checking up on her. Nassir's eyes narrowed slightly. "If you ask me, she's running away and that only makes a predator want to chase, but that's neither here nor there. We have a small window to work with and we're wasting time worrying about Benny's longevity." Nassir didn't mind logic, especially when it worked in his favor. His tone was even and steady when he explained why Benny was allowed in the last place he should be.

I narrowed my eyes at Nassir and snapped, "The only person's longevity I care about is Noe's. It's been two weeks, Gates. Fourteen fucking days. I don't have to tell you what kind of hell she could have endured in that time if she's still alive." I already knew that Goddard liked to hurt women and had no qualms about forcing himself on someone who couldn't fight back. If he did that to Noe, if he let his rich goons defile and degrade her, I was going to take him apart with my bare hands. But I needed to know where she was first, before I could give the fury that was pulsing through me an outlet.

Nassir dipped his chin in acknowledgement. "I am aware that the clock has been ticking every day, Stark. That is why I found Benny." His gold eyes narrowed and his mouth tightened into a line of annoyance as he muttered, "Men who look like Jonathan Goddard, who bleed blue blood and come from where he comes from, do not do business with men who look like me and come from where I come from. There are some doors that even a shitload of dirty money and well-placed threats cannot open. I could not get inside that gilded cage, but Benny, he's been sliding into places he doesn't belong for a very long time."

I felt my eyes widen as I turned to the quiet, bearded man who was watching me thoughtfully. I could tell he wasn't sure what to make of me, but I didn't have time to worry about it. No one was ever really sure if I was friend or foe. That's what happened when you were dead on the inside, when you were robotic and stiff. The best parts of me were dead and buried with my sister, so I could be either friend or foe, depending on the circumstances. Not that the two were much different. I treated pretty much everyone exactly the same. Like they were an annoyance and a distraction. But I wanted to treat Noe differently.

"You know where she is? Is she okay? What's he doing to her?" The questions came out rapid fire, each moving me closer to the man in the flashy suit. By the time I was done asking them, I was right up in his face and I had his lapels clasped in each hand. I pulled him up so that he was balanced on his tiptoes. His fingers wrapped around my wrists, the metal of his rings biting into my skin.

"All right genius, if you shake me to death, you aren't going to get her back, so I need you to take a step in the other direction before you break me." There was a thread of amusement in his tone, but I could also tell he understood that my panic and my fear were completely new to me, and I had no way to control them. Somewhere along the line, Benny Truman had found someone who forced him to think about things other than himself. He actually gave a shit, and that made a man a little bit unhinged. I assumed that was happening to me.

I let him go with more force than necessary and raked my hands through my hair in aggravation. "Sorry, but like I said, it's been two fucking weeks. That's a long time."

Benny smoothed his wrinkled suit and straightened his tie. "I get it, but you can take a breath for the moment. The cop who picked her up tagged her with a Taser. It either knocked her out for a while or she was good at playing possum. Goddard paid some guys to get his stepdaughter's location out of her, and when she came to, she told them that if she didn't check in with Julia every two days, she had instructions to hit the road because it meant something was wrong. She told them that they had a special code, and if they touched her, she would use it and send Julia into the wind. Goddard wants the girl and the baby. He wants to bury the bodies and burn the evidence. He can't do that if your girl won't talk." Benny chuckled a little and rocked back on his heels. "She's smart. They've been playing it pretty easy with her, hoping to trace the calls, pressuring her to get the girl to slip up and drop her location, but she's been playing them."

I grunted and put my hands on my hips as I stared at the floor between my black motorcycle boots. "How do you know all this?"

Benny and Nassir exchanged a look and he ran a hand over his beard. "Goddard is losing patience and getting desperate. He's looking for a pro to get her to talk. Someone who can torture her, hurt her, and get her to give him what he wants. He knows she's from the streets so his usual threats won't work. He needs more fire power. Typically, he would go through Gates to get his hands on a pro, but since he doesn't like to do business with anyone who doesn't bleed blue and has a pedigree that matches his, he put out a call for an outsider to get the job done."

Nassir's narrowed eyes glinted in irritation. "Luckily, no one goes in or out of the Point without my knowing about it. We got word a few days ago that a professional was making his way to the city and I had a welcome committee waiting for him. After we graciously put him up for the night, I retrieved our own professional. Someone Goddard wouldn't question coming in to work the girl over. He thinks Benny is here to make her talk by any means necessary."

Graciously put him up for the night more than likely meant Nassir's guys had maimed and tortured the guy. Given him a taste of his own medicine. He didn't like anyone who wasn't vetted on his streets. He didn't like anyone wandering around who might be as dangerous as he was. He had someone in his life he gave a shit about and he wouldn't let an unknown get anywhere near her. "He didn't even question who Benny was when he showed up at the country club."

I blew out a breath and shifted my gaze between the two of them. "How did he not recognize you?" Like I said, I'd never met him but I knew exactly who he was. The streets used to be under his control.

"Guys like Goddard don't know about guys like me unless they need something. When Novak was pulling the reins, he didn't do white-collar crime. He never saw a use for it. He was much more the rape and pillage type . . . literally. Our paths never crossed and he's watched enough bad cable TV that he's convinced I'm some mobbed-up gangster from the East Coast. He has no idea what a life of crime really looks like . . . which works for us and works for your girl."

I scanned his outfit and his shiny wingtips. "You do kind of look like an extra on the *Sopranos,* except for the beard."

I knew from first-hand experience the guys who made their living breaking the law very rarely looked like the average person thought they did. Sure, there were guys who looked like they loved doing bad things . . . like Bax. But then there was Race, who looked like he owned a yacht and played golf every weekend at Goddard's country club. Nine times out of ten, Race was into more illegal and dirty stuff than Bax, but at first glance, no one would ever know that. Then, there were guys like Nassir. He looked like a successful businessman most days, but there was something about him that screamed his business wasn't anything you wanted to ask him about. His expensive suits never could hide the ruthlessness and raw edge that made him the devil incarnate.

Chuck barked out a laugh and slapped his leg. "Ben's been lost in the woods for the last six months. He's been stuck in flannel and had to learn how to chop wood. He forgot the power of a good suit is in its subtlety. The man used to know how to dress."

Benny swore and Nassir's lips twitched in silent amusement. I wished I could see the humor in the situation, but I felt like I was about to break into pieces. All that would be left of me was the skeleton made of leftover parts and shrapnel.

"So, he thinks you're here to torture her, and if you don't get the info, he'll most likely have you both killed."

I got dual nods from both dark-haired men and a serious look from Chuck. Nassir pulled out his phone when it quietly vibrated and swore softly under his breath. "Either that, or he'll try and sell her. We've had some problems with the Eastern Europeans. Every time I think I've chased them all out of town, they pop back up. If she doesn't talk, he might tell Benny to hand her over to them and they'll move her into their goddamn sex trafficking network. Obviously, we won't let that happen."

"No shit, that isn't going to happen." I growled the words between my teeth. Nassir blinked in surprise at the obvious emotion behind each word but didn't say anything.

His tone was careful when he told me, "We're meeting tonight after midnight at the docks. Goddard has an empty shipping container registered to a shell company that he uses for all his wet work. We didn't have a clue that's where he's been operating until Benny got the meetup info. You can bet the guys running the docks are going to hear from me when this is all over. They're bringing her there so Benny can get the answers from her."

"If she talks?" I knew the answer, but I had to hear someone say it out loud.

"She dies." Nassir said flatly.

"If she doesn't?"

"She dies." Nassir gave me both answers equally with as little emotion as I usually showed.

"I'm going with you." It was a bold declaration, one lacking any of my typical detachment.

Benny immediately shook his head as both Chuck and Nassir sighed. "You can't. Goddard hired a guy who works alone with no questions asked. I can't roll in there with someone else. Your girl will be dead before we step foot on the docks."

"You're too invested. You aren't thinking clearly. Stark, you'll do more harm than good if you involve yourself. You are the brains behind the operation, not the brawn." Nassir's tone left no room for argument and his words were true. I wasn't much of a fighter unless I was pushed. And right now, I felt like I'd been pushed right to the edge and there was no going back. Fourteen long ass days of being suffocated by guilt and remorse. I was choking on it. I was also running scared from a myriad of other emotions I couldn't clearly identify as they swirled under the emotions I did recognize. I hated things I didn't understand. I didn't have the patience or time to be confused and conflicted.

I wanted to fall back to the floor.

I wanted to scream at the ceiling.

I wanted to rip my shirt off and beat my chest like a wild animal.

I felt like I was being consumed by every ugly thing twisting up my insides. Dropping my head, I put my hand on the back of my neck and squeezed so hard that it hurt. Pain was the one feeling I was familiar with. It was an old friend, a comfort. It was the one emotion I knew how to deal with because it was the only one I allowed myself to feel day in and day out.

"Just get her back. I don't care how. I don't care who you have to go through to do it." I closed my eyes and watched Jonathan Goddard's downfall play like a movie behind my eyelids. Once I knew Noe was okay, once she was safe, I was going to take him down.

She wanted to make him pay. I was going to do her one better.

I was going to make him suffer . . . and then, I was going to make sure he could never hurt anyone ever again.

CHAPTER 3

Noe

I WAS GOING TO die.

There were a couple other times in my life when I was pretty sure the end was near, but they were nothing like this. This time, I could feel the end looming. I could feel the tiny window of hope slam shut. I could feel the weight of inevitability pressing down on me so hard that I could barely get a breath in. I'd been stalling, playing games, talking in circles, and lying my ass off. I'd done whatever I had to do to stay alive while I figured out a way to get free from the Mayor and his goons. None of my words or my schemes were working anymore. He wanted his stepdaughter and he was going to kill me if I didn't tell him where to find her.

I couldn't give up Julia's location. I wasn't going to sell her out and put her back in the monster's clutches, the way one of the kids on the street had done to me when the cop flashed his badge and demanded to know where I was. The other runaways knew Nassir had been looking for me and that he'd sent Stark to flush me out.

All the dirty cop had to do was promise that whomever ratted me out would get a get-out-of-jail-free card. Since I had a backbone and was far more loyal than that, I was going to die. But not before the dirty cop who nearly electrocuted me put his hands all over me.

He'd been circling around for the last two weeks. Letting his hands linger. Pinning me with his eyes and taunting me with his words. Goddard told his goons I was off limits until they had a location for his stepdaughter, but they only behaved when he was in the room. When he was gone, they threatened, they touched, they intimidated, and they harassed. My cheek was swollen from being smacked around. My scalp was raw from yanking my head out of grabbing hands, and all my fingernails were broken and bloody from clawing and fighting off unwanted advances. I was disgusted by being pawed and abused, even if I was achingly used to it. The look in the cop's eye was one I was sadly familiar with. He liked it when I fought back, and he was waiting, not so patiently, to get the go ahead from his boss that I was no longer off limits. He'd been telling Goddard that there were other ways to find Julia, that I was just a street-rat without connections to keep the girl hidden for long. He had a very specific way in which he wanted to make me talk, and if Goddard had given him the okay, I would have killed myself before letting him have his way with my body.

I swore to myself when I left home that I would never, ever be powerless like that again. Luckily, the software I set up with basic, pre-recorded responses from Julia meant I could keep the Mayor guessing and the dirty cop on a leash for a little while. I didn't actually know where she was. I never knew. It was safer that way in case something like this happened. I didn't want the temptation to give away information to protect my own self-interest, so I took precautions. But my time ran out today. There were no more distractions and no more delays. Goddard wanted answers I couldn't give him . . . so I was going to die.

For the last two weeks, I'd been trussed up, hands bound behind my back, and confined to some trashy motel that rented rooms by the hour. It was in the heart of the Point—the very worst part. The dirty cop and another guy, who looked like a tired, worn out litigator, took turns trying to cajole me into spilling my guts. The balding, older man, who looked like he gave up on life years ago, made promises I knew he wouldn't keep, and the cop resorted to using his hands. My nipples had been pinched and my ass was squeezed more in the last two weeks than in an entire decade spent living on the streets. He'd tried to poke and prod between my legs, but old memories and long repressed panic gave me the kind of strength he didn't expect me to have after days of eating nothing but crap from the motel's vending machine. Little did these two fools know that life had handed me worse when I'd survived on less.

Even with my hands zip-tied behind my back, I still managed to smash his nose with my forehead and take a chunk out of his cheek with my teeth. It was gory and grisly, bloody and brutal, but after he was done beating the shit out of me for the assault, he left me alone. Goddard was none too pleased when he showed up and saw that I was so battered I could barely speak. I refused to make the fake call to the recorded software for the next two days and flatly told the Mayor if the cop touched me again I was sending his precious package as far away as I possibly could. He didn't know that there was no way for me to get a message to Julia, but I was a good enough liar that he believed me, and the cop had kept his hands to himself . . . until today.

Both he and the skinny, older man showed up in the middle of the night. The crappy motel door was locked from the outside with a padlock and all the windows were lined with bars that couldn't be broken loose. I'd tried the first night they left me alone in this hovel. No one cared if I screamed my fool head off. In fact, the room next to me seemed to be producing even louder, scarier noises. There was no housekeeping, no security. I was well and truly trapped and trying to escape had left me with nothing more than bruises and a raspy voice. I'd gotten used to sleeping at a weird angle because my bound hands wrenched up behind me, making my shoulders stiff. I'd never been much of a heavy sleeper—you couldn't afford to be when you slept under the stars, and I couldn't risk it when I slept under the same roof as my older brother—so I heard my captors outside the door before it swung open.

I sat upright on the ratty bed and blinked against the sudden invasion of neon light from the motel sign. I was going to ask what was going on; however, before the words were out, the nasty cop pulled out something that looked like a black burlap sack and shook it in front of me.

"Boss says it's time to go." He took a step toward me and caught my ankle as I tried to scoot across the bed and away from him.

I screamed as he pulled me across the mattress, evading my kicking feet and chuckling at my protest. The older guy sighed and rubbed a hand over his face.

"Can we hurry this along? The guy God paid costs a fortune and he doesn't like to be kept waiting. We don't have time for you to play with your food."

My eyes went wide as the cop wrapped his hands around my neck and started to squeeze. It made me gag and I kicked and wiggled even harder in his relentless hold. I felt his cheek, the one that needed ten stitches after I bit him, next to mine. He laughed in my ear and his voice sent shivers racing down my spine when he muttered low enough that only I could hear, "That's right, you little bitch. The boss called in a pro. A guy who can make you bleed on the inside so that the pain lasts for hours. You'll be begging to talk by the time he's done with you." I felt him press into my hip as he pulled me up and forced me to my feet. I gagged harder and tried to pull away when he ground his arousal into me. I struggled to get an elbow in his gut, but there was no traction, and I screamed when he pulled on my tied hands. The nerve endings and joints in my arms and shoulders burned from being locked in an unnatural position for so long. "I'm going to ask for an hour with you before they finish you off. The last thing you'll remember is my face." He pressed his ravaged cheek into mine. "The face you fucked up."

I had to breathe through my mouth so I didn't pass out. I was scared. I hated that I couldn't see, but more than anything, I hated that I had no control, no say in what was happening to me or where I was going.

I was no one's rag doll.

I wasn't a *thing* that could be manhandled and tossed around.

I fought back. That's what I always did. That's all I could do.

I dragged my feet. I refused to stand under my own power. I wiggled across the floor when the cop dropped me. I tried to get up and run. I had no idea where I was going but I had to get away. I screamed and screamed and screamed. The older man begged me to keep quiet while the cop laughed and drove one of his boots into my ribs.

I went silent on a gasp and was lifted up and thrown over a shoulder. It dug into my gut. I bounced mercilessly around as I was hauled out of the filthy room and down a set of stairs. The lawyerly looking guy was complaining about the noise and making a scene. The cop placated him by saying he would flash his badge, if necessary. They were so casual about abduction and torture that it made me even more resigned to the fact that this really was the end. They didn't care if anyone saw what they were doing to me because I was about to disappear off the face of the Earth. It didn't matter that they brought in a professional to wring and torment the truth out of me, because I was dead whether or not I talked. I was going to suffer needlessly. I snickered because it wouldn't be the first time. I spent my entire life fighting against people who thought they could break and control me.

My captors tossed me in the trunk of a car like I was luggage and slammed it closed. The cramped space smelled like gasoline and blood, which made my stomach turn. Behind the suffocating hood, I closed my eyes and started to work through my options. Everyone in the Point knew that if someone snatched you, you were far more likely to end up dead if you let them move you to a new location. Well, there was nothing I could do about that. We are on the move and I had no way to stop it. I also knew that I was supposed to look for a release latch or try to kick out one of the taillights and signal for help. The hood prevented me from knowing if I was up or down and my bound hands kept me from maneuvering around. I kicked my legs out in front of me and leaned on my side, groaning as my newly injured ribs screamed at me. My stiff shoulders also protested, but I made contact with something solid and kicked it with my boot. I moved a few inches and tried again. Metal thumped against the sole of my shoe.

I kept kicking, making my way in a half circle when the car suddenly stopped and sent me rolling. I shrieked in surprise and tried to lift myself upright when the trunk was pulled open. Immediately, hard hands latched around my throat and started to shake me. I gagged involuntarily and tried to pull back, but I was stuck firmly in that punishing grasp.

"Do you know what happens if someone stops us or calls the cops because of the racket you're making?" I guess I was lucky he hadn't put me in his patrol car. If he had, he would have been able to blow through lights and stop signs, sirens blaring.

God, I wanted my hands free so I could fight him. I wanted to hurt him. I longed to maim and scar him. I wanted my face to be the last thing he ever saw . . . right before I destroyed him.

"I'm a cop. I show my badge. I flash my gun and we go on our way. All you're doing is making things harder on yourself."

He released me with enough force that I cracked my head on the seam where the trunk opened from the car. I felt a warm river of blood start to trickle down the back of my neck.

"You aren't a cop. You're a lackey on the take. You're a sellout and chump. You let some rich guy up on the Hill pull your strings. You're a puppet and a pawn." I bit the words out and laughed against the pain and dread that was infiltrating every single cell in my body.

A heavy hand landed on my head and I was shoved back into the trunk. "Well, you're fucking dead."

I snorted and screamed, "I'd rather be dead than someone else's toy to play with."

He called me some nasty names but his voice drifted away as the car started to back up and continue the journey to my dismal fate. I stopped wiggling and kicking the interior of the trunk. I needed to keep up as much of my strength and energy as I could on the very off chance that I could get away from the guy they brought in to make me talk. I knew the opportunity for escape was slim to none, but I'd never been the kind of girl who was willing to accept the things that were forced upon me. I did not believe in the inevitable. Nothing was certain until it was, and even though I was pretty sure this was the end of the road for me, I wouldn't give up or give in until my very last breath. I would fight until every single drop of resistance and defiance was dragged out of me. I wasn't going to make this easy on any of the people who had put me in this position, myself included.

After what could have been hours or minutes later, the car came to a stop. The darkness and ache in my head were playing with my sense of time. I had no idea where I was, but I could hear water and the low, deep signals that came from big carrier ships that were constantly coming in and out of the shipping ports on the edge of the Point. I could smell saltwater and oil, so I figured we were down by the docks.

The older guy muttered something in his nervous voice and the dirty cop held me close—hands skimming over my chest and across the front of my pants—and there was a deafening metal shriek and a whoosh of air as a door was opened. I was forced forward and stumbled to my knees. The impact with the ground dug my teeth into my tongue and made my split head pound. I was jerked back to my feet unceremoniously and my shoulders throbbed in protest. I couldn't hold back a yelp of discomfort and was startled when I was pushed into a chair. The metal legs dragged across the ground with a deafening screech and I screamed when hands went around my ankles. I kicked and flailed to keep from being tied to the chair but it didn't do me any good. By the time the gross hood was pulled off of my head, I was trussed up like a Christmas ham and there was no wiggling my way free.

A single, bare light bulb was hanging over my head, and for a minute, I swore I'd stumbled into a Tarantino movie. The Point was bad, dangerous, and ugly. But this, this was a whole different level of depraved and twisted. I couldn't believe this shit rolled down from the Hill. Maybe Stark was right and it was the guys who made the rules who were really the ones we needed to watch out for, not the guys breaking them.

The rusted, weathered metal door to the gigantic shipping container where I was trapped moaned in protest as it was pulled closed behind two new arrivals. It was so ridiculous that they called Mayor Goddard *God* for short. The man had nothing really impressive to speak of. He was average height, average build, and had thinning hair. His face was sharp, his nose hooked and slightly beak-like. His eyes were a washed-out blue that shouldn't be menacing, but I knew what this man was capable of. I knew how little he cared for anyone aside from himself. He looked like a politician, not a monster. Yet somehow, he was both.

The other man looked vaguely familiar. I couldn't place him off the top of my head, but he moved with the same predatory grace and self-assured swagger like all the men with power in the Point. He moved like he expected people to get out of his way and show him respect without knowing a single thing about him. He was big, had a neatly trimmed beard, and was dressed in a pinstriped suit. His tie was loud and blood red. He had rings on his fingers that sparkled in the dim light and a scar across his throat that looked like someone had recently tried to decapitate him. His fog-colored eyes were cold and assessing as they rolled over me from the top of my head to my bound feet. His mouth pulled down in a frown that would've had me taking a step back if I were standing. He was scary in the way only men who killed without conscience could be.

This guy was no joke.

They called him a professional and I could see why. I wasn't sure what he did, but whatever it was, he was the best at it.

"I told you that what I do only works if the subject hasn't been touched. If she has grown accustomed to pain, what I do will be less effective and the results are no longer guaranteed." His voice was sharp and his tone was warning. He moved closer to me and tiny scraps of light from the bare bulb flickered over him. He was far better looking than the guys who had been making my life a living hell for the last two weeks, and I found that incredibly unnerving. Someone that pretty shouldn't be able to do things so ugly. Brutality wasn't meant to be beautiful.

"Our friend with the badge tends to get slightly overzealous when she fights back. I warned him to take it easy on her, but the warning may have come a little later than it should have." Goddard sounded bored. Asshole. Like it was every day he kept a woman against her will and paid someone to bleed information out of her. Remembering Julia, it occurred to me that he did, in fact, torture women on the regular with zero remorse. "He was smart enough not to bring her in the back of a police car. One of those parked down here would have the natives restless."

The guy with the beard stepped closer to me and slowly started to walk around my chair. His eyes picked apart every bruise and mark that was on my face. I felt his gaze burn at the back of my head. It licked over the trashed, torn skin around the zip ties at my wrists and flicked down to my bound ankles.

I gasped when, wordlessly, he lowered himself behind me and grabbed my hands. I told myself not to move, not to make a single sound, but I couldn't bite back a whimper of fear and pain. I heard the snick of a blade springing out of a knife and felt the chill of it against my skin. I sobbed in relief and in agony when my hands were suddenly free. Blood rushed to parts of my body that were starved for it and every muscle in my torso started to tingle with sweet relief. The big man in the flashy suit moved in front of me and kneeled down. He looked at me from under heavy brows and the corners of his lips twitched as I watched him warily. He cut my ankles free with the same precision and efficiency that he had used to release my hands and gave me a little wink that no one else could see.

"I've never had to tie a woman up in order to get what I wanted from her. Sure, I've had a couple beg me to restrain them, but I would say this is overkill." Before I could form a thought or ask him what he was doing, he slid the handle of his switchblade into my hand and curled my fingers around it. In a voice that was so low only I could hear him, he muttered, "It's about to get messy in here, babe. Brace yourself the best you can. Hold onto that and run the minute you have a clear shot at the door."

"I brought you here to get the information I need, not to lecture my men. Your way of extracting the truth might not leave marks, but it is no less violent." The man spoke like this was just another business transaction, and it made my skin crawl when I realized that's exactly what it was. My fingers tightened on the knife as the man with the beard climbed to his feet and put his back to me.

He was taking a big risk. I could easily slip that razor-sharp blade right between his ribs and try and fight my way free while he bled out.

"I told you. She was supposed to be untouched and unharmed. I can't do what I do effectively if your careless thugs already damaged the parts of her that I need to make her talk. I work with the precision of a surgeon. You went in on her like a steamroller."

The Mayor stiffened and crossed his arms over his chest. I could tell he was unhappy and impatient with the man who had armed me. He wasn't expecting pushback or concern about my condition. He wasn't used to anyone defying him, not even a hired killer.

"I wouldn't think I need to remind you just how much I paid for you to be here." He was condescending and haughty. It was almost as if what he paid this man to do to me was distasteful, as if he found the entire thing unsavory even though he was the mastermind behind it all. I would never have known who he was if he hadn't touched his stepdaughter.

"Yeah, I am intimately acquainted with the going rate for torture and punishment. Cruelty has never come cheap. I gotta tell you, it's not enough. It can never be enough."

The cop took a step forward and the lawyer-looking guy shook his head and shifted nervously. Goddard blinked rapidly and opened his mouth like he was going to say something when suddenly, the entire world turned upside down.

Everyone let out a startled sound as the metal container jerked and lurched with an ear-splitting noise. The concrete below the metal wailed in protest as something heavy and hard hit the outside with enough force to send the entire container careening to the side. The light swung wildly from the ceiling. The chair went flying. The dirty cop was flung sideways as the Mayor and the skinny, older man tumbled over one another. The guy with the beard, my savior and current hero, was also tossed heavily through the air. I was thrown around like a rag doll. My banged-up body protesting when the container finally stopped moving and rested on its rusted side. The single light had long since gone out and everything was pitch black. My head was bleeding even more now and the ringing between my ears was loud enough to drown out any other sound.

There was shouting coming from somewhere outside the container and loud pops that were likely gunshots. I wasn't sure what was going on, but I could see a faint light at the end of the tunnel and I was going to run for it. Today was not the day I was going to die.

Clutching the switchblade in my hand, I scrambled to my feet and took off for the far end of the container toward the door. I had no idea if it opened from the inside or not, but I was about to find out.

The Mayor was pointing at me and shouting from where he was lying half under the older man who had helped keep me captive. I was scrambling, slipping and sliding my way to the door, when I was tackled from behind. I knew those hands and I fucking hated them. I didn't even pause before taking the knife and driving it right into the back of one of those grabbing, clutching hands. I heard the cop scream and swear and I took a sick kind of satisfaction in the pain I caused. He let me go like I was made of fire, and in that moment, I wished I could burn him to nothing more than ash.

There was a grunt and the sound of fists hitting flesh, but I didn't stop to see who was fighting whom. All I cared about was getting free. I would throw myself against the door over and over again until I got through or died trying. There was as much yelling and noise happening on the inside of the metal shipping container as there was on the outside. Voices were yelling and there was a distinct pop that rattled off the walls. Someone had a gun and they had fired it at either me or the bearded man who had come to rescue me. I didn't want him to die. I owed him my life, but his heroics wouldn't be worth anything if neither one of us made it out of this oversized tin can.

Head down and frantically feeling my way in the dark, fingers scraping across rough metal and cutting open on unseen hazards, I managed to make it to the sideways door. There was still a commotion going on behind me, and it was technically three against one, but my money was on the guy with the beard. He looked like he could handle himself, and I hoped against hope he could handle the dirty cop and the Mayor, as well.

I tried to find my way out. I pulled and tugged. I pounded and screamed. I couldn't find any kind of lever or latch, and I wasn't sure anyone could hear me on the outside. It sounded like I was banging on the inside of a steel drum; the noise was making my head pound. I was collecting my breath to keep screaming my damn head off but I let it go in a rush when the cock-eyed door suddenly wrenched open. I tumbled out ungracefully and not sure if I was falling into the arms of the enemy or not.

Luckily, as soon as everything stopped spinning and the world finally ended up the right way, I recognized the behemoth of a man who caught me before I landed face first on the concrete. Another bruiser with dark hair, haunted eyes, and a wicked scar that indicated he'd angered some very bad people in his time. Noah Booker worked for Nassir and was no doubt behind the chaos that was currently taking place on the docks. I could see bodies on the ground. I could see blood and spent bullets. I lived a rough life, but this was all new to me, and I could swear I smelled death lingering in the air all around me.

"I got you." His voice was nothing more than a harsh growl.

I let him haul me to my feet and cast a look at the overturned container. "The guy with the beard is still in there. Someone has a gun." I didn't know if they were friends or maybe coworkers of some kind, but I thought he might want to know.

He gave his dark head a shake and the scar that bisected one entire side of his face twitched as he frowned.

"He's on his own. If he makes it out of there in one piece, he gets his life back. He's got a lot on the line so don't worry about him. He's really fucking hard to kill, believe me. Worry about you."

It was good advice and I was going to take it. I pulled my arm free of his hold and shook my head. "Who sent you? Why are you here? Why did you do all of this?" I swept an arm out to indicate the carnage he was walking through like it was a field of flowers. "How did you know where I was?"

He looked like he wanted to strangle me. Admittedly, it wasn't the best time for twenty questions, but I'd had enough of being jerked around and manhandled. I wanted control back. I wanted my power back.

"I go where Nassir tells me to go and I do whatever he needs done." It was said blandly, like laying waste to an entire armed security detail was all in a day's work.

"Why would Nassir care about me? How did he even know the Mayor snatched me up off the street?" I'd met Nassir one time, completely unwillingly on my part. He made it clear he had no use for me beyond the information he wanted at the time, and I couldn't get away from him and his ostentatious office fast enough.

The brute of a man who had just pulled me from certain death cocked his head to the side and considered me silently. His lips twitched and that scar pulled in a way that was oddly endearing. "How do you think Nassir knew you were missing? Who do you know who would be willing to sign his life away in order to get you back?"

I blinked up at him like an owl, sure the gash in my head and the lack of food for the last couple weeks had finally gotten to me. "Stark?" The word squeaked out and once again, the world seemed to spin sickeningly around me.

I asked him for help and he told me no.

It couldn't be.

"The boy genius sent us after you and told us not to come back if you weren't with us. I've never seen him so worked up about anything. Minus the time you cleaned him out. I wasn't sure he knew how to react like a normal human when shit went down."

I blinked again and started to tilt forward. Everything was going fuzzy on the edges and I could hardly hear him over the rushing in my ears. I wasn't sure why I could no longer stand, or why, after everything I'd just been through, it was the knowledge that Snowden Stark did indeed give a shit if I lived or died that took me out.

The last thing I saw was the big, dark man move toward me, swearing and muttering my name, as everything went black.

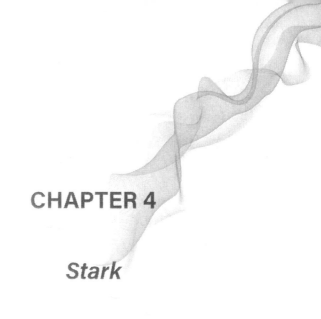

CHAPTER 4

Stark

S HE LOOKED SO SMALL and pale lying against the black sheets that covered Noah Booker's bed. I knew it was irrational and unwarranted to be pissed off at the fact she was unconscious in his bed and not mine, but everything inside of me was struggling against the need to pick her up and carry her off. That's why I hated emotions and feelings. There was no logic in any of it. None of it made any sense.

Booker's place was close to the docks, practically sitting on the water, so it was an obvious choice to bring Noe here when she blacked out on him. It was written on her face and across her skin that the last couple of weeks had not been kind to her. The doctor Nassir blackmailed in order to have him on call had assured both Booker and myself that her wounds were superficial. She had a mild concussion, was extremely dehydrated, and malnourished. Her shoulder was sprained and the cuts at her wrists were infected. She had a couple of bruised ribs and an assortment of injuries that covered her body from head to toe. The physician had asked if we wanted him to do a sexual assault examination, but I couldn't bear the idea of making that call without asking her permission first. She'd been stripped of so much; I couldn't be the guy who took even more from her when she had no voice.

The doctor warned that the longer Noe waited, the worse the consequences could be if she had been assaulted, and it turned my stomach. I wanted to touch her, to smooth her dirty hair back into some semblance of order, and rub my fingers over the purple and blue bruises that covered the entire left side of her face. I wanted to trace the outline of her full but battered and chapped lips. I wanted to crawl up next to her in Booker's black bed and hold her while I promised her that nothing and no one would ever hurt her again.

I didn't do any of it because none of it made any sense. She was safe now and Goddard wasn't going to get anywhere near her again. The guilt that had been eating me alive should have eased, releasing its hold on me, but I was still caught up in the clutches of emotion. There was no reason for me to feel this way, or feel anything other than relief, but I was. I hated that I couldn't bury those foreign feelings with all the other ones I'd fought to bury over the years.

Instead, I paced back and forth at the end of the bed like a caged animal while Booker showed the doctor out and paid him his fee. When he came back to the bedroom, he had changed out of the long-sleeved black thermal he had worn to the docks into a faded band t-shirt that was torn at the collar and had a hole on the side. Booker was usually dressed to the nines like all the guys on Nassir's payroll. I couldn't remember a time when I saw him in anything other than Armani or Tom Ford. Dressed down, with exhaustion and irritation pulling at his normally stony face, he looked more human and a lot older than he typically did. Bullets didn't stop the man, so most of us believed he was invincible. Apparently not.

He dragged a hand over his frown and absently rubbed his thumb along the raised skin of his scar where it cut into the corner of his upper lip. Booker never mentioned where the mark came from and I wasn't sure anyone but Karsen Carter had ever asked. It was a mystery as to whether he filled the pretty teenager in, but if anyone was going to pry the big man's secrets out of him, it was going to be the leggy but too-young blonde. She was the only person, the only thing, that had ever made Noah Booker soft, and again I wondered what had happened to send her running away from him and her home. She'd been persistent and he'd been kind to her and only her. Their dynamic had changed, and I would have liked to know the reason *why* things happened the way they did.

"I know you guys said no cops, but I need to call Titus and let him know one of the goons that had her was on the job," He sounded as tired as he looked, and I wasn't sure if it was from the activities that transpired tonight or the fact that shit like this was commonplace in his life. He'd been shot twice in the short time I'd known him, and I couldn't even begin to count on both my hands the number of times he'd shot someone else.

"How do you know he was a cop? Was he in uniform?" Unable to stand the distance between me and the unconscious girl any longer, I lowered myself to the edge of the bed and lifted her limp hand into my own. Her fingernails were trashed. Her knuckles were split open and crusted over with scabs and dried blood. She had calluses on the pads of her fingers and on her palm. She was a fighter. There was no doubt about it.

I hated the fact that she had to fight at all.

Protective and possessive instincts coiled around my gut and rage felt like it was going to choke me. I was so used to being cold and numb, I didn't know what to do with the fire that was licking at my insides.

"I saw him take her out of the trunk when they got to the docks. He moved like a cop. Not the kind who is there to actually protect and serve, but the kind who pulls you over for no reason and slaps cuffs on you to prove a point. I was locked up for a lot of years, boy genius. I know what a dirty cop looks like. He had a busted-up nose and stitches on the side of his face. Should be pretty easy for Titus to identify him."

Titus King was Bax's half-brother and the only law enforcement officer in the entire city any of us slightly trusted. He was one of the few men the Point hadn't tainted. He was a good guy, trying to do right by the people in our city, and he wouldn't hesitate to throw Goddard's dirty cop under the bus. But I didn't want anyone going after the Mayor. His sadistic ass was all mine.

"Do you think they made it out of the container after you hit it with the truck?" That had been my idea. Nassir was only sending in Booker and Benny to get Noe out, but I didn't think it was enough fire power. Since he refused to let me go, even siccing Chuck on me as a babysitter until the job was done, I made Benny go over the plan with me no less than a hundred times until I came up with a better one. Knocking the container sideways with one of the big semi-trucks that littered the area would give Benny the time he needed to get Noe out and distract the outside security detail enough that Booker could do his thing. It was a risk because the people inside the container—including Noe and Benny—might have ended up injured when the thing flipped, but the odds of them making it out were much higher than if Benny tried to take on everyone on his own.

"If Benny made it out, we won't hear from him again. That was the deal he made with Nassir. He would get your girl and then disappear, so he can go and live happily ever after with his. As for the rest of them," he shrugged, "I guess we'll find out soon enough. Your girl said someone had a gun, so if they were shooting at Benny, he would do whatever he could to make sure they stopped. He's not about to catch a bullet for any of us. I know you want that asshole alive for your own reasons, but honestly, it's better if Benny popped him."

It was better, but it wasn't what I wanted. A bullet between the eyes was way too easy for a guy like Goddard. People would bemoan how bad the Point had become, how Goddard had been a staunch supporter of crime prevention measures. He would die a martyr and a legend. I couldn't stand the thought of that. I wanted who Goddard was, who he really was, out in the open. I wanted his mansion doors flung wide open and every skeleton inside the walls exposed and thrown out on the perfectly manicured lawn for the entire world to see. I hated people who hid behind the law. I hated when men in any position of power got off on using their elevated status to jerk the helpless and hopeless around. Death wasn't the answer. Devastation was.

I closed my eyes and squeezed the cold, still hand that was clasped in mine. Failure weighed heavy on my shoulders and fury lit up my blood like popping and sizzling firecrackers.

"When do we ever end up with anything that's better for us?" That wasn't how the Point worked. That wasn't how we worked.

Booker grunted and I felt him move behind me. "It happens. It doesn't seem like *better* should be able to find a foothold in this place, but despite all odds, it does."

I lifted my head and looked at him over my shoulder. He was staring at the far wall, his thoughts obviously a million miles away from this room.

"And sometimes we get our hands on better and we don't know what to do with it or how to take care of it, so we ruin it."

He shifted his gaze back to me and then let it drift over the still form in his bed. He gave a stiff nod and pushed off the wall. "Sometimes better is better off without this place and the people in it." In that moment, I wasn't sure if he was talking about the situation with Noe or something that had nothing to do with Goddard's proclivities toward his stepdaughter. At the door, he paused and quickly switched the subject to something less soul wrenching and about as normal as anything ever got in the Point, "I'm gonna go order a pizza and pour myself a drink. You want anything?"

I shook my head, unwilling to leave Noe alone until she opened her eyes. "I'm good."

Booker snorted, "No, you're not, and you aren't going to do your girl any good if you end up flat on your face, boy genius. If Goddard made it out alive, this is just the beginning. He's going to come after you and your girl with everything he's got."

I was going to tell him that was exactly what I wanted. It was much better to play offense with guys like Goddard than it was to be forced into a defensive position. I wanted him to come after me. Guys like him thought prestige and money equaled ultimate power, but they had no idea that information was the ultimate weapon in today's wars. I didn't get a chance to reply, because a weak and barely audible, "I'm not his girl. Not anyone's girl," drifted up from the cocoon of black covers.

Noe's fingers twitched in my hold so I forced myself to gently place her hand back on the bed. Booker made his way over and took a spot next to me as we both gazed down at the girl I was willing to rip the world apart for. This was a lot to process for a guy who was used to being numb.

She blinked up at both of us, licked her lips, and let her eyes rove around the very masculine and darkly decorated loft. "Can I get a glass of water? My mouth feels like it's full of cotton."

Booker growled an agreement and disappeared out the door behind me. I couldn't pull my gaze away from her midnight-colored one. I was so glad she was awake. So glad she was here right now and not in the ground. Letting out a sigh that felt like it escaped from the very bottom of my soul, I leaned forward and let my head hit the edge of the bed. My hands curled into fists where they rested on top of my thighs and I could feel some of the tension that had been coiled tightly at the base of my neck release. Maybe now that she was awake, I could put a lid back on everything that was threatening to erupt out of me. I needed my control back. I needed my reason and rationale pushed to the forefront so I could help her. I didn't have the time or luxury to work my way through everything else.

"You're awake." For a guy who usually had no tolerance for asinine observations, it was all I could think of to say. I owed her an apology. I owed her so much more, but I figured it could wait until she had her strength back and could tell me to shove it.

"Appears so. I don't remember passing out. Where am I?" The bed moved as she tried to push herself up into a sitting position. I lifted my head just in time to see a wince of pain tug her delicate features into a fierce frown.

I reached out to help her and bit back a litany of swear words when she flinched away from me and held up a hand in warning not to touch her. I couldn't blame her. I deserved that, but it still stung. "You're at Booker's place. He lives right by the docks. This place is a fortress since Race Hartman lives a few floors up with his woman. It was close when you passed out, and since it's practically impenetrable, it seemed like the best option at the time." I pulled my glasses off my face and rubbed my eyes hard enough to cause double vision for a second. "We had a doctor come and check you out, Noe. He said everything that's wrong with you will heal with time and care."

She dipped her chin and looked at her abused wrists and hands. "I figured none of it was bad enough to kill me. The Mayor wanted me alive so I could tell him where Julia and the baby are."

I blew out a breath and put my glasses back on so that she was in focus when I quietly asked her, "Do you need the doc to come back and do a sexual assault exam? I couldn't give him the go ahead when you were knocked out. That felt like something you should consent to."

She lifted a dark eyebrow in my direction and grimaced at the motion. She lifted her fingers to her forehead and closed her eyes. "He doesn't need to come back."

I gritted my teeth and pushed to my feet so I could continue my pacing. I put a hand to the back of my neck and rubbed at the stiffness that still lingered there, wanting clarification but dreading the rationale of why she didn't want the doctor to return. "Do you not need him to come back because nothing happened, or because you don't want anyone to know what went down while you were being held captive?"

God, I hoped it was the first, but if it was the second, I was going to respect her wishes and let the subject drop. Noe only gave what she wanted someone else to have. Nothing more, nothing less.

She sighed and rolled her eyes so that she was looking up at the ceiling, "Nothing happened, Stark. One of the guys, the cop who grabbed me from your neighborhood, had busy hands, but that's it. I made it clear if any of them forced themselves on me, I would make the girl disappear. They had no idea that I don't know where she is."

I stopped moving long enough to stare at her in a mixture of shock and awe. "You don't know where she is?"

She shook her head slightly, her colorful hair falling into her dark eyes. "I never know. It's safer that way. I use recording software and a dictation program that can pick out keywords and form an intelligent response from a prompt. I was never checking in with Julia, but they didn't know that."

Smart. She was so fucking smart. It made something heavy throb in the center of my chest and the fit of my jeans a little bit tighter. Biting back a hum of appreciation at her brilliance and boldness, I plowed my fingers through my hair and looked at her through the glass that covered my eyes. Lenses were made to bring things into sharp focus when, in reality, her brilliance and overwhelming calm clarified things better than any refractive lens could.

"I should have offered to help." The words were wrenched out of me, broken and twisted with remorse. I was so tired of making mistakes. I was supposed to be a genius, brilliant, and above basic human pitfalls, but they kept happening. I kept tripping over the right thing like I couldn't even see it.

She made a strangled noise low in her throat and lowered her inky lashes so that her eyes and her secrets were hidden from my prying gaze. "You don't know me. We aren't friends. I stole your stuff and don't feel even slightly bad about it. You were my last resort, Snowden. I was disappointed but not surprised you sent me on my way. People don't like to get involved."

I fought a reaction to her use of my real name and shook my head at her. "No one calls me that."

"Snowden? It's your name, isn't it?" She lifted both her eyebrows this time then hissed out a breath between her teeth when it obviously caused her some serious discomfort. She rubbed her fingers across the bridge of her nose and continued to watch me.

"It is, but it's stupid. Snowden Stark sounds like a character straight out of *Game of Thrones*. I've always been Stark." It was too flashy, too whimsical for a guy who had nothing human and living on the inside.

"I like Snowden. Snow and Noe. We rhyme." Her mouth kicked up in a lopsided grin and I could see that her jet-colored eyes were a little glassy and slightly out of focus.

"You have a concussion. You won't think our names sound that cute together once your head is healed up." I doubted she was going to want any part of her attached to any part of me once she was back in fighting form.

Booker came back with a big glass of water and a couple of painkillers that she gladly took. She gazed up at the big man with genuine gratitude as she told him softly, "Thank you for getting me out of there and bringing me somewhere safe."

Booker shrugged one of his massive shoulders and slapped me on the back. "Thank the boy genius. It was his plan and his insistence that we get you out. I only do the heavy lifting and the point and shoot. Are you hungry? I was gonna order pizza."

She put a hand over her stomach as it growled her response. "I guess so. Once I get cleaned up and the room stops spinning, I'll get out of your hair. You don't want me here if Goddard made it out of that showdown alive."

Booker waved her off and pulled a cell phone out of his back pocket. "Don't rush it. This is as good a place as any for you to get back on your feet. No one gets in or out without security's permission, and that includes Goddard. In fact, there's an empty unit across the hall. You might want to see if Race is up for letting you use it as a hideout until you have a handle on this situation."

She muttered, "I can't afford that," at the exact same time I agreed, "That's a great idea."

He let out a whistle and slipped out of the room, his phone pressed to his ear.

Noe and I stared at each other, her eyes searching and mine assessing. She sighed and broke eye contact. "I asked for your help, Stark. Not for you to take care of me. I've been on my own for a long time. The only person I ever count on to show up when I need something is me."

I inclined my chin at her to silently let her know that was probably a smart move on her part. Nothing and no one in the Point was very reliable.

"You need to be somewhere safe until we figure out what players remain in the game. No one will look for you here and Race will let me have the apartment for free. He still owes me from when I helped him figure out someone was digitally spying on his girlfriend."

"And if Goddard is still out there? He's not going to let this slide. He still wants the girl and he's going to want payback for the way things went down tonight."

I grunted and turned my back on her so she couldn't see the rage and uncontrollable hunger for revenge that overtook me. "Goddard isn't your problem anymore. He never should have been your problem in the first place. You worry about getting better. I'll take care of the rest." Like I should have when she showed up on my doorstep.

"Stark?" Her tone was questioning and curious but I didn't turn around.

"I'll have Booker bring up something for you to eat and then, if you're up to it, I'll help you get cleaned up. I can't look at that blood all over you anymore. It makes me want to break things." I had no idea what to do with that. I wasn't the guy who breathed fire and dreamed about revenge. But she turned me into him. In that moment, I realized that my name and actions were more reminiscent of a *Game of Thrones* character than I wanted to truly admit. Revenge and justice being the driving forces behind everything I was doing right now.

She called my name again as I stalked out of the room, beyond confused and so grateful she was alert and awake that I almost fell over. But I never turned around. I left my back to her. The irony not lost on me that turning my back on her was exactly what brought me to this moment.

She wanted my help . . . well, she had it . . . and whatever was left of my broken parts that I could offer her.

CHAPTER 5

Noe

I WAS TIRED AND my head throbbed in time with my heartbeat every time I closed my eyes. The bed with the black sheets and comforter was a far sight cleaner and far more luxurious than the linens from the no-tell-motel. Who would have thought a guy like Noah Booker in all his scarred, glowering fierceness was a guy who gave a shit about thread counts?

All the men who made the Point what it was had things about them I found surprising. I never would have guessed Nassir Gates would get involved in something that he had zero interest in, which meant he *did* have an interest: keeping Stark happy and making sure his tech skills weren't compromised because he was distracted by my abduction. If I had to wager a guess, I would bet that Nassir has a personal investment in helping Stark, as well. I was pretty sure the slick and smooth man they called the Devil was fond of Stark. And everyone knew Nassir didn't have a fondness for many. I noticed it that day when I'd been summoned to his office.

I'd only been around Chuck, the head of Nassir's security, for a brief minute. I remembered him from the bad old days when he was on the streets doing the former crime boss's bidding. Even then, he always had a way about him. He was a good man caught up in some bad things. His lifestyle bothered him. The choices he had to make clearly sat heavy on his strong shoulders. Now that the old boss was gone and Nassir sat on his torched throne, Chuck seemed at peace. He still worked for men who did bad things, sometimes for the right reasons, but more often because that was the only way things went down in the Point. He treated Nassir more like a rebellious son than as his boss. The same went for Race, Bax, and Booker. The man had adopted an entire flock of black sheep and it appeared he couldn't be prouder of himself or them. They were the fibers that held this city—and the people in it—together.

I was also surprised at Booker's willingness to give up his bed to me, knowing exactly what kind of wolves were outside my door. The threat didn't seem to faze him at all, and neither had risking his neck to save a woman who was a complete stranger. I would never go so far as to call any of these men altruistic or moralistic, but there was no denying they all had their own kind of honor and thread of dignity that ran fast and deep. They didn't play by the regular rules that society laid out, but the ones they did play by, they followed to keep the ones they considered their own safe.

Which brought my traitorous thoughts back around to Snowden Stark. His name did sound like something out of *Game of Thrones,* but it also suited him. Equal parts soft and hard. Both unusual and in your face. It would take a guy built like Stark to both physically and mentally withstand the childhood taunting that was bound to come with a name like Snowden. I couldn't picture him as a kid or as a teenager. He was far too serious and way too intense for any vestiges of youth to remain. His cold eyes were aged way beyond his actual years, and his entire demeanor screamed he wasn't the kind of guy who was ever carefree and happy-go-lucky.

When he told me he couldn't stand to see the dried blood that was streaked across my face, caked on my arms and hands, and crusted on my chin and neck, he really meant he couldn't *stand it*. The sight made his hands curl into fists, the corner of his eye twitched behind his glasses, and his entire body vibrated with something that was both scary and reassuring. I'd heard Booker call me *'his girl'* and waited for Stark to deny that we were anything to each other. When he hadn't, it made me shiver under the pain that was coursing through my body, and the confusion was turning my brain inside out. I was the one to set the other man straight, we weren't anything to each other besides an annoyance, but the look in Stark's eyes when I finally managed to look up at him was anything but annoyed. There was so much relief and regret in that steely gaze that it stole my breath for a second.

He hadn't helped me when I needed him and now he looked at me like he was never going to let me out of his sight again.

I was relieved when he walked out of the room a couple of minutes ago, allowing me to gather my wits and take inventory of the situation. I tried to move my arms and my legs. Both responded to the command sluggishly with a fair amount of protest. My entire body felt like a giant, tender bruise. I'd taken a couple good hits when the container flipped over and sent me flying. My head felt like it was on fire, burning from the inside out. I probed at the gash that was now sporting a neat row of tiny metal staples. It hurt, but not as bad as my shoulders did when I contorted to reach the wound. The muscles, bones, and everything in-between were still protesting from being locked in an awkward, uncomfortable position for days on end. The rush of blood to those sensitive areas had me groaning and shifting in agitation under the covers that had fallen down around my waist.

The air felt like it got heavier when Booker entered the room. There was something about men like him, men cut from the same fabric and sewn together with the experiences that came from living in the Point. They made the space around them charged and come alive with something electric and dangerous. The warning that pulsed around them tended to reach a person before the actual man was within touching distance. It was powerful and it was impressive. I also found it reassuring.

The dark-haired man was holding a paper plate that had a giant slice of pizza hanging over the edges and some kind of colored sports drink. He let his gaze slide over me, seemingly pleased with the fact that I was sitting up and still alive.

"The doc said you need electrolytes and probably some vitamins to get you back up to fighting weight. He mentioned it didn't look like you'd had much to eat in the last few days."

I groaned as the scent of the food in his hand hit my nose. My mouth started to water and my stomach made a noise so loud that Booker obviously heard it from across the room. His lopsided grin pulled at his mouth again and I realized he was actually an alarmingly attractive man underneath the intimidation that surrounded him.

"They got me stuff out of the vending machine at the motel once a day. They usually visited in the morning, worked me over the best they could for information and fed me Doritos or Funyuns. They would come back late at night so I was off balance and sometimes they would give me a soda or juice." I gratefully took the plate and sighed when the warmth hit my fingers. I wondered if he would mind if I shoved my face directly into the greasy melted cheese that covered the top.

"If they left you alone, how come you couldn't find a way out of the room? Boy genius seems to think your brain is almost as big as his." Booker slumped down in the seat next to the bed that had been holding Stark's bulk until he ran away from me.

I lifted an eyebrow and blew on the edge of the pizza before sinking my teeth in. I didn't bother to hold back a groan as the spicy tomato sauce hit my tongue. I closed my eyes and savored the bite as if I was eating my last meal.

"I did try. Bars on the windows and no one cared when I broke the glass. The door had a padlock on the outside and the people in the room next to mine were screaming even louder than I was." I took another bite and looked at him over the cheese and crust. "I managed to get the dirty cop in the balls during one visit when he came alone. I was almost to the door. I could see escape, but he caught my ankle and pulled me to the ground. That was the day he thought he could touch me without my permission."

Booker made a noise low in his throat that sounded like a growl, "That the same day you ripped a piece out of his face?"

I nodded and cracked open the drink he brought me, swallowing half of it before adding, "And rearranged his nose." That was also the day my hands ended up tied behind my back, but I didn't share that.

Booker pushed up to his feet and ran a hand over his face. "You might want to keep that part of the story to yourself if Stark starts asking about what happened. He doesn't do well when women get hurt." He let out a bark of laughter that held no humor in it. "None of us do. Stark's strength is his ability to detach and look at a situation coolly and calmly from any angle. The man is a machine, and when something causes a short circuit in his wiring," he shook his head. "That isn't gonna be good for anyone."

"Like I said, I'm not his. I don't belong to anyone. I can take care of myself. I'm no one's responsibility, and what happened to me happened because of the choices I made." Except now, I wasn't so sure how good I was going to be at taking care of myself. I wouldn't be here right now if it wasn't for this man and the one in the other room. "I asked for Stark's help because I didn't have any other choice."

There was a noise from the top of the stairs near the entrance of the bedroom. Stark was standing there watching the two of us through narrowed eyes. There was a glint on his glasses that kept the sharpness of the gray and blue hidden. He cleared his throat and lifted his chin, "I wanted to see if you needed anything, and if you were ready to clean yourself up."

He shifted something in his hands; I gasped and practically fell on my face when I lurched to the side of the bed, reaching for the worn and tattered camo backpack he held. "You have my bag," the words whispered out, and I despised the fact that hot moisture pushed at the back of my eyes. I was used to having nothing.

Nothing to weigh me down.

Nothing to trip over and stub my toe on.

Nothing to keep tidy and neat.

Nothing I would miss if it was suddenly taken from me.

Nothing that I cared about.

The handful of things that did matter were in the bag that Stark was holding like it was made of glass. In this instant, Stark was giving me everything.

I got to the edge of the bed and swung out my legs, belatedly realizing that somewhere along the way, someone had stripped me out of the clothes I'd been wearing for weeks. Now, I was in a soft cotton t-shirt that was way too big and a pair of sweatpants that swallowed my entire lower half in fabric. I didn't want to think about either of these men seeing me naked while I was unconscious, so I foolishly pushed to my feet and tried to take a step toward Stark and my stuff. Immediately, the room tilted and my vision went blurry around the edges. I gasped and felt my knees start to tremble.

I put a hand out to catch myself on the mattress but there was no need. Hard hands caught me around my upper arms and I was softly lowered down to the rumpled bedding. Booker was closer so I looked up to thank him, but it was Stark's stormy gaze that met mine. His mouth was pulled into a tight line as he picked up the backpack from the floor where it had fallen when he caught me. He set it on the bed next to me and looked me over with a tick in his cheek and his back teeth visibly clenched.

"I don't think you're gonna make it to the bathroom. I'll get a washcloth and a bowl of water and undo what damage I can while you lie here." He took a step back, hands clenched at his sides as he looked down to where Booker was watching us both with a speculative gleam in his eyes.

"You don't need to do that. I'm sure I'll be back on my feet in the morning. Cleaning up can wait until then." I really didn't want his hands anywhere near me. My walls had taken a beating lately and I needed time to rebuild them.

Apparently, I was wrong and it couldn't wait because Stark grunted and asked Booker in a clipped tone, "You wanna show me where to get the shit I need to clean that dried blood off of her?"

I could have sworn Booker chuckled, but he didn't really seem like the chuckling type. It was too mundane, too normal for a guy who considered it blasé to describe his occupation as anything more than point and shoot. He climbed out of the chair, picked up the plate and the empty plastic bottle from the bed and nodded.

"Follow me, boy genius."

Stark gave me a look that I was certain was some kind of warning, but I couldn't figure out what it was for. They'd spent every second since I'd opened my eyes telling me I was safe, so I wasn't sure what he was trying to tell me to look out for.

Tired and full, I tugged the backpack onto my lap and wasn't ashamed to give the battered, ugly thing an actual hug. I didn't know how he found it, or how he knew it was mine, but I was so happy he'd instinctively known how important it was. He really was a boy genius.

"You kept one of my computers."

I jolted at the dry statement. He was back with a black washcloth, a towel, and a bowl of water that had a plume of steam rising from it. He walked carefully across the room so as not to spill the water. Everything he did was deliberate and careful.

"You weren't supposed to know that." I told him I pawned them all. It was never a good idea to keep something worth that kind of money on you when you were sleeping on the street.

"Why didn't you pawn it? Why didn't you take the money from the rest of the stuff you stole and get yourself a place to stay? Hell, I know you don't make fake IDs for the Hill kids for free. You have the means to get yourself off the streets, so why don't you? You can't tell me you actually like being homeless." He sounded incredulous and confused. I couldn't blame him. Not many people, even people from the Point, knew what it was like when things were so bad at home that having nothing was preferable.

"People can find you when you have a fixed address." I set the backpack to the side and held out my hands when he asked to see my wrists. He made a strangled noise low in his throat at the sight of the broken, swollen skin but didn't say anything else. "When you have a place, you tend to fill it with stuff, and when it's time to move, time to hide, stuff gets in the way. I don't want to be tied down to anyone or anything."

"So, sleeping on the streets is preferable to being tied down?" He wouldn't understand, even though I could see the wheels in his head turning as he tried.

I winced and tried to pull away when the first sting of the water fell on my wound. I blamed it on the pain when I blurted out, "It's preferable to my family finding me and trying to force me to go back home." I groaned when he moved onto the other wrist and squeezed my eyes shut, even though he was moving slowly and being far gentler than a man his size should be able to. "And I haven't always slept on the street. At one point, I slept in my car. Sometimes, I crash with friends for a few days. The Point has a couple of really well-funded women's shelters that are surprisingly safe and accessible. I don't like to be predictable, which you very well know. That's why you couldn't find me when Nassir sent you after me."

He didn't say anything but his fingers were light and his touch was delicate as he rubbed some kind of oily ointment against the torn skin. Our eyes met as he dipped the corner of the washcloth into the tepid water and brought it up to my face. He swiped it over my chin and across my mouth. I couldn't hold back a gasp when I felt the rough pad of his thumb trace the damp trail left by the dark cloth across my lower lip. I thought I might have imagined it, but then he moved and traced the upper bow, following the tiny dip in my top lip perfectly.

"You know I'm going to ask." His tone was gruff, and his eyes were sharp on mine behind his glasses. Of course, he would ask. He needed to understand just as much as I did. "Why don't you want your family to find you, Noe?"

His dangerous thumb brushed across my bruised cheek and down along the edge of my jaw. My skin throbbed in an altogether alarming way every place his fingers touched. I'd never been so aware of each breath I took, each heartbeat that pounded in my ears. I'd never been so acutely mindful of another person before. I felt like I was memorizing every line of gray and silver striation in his irises, like I was counting each of his dark eyelashes and all the swirls of ink that covered the side of his neck and hollow of his throat. My nostrils flared when he leaned even closer, and I was assaulted with the faint hint of his cologne. Something fresh and clean with a hint of pine. It was masculine without being overwhelmingly so.

He asked about my family and that was enough to act as a bucket of cold water on my suddenly buzzing libido. "Seems odd that a twenty-six-year-old woman should be scared shitless of her family, doesn't it?"

One of his dark eyebrows lifted and the washcloth made its way down the side of my neck. "You don't look like you're twenty-six. You don't look a day over eighteen."

I got that a lot. It was a mixture of my Korean heritage and my size. People always assumed I was much younger than I actually was. This benefited me when I was on the streets. It made the cops rousting the runaways go easy on me and made everyone underestimate my particular skill set. No one knew they were looking for a grown woman when they came looking for me, so it made staying out of sight easier if I wanted.

"Old enough to know better about most things, still young enough to fuck all those things up over and over again." His lips twitched in a reluctant grin, and it made him look almost approachable. I sighed and turned so my back was to him when he asked me to do so. Maybe because I didn't have those intense eyes of his watching me that I managed to choke out, "I was adopted."

The scratch of the washcloth on the back of my neck stilled for a moment, but he didn't say anything as his hand lifted my hair so he could get off all the blood that was keeping several longer strands stuck to my skin.

"Anything you've heard about families not wanting daughters in Asian countries is true. My parents already had one girl, and when I made an appearance, they decided they were plenty happy with the little girl they already had and didn't want to bother with another one. I ended up in an orphanage for girls outside of Seoul. That's in South Korea."

Stark snorted from where he was hovering behind me, and I closed my eyes as I felt him carefully running his damp fingers through my gross hair. "I know where Seoul is, Noe."

I cleared my throat and crossed my arms over my chest. "Yeah, you would. Sometimes it feels like there isn't anywhere else in the world besides the Point. Like nothing outside of here is real. Anyway, I was adopted by a family from the Hill when I was six. I didn't speak any English, had never been anywhere besides the orphanage, had never really seen a white person before. It was all terrifying. I felt like a little doll they dressed up and toted around when they came to Korea to finalize the adoption. I cried so hard on the plane to the States I made myself sick. Mr. and Mrs. Cartwright were appalled and apologized for my behavior endlessly. I didn't know what they were saying, but I could tell they were disappointed. I was so sure they were going to turn the plane around and take me back. I honestly wanted them to, even though the orphanage was overcrowded and underfunded. It was what I knew, and everyone there looked just like I did."

I sighed and closed my eyes as his fingers worked against my scalp. He was good at that. I'd like him to do it when he wasn't trying to pick chunks of dried blood out of my hair.

"The Cartwrights. June and Bradley. They seemed to be nice people. They'd been trying for another kid for a long time with no luck. She really, really wanted a little girl. I'm not sure how they ended up looking at foreign adoptions, but they did and found me. It was a good life for a while. They didn't have a ton of money, but it was enough. I never worried about being hungry or cold. They put me in special classes so I could learn English, and once I picked that up, it was clear I was pretty gifted. They never balked at giving me the kind of education I needed."

He grunted behind me and I felt his fingers work against the base of my skull. It pulled a groan out of me and loosened some of the pressure and pain that had my brain in a stranglehold since I opened my eyes.

"Something went wrong." It wasn't a question. He was smart enough to know a girl didn't give up a sweet deal like that without a very good reason.

"Went way wrong," I snorted and tried to fight back the way those memories made my skin crawl. "June and Bradley had a son who was four years older than me . . . Aaron." I felt the air stir dangerously behind me and I wanted to warn him that he hadn't heard anything yet. "When I was little, he acted like I didn't exist. Classic only child syndrome. He never liked that he had to share his parents, or their time and energy, with me. He was resentful and mean, but the Cartwrights always believed he would grow out of it when he was older. He did, but what he grew into was something much worse."

I shivered and pulled my legs up so I could hug them and rest my cheek on my knees. "When I started to develop, when I started to look like a girl instead of an androgynous blob, people started telling me how pretty I was, how exotic and striking I was. What they meant was how different I looked with my white family. They never thought we were related to begin with, and as I got older, more and more people just assumed I was Aaron's girlfriend and not his sister. It made him proprietary and possessive. He started acting like he really did own me, like I belonged to him in some sort of twisted way."

A familiar fist squeezed tight in my chest as I recalled the first pair of unwanted hands that tugged at me, pulled and pinched. I could remember it so clearly, saying no over and over again until it felt like my throat would bleed.

"I tried to talk to my parents, to the school counselor, to one of my science teachers. They all said the same thing, that I was reading into something that wasn't there. Aaron was just friendly, overly so, and his affection was his way of letting me know that he finally accepted me into the family. The first time he raped me, I was fourteen. I cried so hard when it was over, I made myself sick."

He went still behind me, his hands falling away from my head. The air around us seemed to pulse and vibrate with an energy I couldn't name. It wasn't a fun story to tell.

"The abuse went on for two years. No one listened, no one seemed to care. I thought it would stop when Aaron went away to college, but every weekend he came home, every holiday he came back for, he was all over me, angrier and more violent the older I got. I fought him, God, did I fight, but it never got me anywhere. When I was sixteen, June walked in on us. She heard me crying and saw me trying to get away. She freaked out, but not because her son was raping me, but because she was worried what people would think if it got out her kids were fucking. She was convinced herself I lead him on, that I asked for it. She tried to tell me I was getting what I'd deserved. The next morning, she and Bradley sat me down and explained how I had to keep it quiet. They couldn't imagine how things would look on the outside. They were worried about Aaron's future. I told them over and over that I didn't want him touching me, that he forced me, and they insisted that I was confused and emotional. I waited until the house was empty, when they all went out for dinner, to pack up my stuff. I left the next day."

I exhaled long and slow, the pain inside my chest having nothing to do with the beatings I'd survived the last two weeks. "They found me. The cops picked me up as a runaway and each time I told them what was going on at home, June would show up and say I was sick, that something was wrong with me. She had the cops convinced I was crazy and fabricating the abuse. Time and time again, they found me and brought me back. No one would listen to me. No one would help me. Each time they did, things with Aaron got worse. I was his favorite toy and he never wanted anyone else to play with me. They wouldn't let me go to school anymore, wouldn't let me out of the house. I was a prisoner, but what was worse was that they acted like I should be grateful for what they were doing for me. They reminded me I was in this country without a family and homeless without them."

The bed shifted as he pushed off of it. I could feel him standing at the side, looming like a heavy shadow over my shoulder. "I got away again when I was eighteen and June got diagnosed with multiple sclerosis. They were at the hospital a lot so I managed to escape. I did my best to disappear. I went totally off the grid, started squatting and living on the streets. I got good at being able to disappear. I found a guy who made me a shitty, fake ID and erased the person I was. I thought about leaving the city altogether, but this was the only home I'd ever known. I also realized there was a need for someone like me, someone who wanted no one to know who she was or where she belonged and could do the same for them. The Cartwrights have never heard of Noe Lee and I want to keep it that way forever."

He exhaled long and loud. "Noe, because you said it over and over again. Noe, because no one listened." Again, they weren't questions because he already knew the answers. "Fuck." The word was sharp and sounded like it had been pulled from some dark and painful place inside of him. "I need to get some air. Holler if you need anything."

I knew it was an uncomfortable road to walk, and I had expected his anger when I was done leading him to the end. But I hadn't expected that so much of that anger seemed to be directed inwards. I usually felt like I needed a hug whenever I told anyone about my past, but at the moment, it was my battered body and my uncertain feelings about Stark that kept me from throwing my arms around him instead.

I couldn't figure out Snowden Stark, and it concerned me how much I wanted to tinker with all his pieces to figure out how he worked. They said he was a robot, but they were wrong. He was something far more complex. He was more along the lines of the feared artificial intelligence that always took over the world in science fiction movies.

In those movies, when the AI started to feel, began to grapple with emotion and feelings . . . well, that was when everything fell apart and the humans ended up dead.

I sure hoped Stark's story had a different ending.

CHAPTER 6

Stark

I LOOKED UP FROM a bank of computer monitors when a cup of coffee was set down by my elbow. I tugged off my glasses and rubbed my tired eyes. There was no sleeping after Noe pulled back the curtain and let me peek into her past. I hated her story. I hated even more that it wasn't the first time I'd heard it, or a version of it. I hated that I'd lived inside the less horrible parts of that story myself when I was younger. Trapped somewhere I didn't want to be, caught up in an impossible position I couldn't get out of. It twisted me up inside and I was almost resentful of the fact that Noe was strong enough to get out and rewrite the story with herself as her own hero. In my version, there were no heroes. There was nothing more than a tragic ending and a whole lot of innocence lost. In my story, the heroes were villains, and I was a stupid pawn in a game I still didn't know how to play.

"You been down here all night?" Booker asked the question even though the answer was obvious. I hadn't moved from the security room in the loft's basement for hours. My legs were numb. My back was stiff. My mind was going a thousand miles a minute, but I was oblivious to all of it because a couple of hours ago, reviewing security footage, I'd seen Jonathan Goddard crawl out of that mangled shipping container. A blacked-out SUV had wheeled its way to the wreckage, and the Mayor had managed to limp his way inside. He was alive.

I picked up the coffee and ran a hand over the rough stubble that now covered the lower half of my face. "Yeah. I was watching the container for survivors." Even though Benny wasn't someone I wanted to spend my free time with I realized everything he was risking for to save Noe. I was hoping he made it out of the fray and was on his way to the person that he'd been willing to deal with the Devil for.

Booker grunted as he leaned against the desk. He was back in a severely tailored suit. One cut specifically to hide the bulge of the gun he wore strapped to his side. "It records. You could have fast forwarded through the footage this morning. You didn't need to watch it all night."

I knew that. I was the one who had installed the security system. It was top of the line and had all the bells and whistles. It didn't require any human interaction to operate, but this human couldn't pull himself away. The steady stream of visuals, the low hum of surveillance footage being recorded, soothed some of the wildness that was alive in my blood after listening to Noe explain why being homeless, alone, and hungry was better than being home. The machines did what they were supposed to do; they didn't have stories that made my guts feel like lead, ones that turned my heart inside out and made my head feel like it was caving in. All these feelings were going to bury me. I couldn't breathe through them, couldn't think with them circling around every thought.

"I know. I couldn't sleep, so I figured I would come down here and see if anyone made it out. Benny pulled himself out not long after you got Noe free. He looked pretty banged up, but he was moving under his own steam." I was surprised how relieved I was when I saw the dark-haired man stagger into sight. I knew Benny only went after Noe because Nassir had him by the balls, but he got her out when no one else could. Even if he was a self-serving asshole, I felt like I owed him, and I was glad he hadn't gone down doing this final favor in his hometown.

"If he was moving then he's fine. He's already gone. He has someone waiting on him, and he was anxious as hell to get back to her. Gotta say, I'm glad he's gonna make it. If a shithead like Benny can find a girl willing to wait on him, that means there is hope for the rest of us rejects." He took a sip of the coffee he had clenched in his hand and lifted an eyebrow at me. "Anyone else make it out?"

I dipped my chin in a half nod. "Goddard. Got picked up a little before dawn, but he was barely moving. A clean-up crew showed an hour ago and pulled out the bodies of the cop and some skinny guy. They dumped them in the water along with the security detail you took out and wiped the container clean. They went after the surveillance tapes."

"They freak out when they realized there was none?" Booker sounded slightly amused. Nothing good went down at those docks, and a lot of that nothing good fell under Nassir's watchful eye. The only surveillance that happened on the shady waterfront area came from this building. It was just one more way that Nassir kept his finger on the pulse of everything that went on in his city.

"Yeah. They definitely seemed confused. You would think a guy like Goddard would know more about the place he uses for all his dirty work." Noe was far from the first person to pay a visit to that shipping container.

Booker snorted. "Guys like Goddard think they are above any kind of law. They think they can explain away something like a midnight visit to the docks with a few careful words. He has his supporters snowed. What he declares as the truth they'll believe, even with the facts right in front of them."

Goddard was the kind of politician who ensured the rich got richer and pitted the poor against one another. His supporters were influential and well off. They wouldn't want to rock the boat by questioning why the man who paved their way on easy street was skulking around in the middle of the night, in the slums, with an armed escort. It would take more than a video of Goddard going in and out of that container to push him off his pedestal.

"I know all about guys like Goddard." He was exactly like the men who made me a deal I couldn't refuse. He operated the same way they did. Stripping away choice and putting the vulnerable in impossible situations. It was going to be an absolute pleasure to flip the script and put this asshole in a position that was impossible to wiggle out of. "You tell Titus about the dirty cop?"

Booker nodded. "I did. He was pissed. Guess he won't have to kick ass considering the guy is now fish food. He also mentioned Reeve left a bunch of stuff here when they were using the loft I want to put Noe in. He said she was welcome to any of it."

Reeve Black was the cop's stunning baby-momma. Before they had been parents-to-be, she'd been a witness to a crime and the girl the entire Point despised. Titus was supposed to keep her safe and at a distance. He'd failed at both but got the girl and the bad guy in the end, so he was still a hero. Reeve was all long legs and rocked the body of a stripper before the cop knocked her up. She was still round and stacked in all the right places, but now those places were overshadowed by her baby belly. Anything she left would be the opposite of what Noe typically wore, but I guess it was better than Booker's hand-me-downs, which swallowed her up.

"I'll let her know." I'd checked on her throughout the night. After everything she'd been through, I wasn't surprised that she was exhausted. She didn't move. She slept still as stone, which I figured was unusual for her. She didn't flinch or make a sound when I touched her pulse at the hollow of her throat, and she didn't make a sound when I touched the full curve of her lower lip. I knew it was inappropriate, that I shouldn't have my hands on her in any way when she wasn't aware of it. But I needed to know her heart was still beating. I had to feel her breath on my fingertips to calm the raging inferno that was burning every rational thought and every sane and reasonable part of me to ash.

"She was working on getting up when I headed down here. I told her I was leaving for the day and that you were hiding down here in the Batcave. She didn't want breakfast or coffee, but she did say she wanted a shower." He pushed off the desk and flicked his fingers over the diamond cufflinks that were attached to his shirt. Even badass enforcers liked a little bling here and there, apparently. "You might want to check on her. She looked pale." He reached out and clapped a heavy hand on my shoulder. "And get some sleep, boy genius. You look like shit."

I grumbled a half-hearted agreement and pushed to my feet so I could follow him out of the basement. He paused at the entryway and gave me a look that made my spine stiffen. "If you need a piece, there's a Sig Sauer in the kitchen behind the Froot Loops. There's a Glock in the closet in my bedroom, and there's a ten gauge in the armoire in the guest room." His eyebrows quirked upwards and a small grin tugged at his mouth. "There's a twenty-two hidden underneath the sink in the bathroom, and God forbid you need it, there's an AR-15 in a lockbox under my bed. The key is in the nightstand."

Booker had an arsenal scattered throughout his apartment. I wasn't the least bit surprised, but I was a tad intimidated. I knew my way around a weapon, but I'd never been in the position where I'd ever had to use one to defend myself or someone else before. Usually my hands and the training I received under the tutelage of good ol' Uncle Sam were enough to get the job done. "Good to know, but if someone is badass enough to get through all the security I set up around this place, then they're probably coming in better armed than I'll ever be. I'll get Noe moved over to the other apartment today." I selfishly wanted her out of his bed.

"Give her the nine mil that's behind the cereal." He said it in a way that left no room for argument.

"How do you know she can handle it?" I didn't like how familiar he was with her after such a short time. It bugged me that he acted like he knew her when I had barely scratched the surface.

He lifted a shoulder and let it fall. "Something tells me there isn't much that girl can't handle. She's made of tough stuff." He slipped out the front door before I could agree with him. She was made of tough stuff, the kind of stuff that didn't break no matter what was thrown at it.

I was dragging ass when I took the stairs up to Booker's unit. Typically, I could run up the three flights and not even get winded, but I was running on fumes and the last traces of adrenaline. My brain was fuzzy, and my normally sharp thoughts felt scattered and unruly. The past and the present were at war in my mind, and the battle for which one made me feel worse was raging.

I made my way through the quiet loft listening for any sound that would indicate Noe was up and moving around. When I got closer to the bedroom, I heard the shower running and swear words chasing the steam out of the open door. It was going to be painful for a while when the water sluiced over her wounds. The thought had me squeezing my eyes closed and clenching my hands into fists. Just because tough things didn't break didn't mean they couldn't be damaged, dented, and scratched. The fact Noe was currently suffering so much wear and tear because of me scraped across my skin and dug into my belly like sharp knives.

I was turning to walk out of the room so she could finish in peace when the running water went silent and her swearing ramped up a notch. I heard her banging around in the bathroom and then she yelled, "Booker, I need a towel! I'm dripping all over your floor."

I opened my mouth to tell her Booker was gone and that I would go find her one. I didn't need her poking through his stuff and running across a submachine gun or a rocket launcher. My brain was ping-ponging between annoyance that she'd called for Booker instead of me and the unrelenting image of her, naked, wet, and dripping onto the tile. I wasn't a guy prone to fantasy, but damn if I didn't get all kinds of caught up in the thought of her pretty olive skin glistening with moisture from head to toe. I needed to get away from her. I needed space so I could find a way to wrap armor back around all the soft parts of me she exposed.

I was shaking my head to marshal my thoughts back in order when I heard her swear again. Suddenly, like I conjured her out of a dream, Noe was standing in the pocket doorway of the bathroom wearing nothing more than a scowl of irritation and shimmery, shiny water droplets. Her midnight-colored eyebrows shot up to her hairline, and a bright pink flush stained the top of her chest and crawled up her neck into her face. She didn't lift her hands to cover herself. She stood as still as I was, not moving at all under my furious and hungry gaze.

I wanted to be polite and look away. I told myself it was rude to stare and that the last thing she needed was some guy she barely knew gawking at her like she was a priceless work of art on a museum wall. I berated myself for this invasion of privacy but none of the lecturing or preaching did any good. The only way I could have torn my eyes off that petite frame, with its perfectly perky breasts and slightly rounded hips, was if someone slapped them out of my head. I couldn't blink. I was scared to breathe. I felt like if I moved at all she would bolt like a startled deer, and I needed another second, another minute, another hour, to memorize every single part of her.

She was small, but all the parts added up to perfection. Seeing her like this, stripped bare with nothing to hide behind, I couldn't believe I'd ever been stupid enough to think she was a boy. Everything about her was delicate, feminine, and soft. The hollow of her neck, the elegant curve of her shoulders, the flare of her hips and the fullness of her ass. Her legs weren't long, but they were toned and shapely. She was the very definition of good things coming in small packages and all I wanted to do was wrap her up and put her on a shelf that was too high and too hard to reach for anyone but me.

Choking on possession and a surge of lust unlike anything I'd ever felt, I belatedly turned my back on her and muttered thickly, "I used all the towels in there last night when I cleaned you up. I'll go find where Booker keeps the extras."

She moved. I felt it. The current that ran between us pulsed and throbbed with something hot. I heard her bare feet on the carpet and it took every ounce of willpower I possessed to keep my feet planted and my back turned. She was naked in a room with a very big bed and I was a man who never had such a visceral reaction to anyone . . . ever. If I had a switch, Noe Lee was the only person who had ever come along and flipped it. I was the actual definition of turned on when I had been off for most of my life.

"He told me he was getting ready to head out and that you were downstairs working. I should have asked him before he left. My head was itchy and I decided I couldn't wait. You can turn around now." She sounded slightly amused.

Slowly, I turned to face her. She was wrapped up in the comforter from the bed. Her hair was inky black and blood red where it was slicked back from her face. With the bruise on her cheek and the cuts on her wrist, she resembled a superhero who had just saved the world. I took my glasses off so that she was slightly out of focus. Staring at her was making my heart do some crazy things. I'd never felt it beat so fast. Usually, it ticked slow and even like a metronome.

"I'm so sorry." The words rushed out, blurted with no tact or grace. Realizing in that moment that I wasn't sorry for watching her but for so many other things. I slammed my glasses back on my face and raked my hands over my head in frustration. "I'm sorry I didn't help you. I'm sorry I shut the door in your face. I'm sorry you got taken and that you got hurt. I'm sorry I couldn't find you sooner. I'm sorry you feel safer living on the streets than you did at home. I'm sorry guys like Goddard and your adoptive brother exist, and I'm sorry guys like me aren't better at stopping them. I'm sorry Benny didn't put a bullet between Goddard's eyes so this was all over." I stopped so I could suck in a breath. I lowered my head so I was looking at the floor between my boots. "And I'm sorry there was no towel for you when you got out of the shower. I'll go find one."

I knew good and well there were some things an apology couldn't fix. I also knew just because you gave one didn't mean the person on the receiving end had to take it. This girl didn't seem like she wanted much, and accepting my apology meant she was going to have to hang onto some pretty heavy forgiveness for as long as we were in each other's lives.

I was at the door when she called out my name. I paused and looked over my shoulder at her. She was perched on the edge of the bed and the comforter was barely staying up around her breasts. I knew now that they were a perfect handful, small but tipped with enchanting and delectable looking nipples that were a dusky peach and caramel color. I wanted to taste them. I wanted to put my hands on them. I was so much bigger than she was that it would be easy to smother her, to suffocate her with all the unchecked desire and wild emotion that was rolling off of me. I needed to get myself together. I needed to compartmentalize and organize everything she made me feel, so I could work past it.

"What happened before has nothing to do with you. I didn't give you that piece of my past so you would feel sorry for me. I gave it to you so you would know that nothing that happens or has happened to me would ever crush me. I do what I have to do in order to survive, and I make no apologies for it. When I asked you to help me," she trailed off for a second, her eyes searching mine. "I saw the fear in your eyes. I heard the panic when I mentioned the Mayor was involved. You have your own story and your own reasons for doing what you do. You're just trying to survive, as well. I'm not going to lie, I was very disappointed in you, but I don't blame you, Stark. I'm the one who put myself on Goddard's radar, no one else."

Fear, disappointment, and pain. They were the holy trinity that defined my life. "I'm still sorry for all of it."

She rolled her eyes and pointed to the doorway. "Don't be sorry, be useful. Get me a towel and then come back and tell me your plan to destroy Jonathan Goddard."

I nodded woodenly while trying to stifle a jaw busting yawn. I blinked at her from behind my glasses when she cocked her head to the side to consider me thoughtfully.

"When was the last time you slept?"

I shook my head to clear the fog and grumbled, "A couple of days ago."

"Jeez. No wonder you look like a zombie. New plan, get me a towel, take a nap, and then fill me in on your diabolical plot to ruin the Mayor's life. Why haven't you been sleeping?"

I was surprised she had to ask. I gave her the only answer I could. "Hard to sleep when you're choking on fear and disappointment." She gave a little gasp that I ignored. "I'll be back in a minute with a couple of towels."

I felt her eyes boring into my back as I exited the room, and while they didn't feel like daggers, they still poked and pricked and made me bleed. She saw too much and I was nowhere near ready to give her my story in return. She was strong, unbreakable, and indestructible. There was no way I wanted her to know I was fragile, brittle, and ready to shatter with even the slightest touch. If she knew how just how weak I was, she would never trust me to keep her safe. She wouldn't believe that I could handle Goddard and his perversions. She would go after him herself, because she was a hero.

I never wanted her to know I'd never done anything heroic . . . even when the person I loved the most needed me.

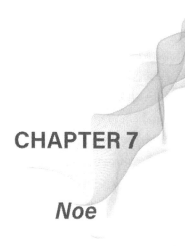

CHAPTER 7

Noe

IT WAS TRUE. THE bigger they were, the harder they fell.

Stark went from being broody, abrupt, and bossy to passed out face down on the couch in the living room of the vacant loft he'd insisted on moving me to. I told him over and over again I didn't need to be under lock and key, but the man was stubborn and only heard what he wanted to hear. I also told him I wasn't interested in taking the scary black gun he forced on me after I admitted I knew how to handle a firearm. I didn't like guns. I resented the false confidence they gave the person who had their finger on the trigger. If you couldn't win a fight fairly, then you shouldn't be fighting in the first place. In the end, I took the stupid thing because he looked like he was about to break.

Those slate eyes of his were full of a brewing storm, one that was getting closer and closer to shore. For a guy who was supposed to be mechanical and methodical, he was all over the place when we were alone together. There was nothing measured or meticulous when he apologized to me, there wasn't any restraint or reserve when his eyes roved over my naked body. There was nothing but heat and appreciation. He didn't look at me like he wanted to figure me out. He looked at me like he wanted to take me apart with his hands and his mouth. He looked hungry.

At first, I was so surprised to see him that I couldn't move, and then it was the gleam in those hard eyes that kept me rooted to the spot, unable to cover up. There was something addicting about having a guy who typically ran so cold and indifferent burn at the sight of you. Snowden Stark might be part machine, but even the Terminator melted when things got hot enough. I wanted to crank up the heat and see what Stark would do. I wanted to know what it would take to turn him liquid and malleable, because I knew, for me, it was nothing more than the quirk of his eyebrow over those glasses and the way he shifted his big body when he was nervous or uncomfortable. He looked like a fighter, not a thinker, and it totally got to me when he put both those things aside and was nothing more than a vulnerable man who didn't have all the answers.

I peeked over the back of the couch and stared at him for a second careful not to make a sound. He went down so hard it was clear he needed the rest, and I didn't want to wake him up even though I was dying to know his plan to take on Goddard. I knew he had to have one.

He was always the man with the plan.

He was also the man who, even in his sleep, looked way too serious and intent. Between his dark eyebrows, there was a deep V of concentration. His glasses were sitting on the coffee table so I could see his sinfully long lashes flutter as he dreamed. The scar on the side of his head looked jagged and rough up close and totally contrasted with the diamond studs that decorated his ears.

The tattoo that crawled along the side of his neck appeared to be an intricate biomechanical design, meant to look like the skin had been peeled away and all his inner workings were gears and wires instead of blood and bone. That same design traveled all the way over his heavy shoulder, underneath his t-shirt, and down his arm. It even covered the back of his hand, and once again, I was reminded of the Terminator. He very well could have been sent from the future to save us all, or he could decide to use his knowledge to bring nothing but doom and destruction to those he deemed the enemy.

He mumbled something in his sleep and shifted so that he was lying on his back, one of his arms hanging over the edge of the couch and touching the floor while his long legs hung over the arm. He didn't fit. I imagined that was a pretty common problem of his since he was so damn big. The thought sent a surprising shiver racing down my spine and my eyes widened at the thought of other places that might be a tight squeeze for him.

When I first left home and hit the streets, I'd gone a little wild. I was so ashamed and frustrated by everything Aaron and the Cartwrights had put me through, I needed some sort of outlet, some way to prove it was my choice who I gave my body to. I burned through boy after boy because I could, and sometimes because it meant I had a safe and warm place to sleep for the night. At the time, I thought it was liberating and redemptive, but when I got older and ended up back in that house of horrors, I realized I was sleeping around to devalue what sex meant all together. I was trying to prove to myself that it was insignificant, to lessen the impact of the way Aaron had forced it on me for so long. When I escaped the second time, I promised myself I would make better choices all around, including the men I picked to spend time with. I understood I was worth more, and that it mattered when I decided to share my body with someone. I very rarely did anymore.

Occasionally, there was an old flame who drifted through the Point on his way to somewhere better, and we would get together. It worked for me because they were familiar and on the move. There was no awkward conversation about how our time together was nothing more than scratching an itch. All I was after was a mutually satisfying encounter with someone I respected and liked, someone who felt the same about me, and didn't mind when I walked away in the morning.

I'd never been attracted to a guy like Stark before. There was nothing easy or predictable about him, and I wasn't sure I liked or respected him after that day he shut the door in my face. I mean, I was totally intrigued by the stories I'd heard about him and the things he'd done, but the reality was completely different. He wouldn't let me or anyone else handle him and he had the kind of secrets that I tended to run from. I didn't like surprises, and he was nothing but one unknown after another. I'd also never been the girl who swooned over muscles and tattoos, but it was impossible not to get caught up in how hot he was. Even if I wasn't invested in his razor-sharp mind, I'd admit to being weak in the knees over the rest of him. I was secretly hoping I'd get a turn to check him out when he was as naked as I'd been. I had a feeling I'd lose my mind and throw myself at him. Just once, I wanted to be with someone who could control me without scaring or threatening me.

Part of me felt that Stark was the only man who could do that because despite everything, I trusted him.

I pushed back from my lurking position and was turning to go to the kitchen where I had left my (his) laptop, when he abruptly made a strangled noise and started babbling, "I'm sorry. I'm so sorry," over and over again. His head was thrashing from side-to-side and his massive chest started to rise and fall rapidly. His mouth was moving without sound and that furrow in his brow dug in deeper. He looked like he was in some serious distress, and I wasn't sure if it was better to let him battle it out himself or if I should try and wake him up. The way he was apologizing over and over again made me think he was dreaming about me and the way he unceremoniously sent me on my way, but then his hands curled into fists and he screamed, "Savina!" It was ripped out of him with such force that I fell back a step and put a startled hand up to my throat.

Stark jack-knifed up into a sitting position, eyes unclear, and panic etched in every line of his face and body. His head swiveled around like he was looking for something, eyes squinting when he realized he couldn't see clearly. He shoved his fingers through his short hair, swung his legs over the edge of the couch, and blindly reached for his glasses. When he got to his feet, tension was rolling off his massive frame in waves. He was clearly unsettled that I'd been watching him and witnessed his memories ripping him apart in his sleep.

"I need some air. I'm gonna step out for a minute. Lock the door behind me." He didn't give me a chance to respond or ask what the hell had happened. He prowled to the door, every line of his body rigid and stiff. He slammed the door shut with more force than was necessary, and when he was gone, it was like a vacuum sucked all the life out of the space. Everything felt vacant and empty. My curiosity was buzzing bright and hot, so I finished making the trip to my laptop and powered it on, making sure the screen was facing the open kitchen so that if Stark suddenly reappeared, he wouldn't get an eyeful of what I was about to Google.

The name Savina wasn't one you heard every day, so I started with that and tacked on the name of the city where the Point and the Hill were located. I blinked when I got pages and pages of results. Savina and Snowden Stark. Fraternal twins that looked hauntingly alike, born to a Conroy and Geneva Stark. Conroy was some kind of nuclear physicist and Geneva was a biochemical engineer; it was no surprise that their kids were almost immediately tagged as gifted and accelerated. Snowden was a mathematical wizard and wrote code when he was only six years old. They called him the second coming of guys like Bill Gates and Steve Jobs. The word prodigy was thrown around liberally when talking about both twins. Savina was a savant. She played the piano and earned a coveted spot at Juilliard when she was only ten. There was article after article about the family's accomplishments and achievements. Stark designed a program that was used to predict highly probable terrorist attack sites, which the government bought for an obscene amount of money when the program accurately predicted the bombings of the subway system in London and the sarin gas attacks in the Tokyo subways in 1995. Not only did it predict the location, but also the type of attack for which officials should be on alert. There were a lot of conspiracy theories that the software would have accurately warned the US government about the attacks on 9–11 if they had been utilizing it properly. He was only twelve when they bought it, and four years after that, he disappeared into a governmental black hole. Some said he went to federal prison, some said he'd been recruited by an unnamed branch of the government. Stark had entire chatrooms and forums dedicated to him; he was a con-spiracy theorist's wet dream.

His sister also had a lot of chatter on the internet. Her chatrooms and forums were incredibly unnerving.

The girl was just as stunning as her brother: tall, dark-haired, and she had the same blue-gray eyes that looked like they were constantly trying to figure out how the entire world worked. Where Stark looked like a younger version of the man he was now, minus all the ink and bulk, his sister looked frail and almost waifish. She looked like prey.

I sucked in a breath as I kept scrolling, each headline screaming something worse than the one before. Geneva Stark was killed in a horrific chemical explosion at the lab where she worked. There was a lot of speculation that the explosion happened from the inside to cover up some kind of top secret research and development program. Conroy Stark was arrested for treason when he was accused of trading information on the US's nuclear program with a foreign intelligence officer. They called him a traitor and a spy. The man was still locked up, and to this day was screaming that he'd been set-up and falsely accused. He swore up one side and down the other he didn't have anything to do with government secrets and claimed that US intelligence wanted his son, that they had killed his wife to get their hands on young Snowden. It sounded like the ravings of a lunatic, but considering how leery Stark was of any kind of government official, I wondered if there was more to it than the rantings of a guilty man.

The worst were the headlines about Savina. She had risen to fame in the orchestral world. She toured and played for the rich and famous. Somewhere along the line, she also picked up more than one stalker. There was all kinds of press about how scared she was, how she considered quitting performing to go into hiding. There were paparazzi shots of the girl looking terrified, her face covered and her body hunched over. In the background of all those pictures was a furious looking Stark. He was trying to shield her from the lights and from so much more.

I wasn't surprised at all when I found an article that had her obituary, which made me put a hand to my chest and blink back a hot rush of moisture that pressed at the back of my eyes. She couldn't take the pressure or the constant threats. She couldn't handle the loss of her mother and her father going to jail. The media was even more in her face after that. The demands of fame and fortune broke her. She took her own life, and the final picture was one of Stark, dressed in a somber, black suit as he threw a handful of dirt into a freshly dug grave. He looked tortured and turned inside out. His pain was obvious in every pixel of the grainy black and white photo. I could feel it, and I hated that.

The door opened with a swoosh and he strode through it looking far more composed than he had when he walked out. I shut the computer and propped a hand on my fist as I watched him walk across the room. He still looked tired, but he was always quick. All it took was a glance at me and at my closed laptop for him to put two and two together. He sighed as he made his way over to where I was leaning against the counter, fingers tapping on the back of the computer.

"Whatever you think you know, you don't." His voice was scratchy and rough.

I lifted an eyebrow and cocked my head to the side. "Is that so?"

He sighed again and dipped his chin in a slight nod. "Google barely scratches the surface. Trust me, you don't want the real story. You don't want anything to weigh you down, and every single part that fills in the blanks is heavy as hell."

I stared at him silently as I worked through the fact that I kind of wanted some of that weight. He was carrying it all, and that had to be exhausting, even with his broad shoulders and strong back. He saved me when he didn't want to. The least I could do was take some of that burden off him if he wanted to hand it over.

"I let you see a lot of the baggage I carry around with me, Stark. I'm here if you ever decide you want to hand off some of yours." I couldn't believe I was offering to take him on, but I really wanted to. In more ways than one. Snowden Stark was the first person in forever who lingered. I was very good at shaking off anyone who seemed like they were trying to get their hooks into me. With this man, I was thoroughly caught and not doing a very good job of wiggling free.

He smirked at me and crossed his arms over his chest. I tried not to ogle the way his muscles bulged and stretched the fabric of his shirt. "I never expected you to be sweet, Noe Lee. Angry, defiant, feisty, and rude. Those I'm prepared for, but sweet is a nice surprise."

I narrowed my eyes at him. I wasn't sure if that was a compliment or not. "You haven't given me a lot of reason to be sweet, Snowden."

He grunted and shifted his gaze away from mine. "You're right. I'll have to work on that. I'm not really a guy who brings out the best in others. I'm not exactly personable."

I slid around the edge of the counter so I was standing directly in front of him. The heat from his body radiated into mine, and it made my breath shudder. The current that pulsed between us had a life of its own as it sparked and popped with electricity that I swore I could almost see and smell.

"You're challenging, Stark. Nothing wrong with that. The things we have to work for are the things we appreciate the most. Nothing that's handed over without some kind of fight is worth holding onto." I'd learned that each time I'd had to make a new life for myself. Each time it had pulled me away from everything I'd ever known. The first time, I'd had to fight to get free from the life I'd been forced into. The second time, I'd had to fight to stay free of the life I'd known. Now, I was fighting for a life that meant something, one that had value and purpose. He was going to be all kinds of effort and exertion. Something told me he was worth every single second of the effort.

"Not everyone likes a challenge." His tone was dry but his eyes were watchful and alert. The pulse at the base of his throat leapt under his tattooed skin because he was a man and not a machine, no matter how hard he tried to fight it and cover it up.

I had to stand on my tiptoes to reach that throbbing vein. I put my fingers over the tender spot and felt his heart race as I leaned closer, eyes locked on his. He could crush me, literally and figuratively, but I trusted him not to. "I do. I thrive on tackling a challenge. The bigger, the better."

His teeth flashed white and his eyes crinkled at the corners as he gave me the first real smile I'd ever seen on his harshly hewn face. It softened him, made him look younger and less world weary. His smile was irresistible and it sealed the deal for me. If he could smile like that when I was sweet, then I would make an effort to be sweet more often, and if I couldn't stick to that plan, then I was just going to kiss the shit out of him every chance I got. I saw his smile brighten and his eyes widen as I threw my much smaller body into his. It was like hitting a wall. I felt the impact vibrate all the way down to my toes. I also felt my heart rate kick up and my nipples tighten as I pressed into the solid strength of his chest.

I had to stretch to get my arms around his neck, and we both gave a quiet groan as the move plastered my entire front to his. Nothing would move him if he didn't want to be moved, but he lowered his head so I could reach his mouth. He tasted like coffee and sleepiness. His stubble was rough against my chin and finger-tips, and I used a finger to trace his chiseled jaw line. I'd never been with anyone who was so overtly masculine before. I'd also never kissed anyone who wore glasses. The way they fogged up and tilted slightly to the side was fucking adorable and had me doing my best to shove my tongue down his throat even though he was taking things nice and easy.

There were no grabbing hands and aggressive teeth with Snowden Stark. The man kissed like he did everything else, deliberate, thorough, slow, and thoughtful. He was turning my head inside out as he traced the curve of my lips with the tip of his tongue, savoring every inch of my mouth. He lifted a hand so he could circle one of my wrists where it was propped up on his shoulder. His thumb gently moved in tiny circles over the abused skin and his simple caress turned my knees to water. I dug my fingers into the back of his neck, nails dragging through his short hair. I enjoyed the prickle of it against my fingertips and the brush of it against my palm.

His free hand smoothed over the curve of my hip and trailed to my backside so he could palm my ass. Everything about him was oversized. I'd never felt more feminine or breakable than I did under his hands. It made me shiver and kiss him even harder. He made a noise as I nipped at his lower lip with my teeth, but relented when I soothed the bite with a flick of my tongue that demanded he let me inside the warm cavern of his mouth. He complied with a soft chuckle that I felt between my legs. I shifted anxiously on my toes as my center throbbed and pressed involuntarily against the rigid length that was making itself known against my stomach. He was hot and huge. Like seriously, the thing was intimidating on its own without the rest of him that loomed in front of me.

Twining and twisting my tongue around the heat of his, I gasped into his mouth when I felt his other hand land on my ass. He used his hold to hoist me up as if I weighed nothing. I wrapped my legs around his lean waist and circled his neck in a death grip. I didn't think he was going to drop me, but if he suddenly realized we were the worst two people in the world to be getting all tangled up in one another, he might. The boy was nothing if not logical, and eventually he was going to remember that we were a bad idea, nothing short of a bona fide disaster waiting to happen. For now, he kissed me back with as much enthusiasm as I had while I tried to devour him.

I knew what it was like to be hungry, so hungry you thought you might starve. When you finally got a bite, no matter how big or small it was, you inhaled it like you might never eat again. That's what I was doing with Stark. I was taking as much as I could, since I didn't know if I was ever going to get another taste.

I moaned and pressed my breasts into his chest when he used his hold on my hips to grind my soft, wet center against that straining erection that was like a steel pole between us. The friction made me squirm and had my thighs quivering. I couldn't remember ever being this sensitive and this quick to turn liquid and ready before. That ever-present electrical current wrapped around every nerve pulsed with need. I could feel his heart pounding and the iron control he was exerting as he accepted what I gave but made no demands of his own. I wiggled in his hands, pressing closer, grinding down on his cock in frustration. I wanted the clothes between us to be gone, and I wanted him to want me with the same kind of uncontrolled fierceness I had for him. He made me reckless and it bothered me that he handled me so carefully.

I dragged my rough and uneven nails down the side of his neck and swallowed the moan that vibrated against my lips. I felt his fingers press into my backside and his chest rise and fall like he was struggling to breathe. He was on the edge and it wouldn't take much to push him over. I pulled back a little bit so we were eye to eye, considering each other as we panted and pressed into one another. I was planning my attack. I wanted to push him. I wanted to prod him until he short-circuited like Booker warned me he would.

I never got the chance. As soon as we came up for air, his phone started to ring in his back pocket and he carefully set me down on my feet, hands lifting to my waist and setting me back a safe distance. He looked at his phone and told me he had to take the call, and although he didn't tell me who had interrupted us, I saw Nassir's face flash on the screen.

I rubbed my fingers over my swollen mouth and across the tender spots on my face where his whiskers had rubbed my skin raw. "I told you I could be sweet." I smirked up at him and was surprised when he tossed back his head and let out a rusty, cracked laugh.

When he looked back at me, his eyes were glimmering with promise and so much potential for more unexpected moments of *sweetness* that it stole my breath.

"No one has ever been sweeter."

He said it like he meant it and I knew I was in trouble. I didn't have any room for him and his secrets, but somehow, I was already clearing space. Something told me I was going to have to get rid of everything that cluttered up my insides because Snowden Stark was about to fill up every nook and cranny. He would weigh me down more than any of the baggage from my past ever could. I knew that was going to be okay, that together we both would be okay.

CHAPTER 8

Stark

A CLIENT WHO HAD a standing date with one of Nassir's working girls claimed he was being blackmailed by the escort. He was up in arms because the girl had threatened to out the John to his wife and the rest of his very conservative family. The man claimed she demanded twenty thousand dollars in cash and had already sent a threatening text message to the man's spouse that had her questioning where he spent his Wednesday nights. Nassir was calling bullshit on the man's story. His girls had rules, and they knew not to break them if they wanted to stay on the Devil's good side and on his very lucrative payroll. He kept them safe. He vetted all the clients and wouldn't let anyone near his business unless they knew how to keep quiet and treat the girls well. He didn't tolerate any kind of nonsense, and his wife was even more fiercely protective of the women who earned their living in such a timeless and dangerous way. She didn't tolerate any disrespect when it came to the working girls, and it was no surprise that Nassir was on the warpath if Keelyn was upset. He moved mountains and leveled entire cities to make things right for his woman. She was the only thing on Earth he cared about more than power and control.

I told the man who pulled my strings that I would run a background check on the John, pick through his finances, and trace where the text to the wife originated. I also promised to dig up whatever I could on the hooker. I refrained from calling her that because I didn't have the time or the patience for a lecture on how people did what they had to do to survive in the Point, and no one should judge those choices. It was a common refrain in this city. People were always *something more* than a simple label. There was always a story behind how they had earned that title, but I wasn't the kind of guy who ever cared about the story. Probably because I spent so much of my time trying to forget my own. I wanted to be the big, broody guy who was good with computers, nothing more and nothing less. Simple. However, since I'd started tangling with Noe, it was clear some stories couldn't remain unspoken. Sometimes they were told without words. History and memories were shared through unblinking looks, soft touches, and surprising sweetness. She'd barely scratched the surface of where I'd been or what I'd done, but she was a girl who had the skills to look deeper, unearthing the truth. I couldn't be anything but who I was with her, because she was the one person who could uncover the lies I'd been living for so long.

When I made my way back into the borrowed loft, she was on the computer again and didn't bother to look up when I entered. She was scowling at something on the screen, her eyes flicking in my direction as I got closer.

"The motel where Goddard's goons held me just burned to the

ground. It's all over the local news. Three people died because the fire suppression system didn't come on—shocker—and because of those fucking bars on the windows. He's covering his tracks. He even released a statement saying the loss of life is a tragedy and his heart goes out to the victims' families. He's such a prick. He followed that garbage up with the fact that losing such a disreputable business is no great loss to the community." Her mouth was pulled into a furious, tight line and her dark eyes were alight with anger. "I can't believe anyone re-elected him."

I braced my hands on the edge of the marble counter and looked at her with grim determination. "That's why we have to stop him."

She let out a bitter laugh and pushed the red part of her hair off her forehead. "I'm all atwitter with anticipation to hear exactly how you plan to do that, Stark. The more I think about it, the more he seems untouchable. The man killed three innocent people to cover up the fact he kidnapped me. He's ruthless."

"He's greedy. He wants to keep his standing in the community, his good name. He wants to keep his title and his money. But more than any of that, he wants to keep his secrets. We're going to take each and every one of those things from him. We're going to burn his entire world from the inside out." My hands curled into fists on top of the marble; her eyes widened a fraction as she stared at me. My anger was happy to finally have a clear target, a pointed direction to blow. The heated vengeance wasn't curling wildly and furiously around everything in my path anymore. It had a goal, a purpose, and I no longer felt like I needed to get a grip on it. I wanted to let it run wild and see what it would do.

"How?" The word escaped on a breath, and I couldn't blame her for needing details and not having blind faith in my ability to come through for her. I'd already let her down.

I cocked my head to the side and watched her carefully as I told her, "You know what's worse than death for a man like Goddard?" She shook her head, eyes curious, mouth still frowning and unsure. "The worst thing a man like Goddard can imagine is being invisible, being irrelevant. It's torture for a man like him not to have the world falling at his feet, to have everything he's ever wanted within reach but not able to touch any of it. We're going to leave the walls of his empire standing but turn everything on the inside to ash. We're going to kill him . . . digitally." We were going to wipe any trace of the man off the face of the Earth but leave the old, tired, helpless vessel afloat in his sea of corruption, constantly searching for a life raft from his previous conquests but unable to get a hold on any of them.

She blinked at me for a second and then cocked her head to the opposite side of mine. "Like steal his identity?"

I grunted, "Oh, so much more than that just taking his identify. We are going to electronically wipe him out of his life. Not before we take his money and ruin his reputation. We're going to ensure Goddard has a sizeable life insurance policy, naming his stepdaughter as the sole beneficiary. We're going to expose every bribe, payout, and misappropriated use of taxpayer money he's ever touched during his time in office. Once we do that, we're going to make sure the city and the rest of the world knows that he likes to play grab ass with young girls, proving he's not the man they think he is. Once we have him on the ropes, we pull the cyber trigger and end his digital life. A signed death certificate trumps all other forms of identification. Goddard can show his ID, flash his passport, he can scream from the top of his lungs that he's alive, but if there's a death certificate on file, it doesn't matter. That piece of paper means you're dead, which means no access to your money, no credit, no travel, no mortgage, no marriage . . . no anything. You don't exist, even if you are someone important. WE bring his life to a total standstill so that even while he's in the public eye, he loses control of everything. We take it all away from him. We put him on the streets and teach him what it's like to have no options and no power." He was going to live the way Noe did, frightened and alone. I wanted him as desperate and afraid as she had been when she first sought me out for help.

Noe slowly reached out to close the computer in front of her and delicately cleared her throat. She tapped her bare, broken fingernails on the counter and watched me with unwavering eyes. "That's . . . ambitious. Wouldn't it be a whole lot easier to let one of those guys you work with take care of the problem? Couldn't Nassir make Goddard go away with a whole lot less work?"

I bristled a little at the implication that I wasn't capable of getting my hands dirty but took a deep breath and reminded myself I had yet to prove to her just how capable I could be. I'd had to prove myself before and I hated every second of it. Showing her I could fix this for her was a challenge that made a strange heat work through me and some sort of foreign anticipation course under my skin. They were new feelings, but unlike the anger and helplessness I'd felt before when dealing with her, these emotions weren't unpleasant at all. This was what I was made to do, and vengeance was definitely going to be mine.

Her question was valid but shortsighted. "If I thought a bullet between the eyes was the right answer, I would be the one pulling the trigger. We can put Goddard in the ground, but then whomever comes behind him is going to be more careful, more watchful, and even better at keeping his secrets hidden. If we take Goddard down my way, he's here, a walking reminder of what happens when you mess with the kind of people who can be just as ruthless and cold-blooded as most politicians tend to be. If we strip Goddard bare in front of the entire city, we set a precedent. We show everyone who is really calling the shots and it sure as hell isn't anyone they voted for. That man and the promises he made don't exist. And with our skills, he won't exist."

I couldn't keep the edge out of my tone, the harshness. Of course, Noe picked it up and, of course, she remembered what I told her about my reluctance to tangle with any kind of government when I refused to help her.

God, what I wouldn't give to do that entire day over again. I would be more careful with what I told her, more careful with her, in general. After our kiss, I knew she was all kinds of soft and sweet under her prickly shell. She was just as vulnerable as I was, and it was clear neither one of us was very good at keeping our battered armor in place when we were around each other. In fact, if she kept looking at me like I was the answer to every single question she ever had, there was a chance there would be nothing between us at all before the day was done. The image of her dripping wet, wearing nothing but defiance and bravery, tripped unwanted and unstoppable through my mind. It was my favorite memory to date, but it bothered me to no end that it was more powerful than the task at hand I needed to focus on. I needed to get shit done, not get my dick wet. That could come after we took Goddard down.

I'd never had to struggle to concentrate on one and not the other before. She was messing with the way I was wired and it didn't feel much like an improvement.

"You mentioned not picking fights you weren't sure you could win when I asked you for help with Goddard. What makes you so sure we can do this? What makes you think this is a fight we can win?" She didn't sound doubtful, just careful and curious.

I blew out a long breath and closed my eyes so her earnest expression was blacked out. "Because I can't afford to lose again." Last time I lost it cost me everything. My freedom. My family. My sense of self. "I'm a whole lot smarter and stronger now, thanks to the guys I lost to last time." They took me. They trained me. They changed me. I knew about winning at all costs thanks to them.

"Does that have to do with why you hacked into the Department of Defense and disappeared? Were they the ones you lost to?" She'd heard the stories, but just like Google, those rumors only scratched the surface of everything that had really happened. My life had never been easy. Most kids were born and their parents told them that they could change the world if they tried hard enough. When I was born, it was obvious I *would* change the world and my parents were just waiting for the moment when. I was special, both Savina and I were, but that also made us more than just twins. It made us something more than children. We were a gift, treasured and cherished. We were never treated like typical kids and we only had each other. She was the only one who understood how hard it was when all eyes were on you before you'd even lost all your baby teeth. She was the only one who got it when I wanted to play baseball instead of work on Millennium Prize Problems.

I lifted a hand and rubbed it over my short hair. My fingers were shaking and I hoped she couldn't see the tremor. I wanted her to trust me. I wanted her to believe in me. I wanted to pretend like I was invincible and unbreakable, just like she was.

"I hacked into the DoD because they killed my mother and I was looking for proof." That was before I could control my impulses. That was before I'd learned to shut everything inside of me off. That was before I'd been honed into a hard, cold thing at the hands of the men who made me. I wanted to make them pay. I wanted to clear my father's name. I wanted to save my family, but all I did was put everyone I loved right in the crosshairs of something so much bigger than any of us could have imagined. I heard my voice break and felt the way all of my muscles started to lock. It was fight or flight, and when I'd fallen into the wrong hands, the only choice I'd been given was fight. That conditioning was hard to shake even after all these years.

"That's what your father said. He blames the government for her death and thinks they framed him and sent him to prison so they could get their hands on you." It sounded outrageous, fictitious, and paranoid.

I believed with every fiber of my being that all of it was true.

I peeled my eyes open and blinked in surprise when I realized she was standing directly in front of me, close enough to touch. Without even trying, those knowing eyes of hers stripped away all the layers I'd spent years wrapping myself up in.

"When I wrote that predictive program that the military bought, I thought that would be the end of it. I thought they would use it to make the world a safer place, that they would utilize it to bring peace to places in the world that have been war-torn since before either of us were born. It was solid code that was adaptive. The program was designed to save lives, but our government used it to take them. They tweaked the code so that the algorithm predicted where it was most likely to find terrorist camps instead of possible targets. They called it preemptive measures. They wanted to stop the people behind the attacks rather than the attacks themselves. It was never about helping victims but about declaring war and waving their dicks around. My program made it possible for them to make sure they always had the most inches. They sent drones in and wiped out entire families, complete villages, without proper research. They didn't have enough evidence to prove if the program was accurate or not, but they used it anyway. I have no idea how many innocent people died because of me, or how many more will. I know it's a lot, but knowing the actual number might cripple me." I wasn't exaggerating.

"Last I heard, they were still using it. Hit or miss, if they take out the bad guys or not." They wanted to take out the offenders, not save the innocent. Our goals had never been the same. From the beginning, what I had intended was bastardized and tainted. As a result, new terror groups got their legs under them and had moved to hiding in plain sight. More people have died for no reason, people simply trying to commute to work, or enjoying coffee with friends, people gathering in a crowd on a street minding their own business. It was possible my program would have pinpointed those exact locations, that it would have stopped those needless slaughters, but we would never know, because the powers that be instead used it to justify dropping bombs on undisclosed locations in the desert. All of it left a bitter, nasty taste in my mouth.

"They wanted you to write more software they could use against anyone they considered a threat to American soil, didn't they?" She sounded so understanding. The reason I never talked about my past was because it hurt. The pain was always amplified when I realized whomever was hearing my story looked like they were struggling to believe it.

"That's the problem with being smart. People think that intelligence is an unending commodity, that the well never runs dry. They wanted to pick my brain clean, but my mom insisted that Savina and I use our gifts to give back to society. She was convinced we were going to be part of a new Renaissance. She honestly thought my sister and I were going to change the world. She refused to let them tie me up in all their governmental red tape. She told them one program was enough, and if they wanted more, they could approach me when I was eighteen. She knew I was too scattered, too adventurous to tie myself to any one kind of programing. I wasn't interested in warfare or military strategy." I jolted when her hand landed on the center of my chest, her fingers smoothing over the cotton of my t-shirt like she was trying to soothe the erratic beat of my heart. I leaned into her like her small frame could keep me up when I was ready to collapse under memories and regret. "If I had given them what they wanted, something that would have taken no time and almost no effort on my part, maybe my mom would still be alive. She told the men who came for me no and her lab blew up the next week. My dad was arrested a month later, and they picked me up for the hack a month after that. My sister was left on her own, unprotected and vulnerable. The DoD told me if I did what they asked, if I let them completely own my body and mind, they wouldn't lock me up next to my father. They promised they would train me and give me the tools I needed to excel physically and mentally, all while keeping Savina safe. They knew she was all that I had left. I was obsessed with her safety and they used it to gain my compliance. They knew I would do whatever they wanted as long as no one touched her." My jaw clenched and there was a familiar burn at the back of my eyes. My hands curled into fists and my throat felt like it was going to close in on itself. It hurt. Talking about the past, remembering my sister. I never let that pain out. I kept it locked down with everything else, contained it and controlled it. She was the only person I'd ever shared it with, and that hurt in a different way, one that left me confused on top of everything else.

"What they wanted was for me to be a mass murderer. They wanted me to create weapons and strategy that would wipe out entire countries in the blink of an eye. They wanted me to change the world in an entirely different way than what my mother envisioned for her children, and they wanted me to do it while they pulled my strings and fiercely controlled my creativity and ingenuity. They swore up one side and down the other it was for the best. If I fell into the wrong hands, enemy hands, then I would be declared an enemy of the state, and the honey pot that was my mind would be considered a weapon of mass destruction. Then my own government, the men who were training me, molding me, challenging me, would have no choice but to end me."

It burned like acid in my gut to admit that I'd been so easily manipulated. It made my teeth grind together and my jaw tighten when I thought about how malleable I'd been. I'd played right into their hands. I'd lost the game before I even knew we were playing. They set a trap and I walked right in like the naïve, unassuming child I was.

"They wanted you to be Captain America? A super soldier?" Noe sounded both horrified and amused.

If we were talking about anything else, I would have laughed. There was a moment when they had had me running drills and training with weapons that I wondered the same thing. I could do PT with the best of them and would probably make it through BUDs Seal training, if I had to. There wasn't much I didn't know how to do with my mind, and the government made it so the same was true with my body. The truth was, they only wanted me skilled enough to protect myself if someone else came after the unbelievable asset that was my mind. They wanted to keep their prized possession safe and out of enemy hands, and the first step in that was making sure I could kick ass and throw down if anyone they deemed a threat came after me. They wanted me to be able to take care of myself but rely on them . . . and I had. Much longer than I liked to think about.

"I'm no hero and I'm not interested in trying to save the world anymore. I just wanted to save my sister." And I failed. Hard.

"They did a shit job of keeping her safe. She had more than one stalker according to the articles I read. She was constantly in the news and the public eye," Noe sounded angry, and I remembered how hot and turbulent it felt when anger was the only thing keeping me going.

I wrapped my fingers around her tiny wrist and felt her pulse flutter rapidly against the touch. The frantic beat matched the one pounding between my ears, it was a fight song only she and I could hear. My frozen heart struggled to keep up with the powerful rhythm.

"I never realized they needed to protect her from herself. The stalkers never got close to her, but she was lonely, isolated by fame and her incredible gift. I was her only friend, the only one who understood her, and when I was taken away, she lost her hold on reality. She lost the only person she related to. We were more than close." Twins had a connection that went deeper than most siblings. She was my other half. She was the best parts of me and she was the one who was special because of who she was, not because of what she could do.

I swallowed past the lump in my throat and squeezed my fingers around Noe's wrist hard enough that she let out a low gasp. I was looking into her dark eyes, but I wasn't seeing anything but my sister's casket getting lowered into the ground. "When she committed suicide, she set me free. The DoD knew they didn't have anything else to hold over my head when her safety was no longer an issue. They didn't have anything that kept me compliant, and with all the training they'd given me, I was far more dangerous than when they took me. They lost the only bargaining chip they had, and now I really was a weapon of mass destruction. They threatened to lock me up, but after Savina was gone, I didn't care. I thought I was going to die. I wanted to." They'd been training me to compartmentalize my feelings for years. They wanted me to separate how I felt about what needed to be done from the very logical questions and reasons for *why* those things had to be done. There was no place for emotion in war. It was all tactical and strategic, but when Savina died, there was nothing. There was no emotion and no reasoning. I disappeared into the void she left behind. I was practically catatonic and I felt like I had lost a limb.

"No," She whispered the word out and leaned forward so that her forehead was planted in the center of my chest.

"I did. I was unresponsive. I stopped eating. I stopped drinking. I didn't care about anything. The guys at the DoD tried all kinds of shit to get me back: therapy, drugs, torture. They tried to bribe me, promised to let my dad out of prison if I would snap out of it. They could control me, but they couldn't control the grief." I shook my head and lifted a hand so I could thread it through the silky strands of her hair resting on the back of her neck. "I was broken, so they let me go. They had no use for a weapon that was bound to misfire when they needed it most."

She lifted her head, eyebrows raised, and a million questions crowding her eyes. "Just like that?"

I shook my head in the negative and heaved a sigh that felt like it weighed a thousand pounds. "No, not just like that." Nothing was ever that easy. "They keep eyes on me at all times, waiting for the day I slip up and let them know I've learned to function again. I spend every minute of every day making sure I don't do anything special, that I'm nothing more than an ordinary guy who is good with computers. I've spent the last several years working for criminals and killers. Something they know would make my mother turn over in her grave. I don't do anything remarkable. I don't create anything that would ever make them think they want me back. I live my life in the dark. I use a fraction of my brain, and I live with the knowledge that I'm the reason my entire family was destroyed. I could go back, could let them use me as they see fit so my father is freed, but I don't. I play dumb and feel helpless. I couldn't help you because I don't even know how to help myself."

It was a good thing Nassir and Benny hadn't let me go after her when she was at the docks. There would be no hiding the things I knew how to do when I took whomever was in my way out of the picture trying to get to her. I could be just as effective as Booker when it came to the point and shoot. It wasn't in my nature the way it was in his, but in order to get to her, I would have spilled my secrets and Nassir, as well as the ever-watchful eye of Big Brother, would know exactly what I was capable of. I was a dangerous man, one with nothing to lose.

I was in so deep that drowning had become comfortable.

We stared at each other silently for a long, drawn-out minute. I waited for her to tell me how disappointed she was in me, how I had shattered her illusion of the man I was. I waited for her to spit in my face and look at me with undisguised repulsion. She was so much stronger than I was, so much better at taking care of herself. I was a broken toy with no one to mend my pieces.

I stopped breathing when she lifted a hand and gently ran her finger over the curve of my bottom lip. "Sounds like you know your way around a pretty impossible situation, Stark. If anyone can take Goddard down, it's going to be you."

I was so far from cold it wasn't funny. All that emptiness inside of me suddenly felt full. There was so much pressure inside of my chest I couldn't get a breath around it. My hands curled on the counter so I didn't touch her. I'd never had to fight down the urge to keep my hands to myself before. Everything about this woman was a battle. I fought everything about her and how she made me feel.

She was wrong about Goddard. I couldn't do shit to him on my own because I was fucked up and frayed at the end of all my wires. Short circuiting without the tools to stop the sizzle. It was going to be us . . . had to be us . . . together . . . because she would fight, and I was going to give her all the ammunition she needed to take the bastard down.

CHAPTER 9

Noe

H IS STORY WAS CRAZY . . . but then again, so was mine.
I'd spent forever trying to get anyone to believe me
when I told them what was going on behind closed
doors in the fancy house on the Hill, and no one would listen. It
would be easy to dismiss Stark's wild tale as the product of a paranoid mind, a story only a genius could craft and was impossible
to prove. However, I saw the way his typical reserve cracked when
he talked about losing his sister. I saw how he believed every word
he spoke when he declared himself broken and malfunctioning. I
could feel the way guilt and something bigger, something heavier,
held him down when he blamed himself for his father's lack of
freedom. It was a backstory that belonged to a superhero . . . or
an evil mastermind hell bent on world domination. I decided that
Snowden Stark had a little bit of each in his eyes.

He hadn't quite figured out if he was one of the good guys or
one of the bad ones yet. The truth was he hovered somewhere in

between the two.

His fingers circled my wrist where my hand was still resting on the center of his wide chest. I expected his heartbeat to slow when he was done talking, but it sped up as soon as his fingers found my pulse.

"I've never been distracted by a woman before," His words were soft, low, and slightly angry. The storm in his eyes built as did the tension that always seemed to be coiled so tightly around the two of us when we were within touching distance of one another.

I scoffed lightly and let him draw me closer. I had to crane my neck back in order to meet his gaze and his eyes followed the movement intently. They locked onto the exposed column of my throat, and I wondered if he could see my pulse fluttering like a trapped bird underneath the skin. "The way you look, I find that hard to believe. I'm willing to bet women go out of their way to distract you on a regular basis." I'd seen the beautiful girls Nassir hired to work for him in his clubs and elsewhere. There was no shortage of distractions in the circles this man ran in.

His dark eyebrows lowered and his eyes sharpened behind the lenses of his glasses. He always looked like he was trying to figure out something important, something that would fix everything. He always looked like he was seeking out answers to questions that hadn't been asked yet. It was beautiful. He was beautiful in his own, unusual way.

"I told you, I'm not exactly personable. I'm not good with people, women, in particular. They don't know what to do with me, and I don't know what to do with them outside of the bedroom. Most don't like much about me beyond the way I look." He frowned and his next words made me suck in an audible breath. "I like the way some of them look. I like the way some of them talk. I like the way a couple of them move. I like the way a few of them think, but I've never met one that I like everything about. Spending time with most of them is boring and useless."

His eyes lifted to mine and I swore I could feel myself being swept up in the tempest and temptation that lurked there. I moved closer still and almost groaned when his big, rough hands settled on my hips.

"Never met a woman I wanted to spend more time with until you, Noe Lee. I like the way you look, the way you talk, the way you move, and the way you think. You are never boring, and for the life of me, I can't figure you out." His voice dropped even lower and I let out a strangled sound of surprise when he used his hold on my waist to lift me like I was nothing so that I was planted on the countertop in front of him, legs dangling on either side of his lean hips. I shifted my hold to his shoulders and refused to pull away as his slate gaze bore into mine. I was the problem he was looking for a solution to and I wasn't about to tell him that there wasn't one. If he put all the pieces of the puzzle that was me and my fucked-up life together, he would get bored and move on. I wasn't ready to be unraveled just yet.

"Stop trying. Take what I give you at face value and understand it's far more than I've given anyone else." So much more. He knew the whole story and was smart enough to know how it had changed me. No one else got that. I didn't trust anyone else with my truth and honesty. Never allowing the scattered pieces of myself to be exposed for anyone to see.

He stepped closer to me, forcing my legs to open wider. I was still in borrowed clothes, which were way too big, but I could feel his heat and his hardness between my legs. It made me lightheaded and had my skin warming and my pulse pounding. He was so big it was easy to get overwhelmed by him, but it was his eyes and the way they were trying to take me apart that had me shivering. The man seemed like he could peer directly into my soul, and he didn't appear to mind all the grime and filth that clung to it. In fact, the tattered conditions of my insides were nothing compared to the ravages of his. I'd held onto what was left with both hands, he'd let his go entirely and was just now starting to notice the loss.

"What if I want more than what you give me?" He hadn't had much of anything since his sister died. If I wasn't careful, he would take all I had and leave me with nothing. I couldn't let that happen again. I felt the heat of the words as he touched my mouth. Perched up on the counter, I was almost eye level with him, and all of my most interested parts were lined up perfectly with the parts of him that felt just as attentive. The press of his hardness between my legs was making my breath shaky and nipples hard.

"Don't be greedy. You can always ask for more if you aren't satisfied." The double entendre made his lips twitch and I moved my fingers from the back of his neck so that I could trace the scar on the side of his head. He watched me silently as my touch moved to the barcode inked behind his ear. His skin was hot and the gentle caress made his entire massive frame stiffen in front of me. I blinked and told him quietly, "You're distracting, too, Snow." I liked his first name. It made him more human. There was nothing cold or distant about him now that he was pressed against me.

He grunted a response and bent so he could close the last inch or so that separated his mouth from mine. My fingers raked across the short hair at the back of his head and my legs automatically wrapped around his waist. I let out a moan that he promptly swallowed. His tongue darted between my open lips and touched mine with purpose and intent. His hands landed on the small swell of my ass and tugged until there was no space left between his hips and mine. My thighs clenched around his waist and I involuntarily ground myself against that rigid length trapped behind his jeans. He felt unbelievably good, even though the fit wasn't exactly right. If I wasn't careful, if he didn't watch himself, he really could hurt me . . . in all kinds of ways.

He had to bend and I had to lift. I had to hold on and he had to hold me. It meant a lot of grabbing hands to go along with the twisting tongues, but it was hot, and I definitely wasn't complaining about any of it.

One of his hands skated over my hip and found the hem of my borrowed t-shirt. The width of his palm covered my ribcage and the edge of his thumb brushed along the underside of my breast. My already hard nipple tightened even more, and I tried to pull him closer even though there was no space separating us. I wiggled myself against his straining erection and felt my eyes flutter closed at the hard pressure straining against the soft place at the apex of my thighs, warm and wet. It usually took more than a little foreplay to get me going. I usually needed the time to get out of my head and to lock away old memories, oftentimes nightmares.

Not with Stark.

All it took with him was a little pressure, a barely there caress, and I was ready to jump out of my skin. I wanted to pull his shirt off and sink my teeth into those tattoos winding around his torso. I wanted to pop the button on his jeans and sink to the floor in front of him, so I could face that beast I was rocking against. I wanted him to cover me, to block out anything but him, and lose us both in the storm he always seemed caught in. I wanted his hands all over me and inside of me. I wanted to give him a real reason to be distracted, so distracted he was thinking of me long after I walked away from him. Long after this seemingly impossible quest for revenge ended.

I choked out his name as his thumb found my aching nipple and slowly started to circle it. His touch was a little tough, slightly uneven, but I liked it. I liked that he didn't have all the answers to all the things, and I smiled because I realized I might just know a little bit more about something than he did. Even if the something I knew more about was as carnal and as basic as sex. I arched my back and thrust my throbbing peak more firmly into his hand and groaned when he shifted from stroking to lightly tugging on the tender tip. I could feel a tremor working its way from my core outward and I gasped as hot pleasure tripped along every nerve ending.

We were still fully clothed, had barely rounded second base, and I was as close to coming as I would be if he had his mouth between my legs. The thought evoked images of his surprisingly rough hand and unsmiling mouth doing decadent things to me. It made me shiver and dig my fingernails into the tendons on the back of his neck hard enough to make him growl.

The sound vibrated against my parted lips and I sank my teeth into the bottom curve of his. His glasses were slightly askew and it was adorable. I wanted to rip them off his face and demand that he fuck me. Dry humping was nice and all, but I wanted my hands all over what he was working with. I felt like a kid at Christmas who knew she was getting exactly what she asked for from Santa. I needed the wrapping paper out of the way so I could play with what was inside.

The hand he had on my ass tightened as I thrust my hips against his hard cock. His heat scaled and the pressure against all my most sensitive parts felt really, really good. In fact, if I slid a hand down the front of the baggy sweatpants I was wearing and touched myself, just barely, it would be enough to send me over the edge.

But it wasn't my fingers I wanted. It was his.

"I need you to touch me, Snow." The words escaped choppy and breathless, pleading and insistent. I had had hands all over me the last few days that I didn't want and didn't ask for. I'd been touched when it was the last thing I wanted. I'd been hurt and manhandled. I needed his hands. The ones I'd asked for, the ones I was ready to beg for, the ones I put myself willingly into to remind myself this was up to me . . . he only got what I was willing to give. I didn't want to think about how much that was. The man was tempting and dangerous. If I wasn't careful, I would hand over my heart without a fight. Even though he'd never given any indication he wanted it.

He lifted his head from where he was tracing the sensitive shell of my ear with his tongue and looked at me through hooded eyes. "I am touching you." He gave the nipple trapped between his fingers a hard tug that I felt all the way through my body, and his fingers dug deeper into my ass.

For a smart man, he could be incredibly dense. I put my hands on his cheeks, his stubble rubbing against my fingertips, and buried my heels in his backside. "No. I need you to *touch* me."

He stilled and stared at me for a long second. He watched as I waited. Our breaths were the only sound competing with the pounding of my heart in the quiet apartment. I was giving him more than he asked for and I felt like I was balancing on the edge of something huge and scary, waiting to see if he was going to join me.

He blinked behind the lenses and then an animalistic, possessive, raw sound was ripped out of the center of his broad chest. There was nothing robotic or practiced about it. He was nothing more than a man who had his hands on a woman, who wanted him so much she couldn't think straight. He was just as human and as hungry as the rest of us. He was better at hiding it, but not from me.

The hand that was holding onto my ass slipped over my hip and brushed over my lower stomach. His fingers were long and strong, the tips rough against my skin. He paused to trace the bruises that were left from my ordeal at the hands of Goddard's goons, and I could see the anger that chased the passion in his eyes. In order to keep him on track, I attacked the side of his neck with my teeth and worked my hand under the hem of his t-shirt so I could trace the corrugated lines of his tight abs with my fingers. The guy was a monster and I loved everything about being pinned and held against all that strength. It was straight up fantasy material, even if he wasn't anyone's idea of a dream guy.

His fingers disappeared into the top of my sweatpants and both of us stilled when he realized I wasn't wearing any underwear. That wasn't something Booker had on hand for me to borrow and I hadn't gotten around to seeing what the woman who used the apartment as a safe house before me left behind. I moved a hand to circle his thick wrist and opened my mouth to let out a silent sound when the tip of his middle finger slid down through the dampness that was already collected and made my inner thighs wet.

His nostrils flared and his jaw ticked furiously as my body pulsed around him.

"Hot." The word seemed like it was wrenched out of him.

"Yes." Mine was barely audible and strangled.

His tricky digit slid farther down, tracing sweet folds and slipping through liquid pleasure.

"So wet." Obviously.

I choked out a laugh. "Are you surprised?" How could he be? I was wrapped around him, practically melting into him.

My eyes snapped shut as his middle finger found entrance at

the exact same time his thumb rolled across my clit. I groaned and tightened my hold on his wrist and I rubbed myself against his touch like a cat.

"I . . . maybe a little." I'd heard Stark sound a lot of ways but unsure wasn't one of them. I had no idea how he could doubt I wanted him when I was the one chasing after him.

I wanted to reassure him that this was exactly what was supposed to be happening between us. I gave him my truth and he gave me his. Both were messed up, ugly, and hard to hear, but we were still standing. His past was darker than mine, cloudier and convoluted, but somehow even with all those shadows in the way, we managed to see each other. We managed to find the only other person in the world who would believe, the only one who would trust. I couldn't say anything because his finger was pumping in and out of my soaking center and his thumb was stroking my clit relentlessly. All I could do was throw my head back and ride the wave of pleasure that was crashing through me. It rushed around me, coating his fingers and leaving me shaken and breathless in his hold. His tongue traced along the line of my neck and I could feel his appreciative sigh against my skin as my body tugged and quaked uncontrollably around him. His fingers dragged wetness across my skin when he pulled from my body. I thought I was going to come again when he lifted them to his mouth and flicked his tongue across the shiny surface. His eyebrows arched and that sound that wasn't close to human rumbled out of his chest again.

I knew it wasn't going to take much. A little bit of Stark went a long way.

My legs fell weakly from his hips and I slumped backwards so I was sprawled bonelessly across the top of the counter. My chest was heaving and my heart was thudding, but I'd never felt better. I couldn't remember when having a man's hand on me had ever felt as right, as destined, and as perfect as his did.

I could still feel his erection throbbing between my legs. Before I could offer to do something about it, he stepped away, pulled off his glasses, and rubbed his hand over his face.

"Like I said, distracting. I like the way you come, Noe." His voice wasn't exactly steady, thrilling the secret, soft part of me that I liked to pretend I didn't have. "We need to talk about what our next step with Goddard is before we get interrupted . . . or distracted again."

I stared up at the ceiling wondering how he could ignore the electric heat that was still swirling around us like a living, breathing thing. I heaved a sigh and pushed myself to a sitting position. He moved a couple of steps away but I could still clearly see the outline of his cock behind the taut line of his zipper.

"Goddard will still be there after I suck your cock, Snowden." I really wanted to know how he tasted, how he looked when he finally lost control. I hopped off the counter and started to move toward him.

His eyes widened and then narrowed as he held up a hand and took another step away from me. His jaw tightened and I saw his cheek twitch as he told me harshly, "I need to think. I need to plan. I need to keep you safe, and I can't do any of that if all I'm thinking about is how your lips would look wrapped around my dick. I'm going to take care of you, Noe."

I paused mid-step and cocked my head to the side so I could consider his words without losing my shit. I didn't need him to take care of me. I was just fine taking care of myself in most things, but in this one instance, I really wanted him to have a hand in it. I didn't want to take care of the hollow ache between my legs by myself, and I didn't want him to touch the seriously impressive length that was making the front of his jeans obscenely tight. That was all mine. I understood his reluctance wasn't about rejection. It was about him having to prove something. He wasn't going to budge. I could see it in every stiff line of his big body. and I had to admit it sent a different kind of thrill shooting through me when I realized he really meant what he said. He was going to take care of me.

"Maybe you are part robot after all. No man I've ever come across would rather talk strategy than get his dick sucked." I sounded a little petulant. I really wanted to show him I could make him feel as good as he made me feel. I wanted him to realize I was a woman who knew exactly what to do with him in the bedroom and out of it.

I could handle Snowden Stark. The part of him who was a tortured genius and the part of him who was a broken brother.

"Getting my dick sucked won't keep you alive. Strategy will." He huffed out a breath and rolled his heavy shoulders. "Can we stop talking about my dick? I'm trying to think."

I snorted out a laugh and turned to walk to my spot in the kitchen. "As long as you realize I reserve the right to bring your dick back up at a more opportune time." I wiggled my eyebrows at the sly play on words.

He put his glasses back on and looked up at the ceiling like he was looking for help from the heavens. "Fine. Once Goddard is gone, we can talk about my dick whenever you want, but right now I want to talk about the first part of taking the Mayor down. I need to get into his computer. I need a backdoor so we have access to everything we need."

I rested my elbow on the marble next to my laptop, his laptop, resting my chin in my hand. I lifted an eyebrow back at him. "How do you plan to get close enough to install the software you need? It's not like you can waltz into his office in City Hall. You're pretty memorable." He was too big and too tattooed to forget.

"I can't walk in and I'm not letting you get anywhere near him, but I know someone who can get close without any questions."

I smirked at him. "For a guy who claims to be bad with people, you sure have a lot of them willing to help you out."

He blinked at me while assessing my words. I wondered if he was so fixated on what he'd lost that he couldn't see what he had standing right in front of him.

I gave him a grin and waved a hand in the air. "Go ahead and dazzle me with your mind, Stark, but don't think for a second that you didn't dazzle me with your hands or your mouth a minute ago."

I wasn't sure, but I could have sworn he breathed a sigh of relief.

I wanted Snowden Stark. However, the moment I listened to him talk about the methodical, meticulous way he planned to destroy Jonathan Goddard, I realized I never wanted him as an enemy.

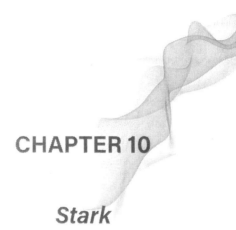

CHAPTER 10

Stark

IN A PERFECT WORLD, which this was not, I would have been able to get all my ducks in a row and have everything moving forward as soon as I got my wayward body under control and tamped down the overwhelming need to possess, to own . . . to conquer what Noe Lee sent spiraling through me. As it was, it took longer to get my head back in the game than I thought, and Nassir called wanting an update on the situation with his girl.

Since I owed him more than I would ever be able to repay, I spent the rest of the afternoon tracking down the information he wanted instead of destroying the Mayor. The hooker was clean. She didn't show any influx of sudden income in her accounts and the messages to his wife hadn't come from her but rather a burner phone that was untraceable. Upon further examination, I was slightly surprised to find that the man's wife was hemorrhaging money. She had an unhealthy addiction to online gambling and was a lot smarter than her husband gave her credit for. She was well aware of his standing date with Nassir's girl, and instead of being pissed about it, she was the one blackmailing him for the twenty grand. It looked like she had drained their kid's college fund and was desperate to replace the money before graduation. She wasn't very sneaky, leaving proof of her addiction all over the family's home computer. I wasn't surprised the site she used to waste her money was one that Race ran. The man was crafty when it came to robbing people blind, and he made sure the house always won. The poor woman didn't stand a chance, so it was no wonder she resorted to both revenge and blackmail. I was just glad Nassir's girl was in the clear because it made me uncomfortable to think about how things would have worked out for her if she had violated the Devil's standing orders. Nassir didn't tolerate insubordination. He didn't tolerate much of anything.

The second hurdle was Titus being a stubborn asshole. I'd called him three times and each and every time, he'd hung up on me before I could explain exactly why I needed him to march into Goddard's office and plug a loaded USB into the man's computer. I also wanted him to sync my phone to the Mayor's, but that might be a reach since Titus was flat-out refusing to help. He was the only person who could walk into City Hall without drawing suspicion. No one would question why a decorated detective, who was as tough on crime as the Mayor claimed to be, wanted to meet with the corrupt bastard. Plus, there was the dead, dirty cop in the water off the docks. It wouldn't seem suspicious if Titus wanted to talk to the Mayor about that. Titus wasn't budging.

He told me he refused to get caught up in any of Nassir's games, and that even though his girl worked for the man, he did his best to keep clear of anything the Devil deemed worth his time. He repeated over and over again there was no report of sexual abuse from the stepdaughter, no proof Noe had been kidnapped, because the tapes only showed the dirty cop hauling her to that shipping container and in this town, that could mean anything. He needed something solid if he was going knocking on the Mayor's door. That's the way things worked. I tried to explain that I needed his help for me and not for anything to do with Nassir, that he didn't have the entire story, but Titus shut me down by telling me, "You can judge a man by the company he keeps."

I refrained from pointing out that his baby-mama had a hand in getting his brother's girlfriend kidnapped, and that said brother was an ex-con and unrepentant car thief. I was trying to get the guy to hear me out, not piss him off even further.

It was actually Noe who came to the rescue. Tired of waiting around for justice to go unanswered, she was the one who suggested we offer the cop something in the deal he wouldn't be able to refuse. We needed to appeal to his ingrained sense of right and wrong and his zealous need to keep his streets and department clean. She was the one who mentioned that Booker said Titus went off the deep end when he told him about the dirty cop. It was no secret the Point had their fair share of corruption in the police department, but Titus had been working closely with Internal Affairs to shut down as much of it as he could. You couldn't keep the streets safe if you knew the good guys working them broke the rules as often as the bad guys. She cleverly pointed out that if we were going after Goddard's money, we were more than likely going to find the names of the people on his payroll, including the cops. Titus King could do a lot of damage with such a list. He could get his department back and get the wolves wearing sheep's clothing away from the flock he was so desperate to protect.

It was the obvious answer. One that shouldn't have taken me so long to see. She was messing with more than my dick, and I didn't like it. I'd been pretending to be an idiot for a long time; actually being one was far less fun and it made my skin feel too tight. I lost everything that mattered to me. The only thing I had left was my ability to outthink everyone around me, everyone except for Noe Lee, apparently.

Reluctantly, Titus agreed to get me into Goddard's computer. He couldn't resist the lure of returning hard won dignity to the badge, and begrudgingly, he admitted that it really bothered him he couldn't do anything for Noe or Julia Grace. Sometimes being law abiding sucked, especially in a place that ate rules and regulations for breakfast. He did warn that if Goddard caught on to what was going down, he was going to disavow knowing anything about it. There was only one criminal he was willing to put his ass on the line for, and she was getting ready to have his baby.

I told him the only way he was going to get caught was if Goddard noticed him putting the flash drive into the computer or noticed him setting my phone down next to his. In order to make sure neither of those things happened, Noe was going to make sure Goddard had to step out of the office while Titus was there for their meeting. She was going to call in and use the recording software she had used to fool him before, make him think his stepdaughter was reaching out. We were all hoping the man had enough sense of self-preservation to excuse himself and take the call away from the prying eyes of the police. If he didn't, I was going old school: running into the fucking building and pulling the damn fire alarm. It was far less technical but it would get the job done in a pinch.

I was twitchy and anxious leaning against the side of the cop's cherry GTO. It was one of the few things he had in common with his felonious younger brother. They were both big, badass dudes who liked old muscle cars that were loud and looked mean. He'd parked it a few blocks away from City Hall and told me not to move a muscle. I had my laptop open on the roof of the car, waiting to see if Titus came through and made the connection. While I paced aimlessly on the sidewalk, Noe was busy making me an ID that declared I was none other than Jonathan Goddard. Once I had all his personal information, I was headed to the closest, no questions asked insurance office to take out a policy that would freeze every account he had when that death certificate was handed over. That was one good thing about the Point. There were plenty of places willing to turn a blind eye to obviously shady dealings for the right price.

My computer binged with an alert and my head whipped around as the screen lit up with green code. The first thing I did, as I started frantically typing on the keyboard, was to turn on the microphone so that anything and everything Goddard said while he was near the computer was recorded and transmitted back to mine. I turned on the webcam for the same reason and set up the shadow software so that every website he visited, every word he typed, was tracked and relayed to me. I didn't want to move too fast, or make him suspicious right off the bat, so I started small by rooting out all his vital information: birth date, social security number, and mother's maiden name from his personnel file. I snorted at how easy it all was and sent the info in an email to Noe so she could have the ID ready for me when I got back to the house.

Since she didn't know where Julia was and didn't want the teenager involved in any of this, Goddard's money was going into a trust fund for the girl so that she could access it whenever she was ready. I told Noe that Nassir had a PI on his payroll who could track the girl down at a later date. Chances were, she was still using the identity Noe created for her, and that was as good enough place as any to start.

She replied with an email that stated no one in their right mind was ever going to believe I was in my mid-fifties. I told her all that mattered was that our information matched, not our faces. The place I was going for the forged documents wasn't going to look too closely at either after I slid them a fistful of cash to look the other way. But before I did any of that, I was going to have to find where the man hid his dirty money, because I knew for a fact it wasn't sitting in an account at any bank on the Hill. Guys like Goddard could teach guys like Race and Nassir a trick or two about hiding ill-gotten gains. Legislators were the best at keeping the bad things they did on the downlow.

I was poking at the keys on the keyboard and frowning at some of the extra security measures Goddard had installed when a heavy hand landed on my shoulder and my phone was shoved back into my hand. The screen was glowing green and the cloning app I'd asked Titus to sync to the Mayor's phone was already working. He was texting someone about Titus and his unexpected visit. The words were harsh and demanded that whomever he was texting get the decorated detective on a leash. I sucked in a breath when Goddard typed that an accident might be required if Titus didn't back off.

I held the phone out to the dark-haired man who stood eye to eye with me. Titus King was an intimidating man. His eyes were too sharp and he carried himself like the immovable monolith he was. The white streak in his hair made him look distinguished and slightly older than he actually was. Trying to protect this city and the people who called it home had taken its toll on the man, making him one of the few people I'd run across since the government set me loose who I wouldn't want to throw-down with. I was bigger, but he had more to lose and that always made a man dangerous.

"Can you tell me who he's sending that text to?" He sounded pissed, and I couldn't blame him.

I rubbed my thumb against the corner of my mouth and nodded. "Give me a sec. I told you we were dealing with a bad dude."

The big man sighed and ran a hand over his hair. "He didn't even blink when I asked about the dead cop or the torched motel. He gave me some song and dance about the crime rates in the Point being on the rise and needing a firm hand to deal with the offenders." He snorted and shifted so he was resting his hands on his hips as he watched me through narrowed eyes. "He turned white as a ghost when his receptionist came in and told him he had a call from Julia. How has no one in that house reported the fact she's missing? If they reported her as a runaway, law enforcement would be obligated to bring her back if they ran across her. Not to mention the kind of media coverage they would get."

I tapped the screen of the phone and scrolled through the replicated contact list until I found the name the threatening text had been sent to. "I told you the girl is pregnant. He knocked her up and by now she's more than likely showing. That's hard to cover up if she doesn't play along." I turned the phone to face Titus. "You know someone named Bullock? That's who he's texting."

"Motherfucker!" The cop reached up and pulled off his tie, tossing it furiously into the open window of the GTO. His face flushed with angry heat and he started to pace in front of me with short, quick steps. "Garett Bullock is the Assistant Commissioner. He's the one who's the go between us and City Hall. He's on Goddard's payroll?"

I shrugged. "It looks like. I'll know more once I find the money and see where it's going, but I would watch my back if I were you."

He swore again and looked up at the gray sky. "I give my girl shit about working for a criminal on a daily basis. How am I supposed to tell her I'm not any better? That the guys I work for are actually worse because they hide what they are? At least with Nassir, you know exactly what you're getting. All I ever wanted was to do right by the people who deserve it."

I dipped my chin in silent agreement. I knew all about wanting to help but feeling like your hands were tied. "You don't work for the guys who were elected, King. You work for the people who need you to protect and serve. You make a difference; anyone above you is only making money."

He grunted and lowered his eyes to the cement between his feet. "It never feels like enough."

I also knew that feeling well. I gave everything I had and it still wasn't enough to keep my sister alive. It wasn't enough to change lives and make the world a better place. I wasn't enough, but I couldn't let that happen again. I *had* to come through for Noe. No one else had showed up for her, and I refused to be another name on that list.

"Maybe it's not about what we can't do. Maybe it's about the fact you tried to do something in the first place. What you do might not be enough, but who you are sure as hell is enough, Detective. There are a lot of people willing to look the other way when something isn't right. They sweep things they know aren't right under the rug. We need men like you to face the wrong and to shake the rug out. Everything in life needs a series of checks and balances. Without you, everything is uneven." I'd tried to be one of the guys who evened things out, but the scales had tipped so drastically in the negative that the entire thing fell over. I didn't care about right and wrong anymore. I didn't care about anything . . . until Noe Lee.

I cared a whole fuck of a lot about her.

The minute I realized I regretted sending her away and that I wanted—no, needed—her back, it was like someone had turned on a faucet inside of me. All the sentiment that I'd shut off when my sister died rushed through my arid veins. I couldn't stop caring now, even if it would be better for both of us. I didn't have anything to offer her, not that she was the type of woman who collected hearts and feelings. She liked to keep her hands free so that she could make a quick getaway, and I was well aware of the fact that once she was free, once she didn't have to look over her shoulder anymore, she was going to ghost me. She was going to take what she needed and hit the road and I was going back to my cold, predictable life. Well, as predictable as working for a guy like Nassir could be.

Titus grumbled something under his breath and met my gaze with a pointed one of his own. "I could use some weight on my side of the scale, Stark." I knew he wasn't talking about my size, but about what I could do to help the people of the Point if I made the effort.

I shut down my laptop and sent Noe a text to tell her we were up and running on all fronts. "Never been the kind of guy who likes to throw my weight around, Detective."

He lifted a black eyebrow at me and the hard line of his mouth lifted into a smirk that almost made him look friendly. "No, but you aren't shy about shaking the rug when you think no one is looking."

I did my best not to flinch. I knew people talked about the hack into the sex offender registry and the sex trafficking cyber market I shut down. I had no idea anyone on the right side of the law was applauding my late-night missions to right the kind of wrongs I couldn't stomach. I hated when victims were voiceless and I hated it even more when no one listened when they did speak. Basically, everything that Noe had been battling before she showed up on my doorstep.

Wordlessly, I slid back into the GTO and wondered if I would be unable to help myself from righting any wrong I stumbled across now that Noe had turned my soul molten and rattled all the impenetrable things I kept locked around my insides. I'd always been more of a thinker than a doer, but something about her made me want to be both.

Maybe it was about time I put everything I learned from everyone—my altruistic mother, my overzealous father, my sweet sister, the manipulative, unscrupulous men who made me, the ruthless men who trusted me, the independent woman who needed me, and this good man who believed in me—to good use. Maybe it was time to be the man they thought I was and not the one who was so sure he had nothing and no one to live for.

CHAPTER 11

Noe

IT BECAME INCREASINGLY CLEAR that all Stark's plans to bring the Mayor down, as precise and intricate as they were, did not include me. He refused to let me go with him when he took the fabricated ID to get the fake insurance policy. He refused to let me tag along when he handed over the list of names that showed all the city officials and beat cops who had been taking payouts to look the other way while Goddard robbed the city blind and committed atrocious crimes against young women. As soon as Stark started poking around Goddard's computer, it became clear that Nassir couldn't get a handle on the sex trafficking and the Eastern Europeans because Goddard had a vested interest in keeping them in the Point. As it turned out, he didn't turn his nose up at doing business with people who didn't look like him when they were providing something he wanted, and what Goddard wanted was access to girls. Really, really young girls.

It was horrifying, but instead of talking to me about it or

working through how he planned to stop it, Stark had disappeared inside himself, just him and his laptop. It was like I didn't exist. I was pretty sure I could have paraded around the loft naked and he wouldn't even blink. I was tempted to try, but the idea that he really might not notice, or that he honestly might be able to resist my limited charms, kept me clothed. I was confident when it came to my appeal to men, but Stark was a different breed. The man was complex and unpredictable. He also wasn't sleeping. He wasn't eating. He was in the same room as I was but so far away that it felt like he was on another planet entirely. When I asked him questions or offered up suggestions, all I got in return was a monosyllabic response. If this was what it was like to watch a genius at work, I hated it. I wanted the broken Brainiac back. The one who watched me with heat and curiosity in his eyes. The one who wanted me just as badly as I wanted him.

On the third day of living in the vacuum where he sucked all the life out of everything, I decided I'd had enough. I appreciated that he was hell bent on destruction, but somewhere along the way he seemed to have forgotten that the reason he was so invested in vengeance was standing right beside him. I didn't like how easy it was for him to disconnect from me and from how all of this had to make him feel.

He was well on his way to completing the first step of the plan: taking Goddard's money. The man had offshore accounts in every island nation from here to the Philippines, but Stark had found them all. He'd also sniffed out the secret account Goddard opened under his stepdaughter's name that he used for most of his illicit dealing. He was also using an account he set up under the guise of a nonprofit after-school program that claimed to be directed toward supporting at-risk youth. There was money going in the account from investors and donations, but according to Stark, that money wasn't going back into the program, but being taken out in small chunks of cash. He mumbled that it was a different kind of payout than the huge transfers he traced through the fake account in Julia's name.

He didn't seem overly interested in that little blip. He was more focused on tracking down the list of the Mayor's top donors. As soon as he had the names, he was firing off email after email letting them know exactly where their hard-earned money was going. They were backing a criminal, and even if they didn't care about the kind of man they had put in office, the media would. Anonymously, he was already leaking bits and pieces of the information he uncovered. They were going to have a field day when the whole truth came out. Everyone loved a juicy, political scandal and this one was ready to leak all over the place.

I wanted to know where that money was going. I wanted to know why a man with so much to hide and so little regard for the people of his city had bothered to set up a program that was aimed specifically at the unfortunate youth of the Point. Something about the set up didn't sit right with me. Not too long ago, I was a teenager sleeping on the streets, trying to make it on my own, worried when it got cold and miserable and I couldn't scrounge up enough change for something to eat. I knew that desperation brought on the willingness to accept terrible things as the status quo. I would have been tempted to take any shelter that was offered and I may have been willing to look the other way to have a roof over my head and something warm to eat, but now I refused to ignore the fact that someone else might be stuck in that same awful position. If Goddard was exploiting the young and the poor, which I had zero trouble imagining him doing, then it needed to stop. Those without deserved the same justice as those who had everything.

I told Stark I was going out. I was sick of wearing clothes that didn't fit. Booker's pieces covered me up and swallowed me whole. Reeve's were too tight and too revealing, not that he noticed when I switched from one to the other. He barely lifted his head from his work when I started for the door. It wasn't until I hit the hallway and was waiting in front of the elevator that he must have realized I meant I was leaving the safety of the apartment. Just as the metal doors swished open, I felt a hand on my elbow and was turned around.

His eyes were bloodshot behind his glasses and he had dark, deep shadows in all the hollows of his handsome face. His stubble had moved from scruff to the start of a short beard, making him look rougher and tougher than he already did. I wasn't scared of him, but the look in his eyes and the tension rolling off his big body was scary.

"It's not safe out there. Goddard is still looking for you. You can't go prancing down the street like nothing happened the last couple of weeks. Next time he gets his hands on you, he's going to kill you to keep you from talking. You're as much of a liability as the girl is now." That logic of his was always right on point, but I couldn't sit by while he dismantled the Mayor's life anymore. I'd always been the type of person who was hands on, the type of person who made things happen instead of letting them happen to me. The vengeance he was orchestrating was mine, and I refused to let him write the song without me. I was the one who needed to sing it.

I tugged on my arm until he got the hint and let me go. It was getting old, him only noticing me when I wasn't around. I slipped my backpack off my shoulder and pulled a wool beanie out of the front pocket. I slipped it over my head, made sure all my hair was tucked underneath it, and scowled at him from under my eyebrows. "I know the danger I'm in. I'm the one who was tied up and knocked around. He won't be looking for a boy . . . you weren't when you were looking for me." He frowned even harder at the reminder I'd already been overlooked under his nose once. "I can't sit in that loft doing nothing while you dissect every single thing on Goddard's computer. I need to *do* something. I'm as much a part of this as you are, even if you can't see me standing here in front of you."

He rocked back on his heels and lifted his hands like he was trying to deflect the truth in my words. "I see you, Noe. I also see everything bad that can happen to you if you're not careful. When I close my eyes, all I picture is lowering you into the ground right next to my sister."

I swore under my breath because he wasn't playing fair. "I'm sick of living inside someone else's life and clothes. I can't be whoever this is forever. I need to get back to being me." I waved a hand over the gigantic, heavy metal t-shirt that hung to my knees and the baggy sweatpants that were rolled up so I could walk without tripping over the them. The outfit worked for my haphazard disguise, but it was no longer working for me. I wanted to feel like I was back in my own skin and back in control of my life.

He stared at me silently, those gears turning and grinding furiously behind his stormy gaze. He opened his mouth as if he was going to argue with me, then snapped it shut and looked back toward the open door of the expensive loft. "Let me finish pulling Goddard's tax returns for last year and I'll go with you, wherever you want to go."

I should have known he wasn't going to risk me getting snatched again. He was a minute too late the last time I needed him and he didn't want to drop the ball again, but I wasn't his responsibility. I wasn't his to take care of or to protect, even though a tiny part of me screamed in protest when I reminded myself of that.

"I'm going alone. I want to see what's going on at that nonprofit. Something isn't right and the kind of kids who would utilize that place aren't going to talk to you. They won't trust someone who doesn't know what it's like to have nothing. That kind of despair clings to you. It leaves a mark." He was too big and radiated too much power for skittish street kids to feel safe in his presence. They would clam up and hit the road the second they saw him coming. I would be able to slide through the ranks unnoticed and unquestioned in a way he never would.

His head jerked back and his chin lifted. "What do you think I have, Noe?" His tone was brittle and raspy reminding me his family was gone and the one thing he's always had, his mind, was locked away like the dangerous weapon it was. The safety was on and he'd only put his finger back on the trigger when I needed help.

I sucked a breath through my teeth and pulled my gaze away from his. That gray was as sharp as the edge of a knife. I was talking about his nice house and his designer jeans and boots. I was thinking about the fact that he was covered in obviously expensive artwork. Those diamond studs he wore in his ears were no joke and any kid who was hungry and homeless would resent the hell out of them. I didn't mean to diminish the fact he'd lost just as much as I had. I only meant it was obvious he was living a pretty cushy and comfortable kind of life, and that wasn't the case for most of the people where I was going.

I touched my ear where it was covered by the hat. "You have those shiny rocks in your ears and your glasses say Gucci. Anyone who has to find their dinner in a dumpster or goes without dinner altogether is going to notice those things, Stark."

He mirrored my action, his fingers brushing over the bigger set of jewels and the second smaller set. They were an oddly feminine choice for such an overtly masculine man to make, but on him they worked. "One set was my mother's. The other one belonged to Savina. I never take them off."

Well, shit. If that wasn't a kick right in the gut. I reached out a hand to touch him, to soothe, but he backed away, eyes hard. If my words had wounded him, he'd taken the pain and locked it away, somewhere deep and dark. He had an uncanny ability to go glacial when it suited him. His armor wasn't on the outside, it was wrapped around his insides, tight and impenetrable.

"Snowden." I took a step toward him but halted when he held up a wide hand and shook his head, telling me without words to stay where I was.

"I'm going to go with you." It was a statement, one that left no room for argument or negotiation. "Once we get wherever it is you're determined to go, I'll wait outside."

It wasn't the best option, but it was the only one he seemed willing to give me. He told me to wait for him while he grabbed something from the apartment and I debated bolting for the stairs and taking off on him anyway. I wasn't used to having anyone push back when I laid down the law, and I wasn't sure I appreciated his high-handed attitude, even though it was clear he believed he was acting in my best interest.

When he headed in my direction, I noticed he'd added a battered, black baseball cap to his outfit and had tossed on a well-worn hoodie that covered up his massive bulk. He still wouldn't blend in, but he looked more like the typical kind of guy you found walking the streets of the Point and less like an eccentric genius who could make his own rules. When he reached around me to call the elevator, the bottom of the heavy sweatshirt lifted and I caught a glimpse of the nine millimeter he'd forced me to take from Booker's apartment. The gun had remained untouched and unwanted, but seeing it tucked into Stark's waistband was a vivid reminder that danger was all around, and maybe I had been foolish in my rush to involve myself in the plans to ruin Goddard. I wasn't used to being idle. When I stopped moving and stopped doing, all the memories and recollections I swore I left behind had time to catch up to me. Being alone with my thoughts was never fun. Being alone with my thoughts and Stark's silence was even less fun, so I did what I always did: I ran away from it.

We shuffled into the elevator and immediately became engulfed in a suffocating quiet. The only sound between either of us was the sound of our breath. Mine were slow and steady as I tried to calm my racing heart and nervous twitches. His were low and furious. He was breathing fire, and again I wondered how one man could have cold inside of him, when he also ran so hot. I could feel his frustration pulsing in the air around us, but he didn't say a word until I started for the front doors of the complex. He grabbed my elbow again and told me his truck was in the parking garage on the lower level.

I shook my head so hard I almost lost the beanie that was hiding my hair. "We're taking the bus." The kids I wanted to talk to could spot a fake from a mile away so there was no way in hell I was going to blow my shot at information before I even made it to the center by rolling up in an unmissable 4x4.

When Stark made a face that clearly displayed his opinion on public transportation without saying a word, I calmly pointed out, "The cops won't pull a bus over. If Goddard still has people looking for me, they won't be looking on a bus."

He snorted in response but followed me out the front door anyway. "Buses have cameras. If Goddard has someone in tech working for him, they can track you using facial recognition software. It won't matter that you're dressed like a boy; your face is still the same."

Stupid, smart man. Always had to have an argument for everything. I sighed and looked at him out of the corner of my eye. It was time I leveled with him if I wanted him to understand why checking out the fishy nonprofit was so important to me. He might have a difficult time navigating his own emotions, but he had been nothing but reasonable when it came to dealing with mine. "I need the kids who use Goddard's program to talk to me, Stark. The things he did to Julia," I shook my head in disgust. "You know she wasn't his first victim. He didn't marry her mother until a couple of years ago. Before he had someone in his own home he could violate, he had to find victims elsewhere. I'm willing to bet he started the nonprofit for no other reason than to have an endless pool of desperate, hopeless victims. When you're in that situation, young, alone, and scared, there is no end to the risks you're willing to take when someone offers you something that seems too good to be true. I imagine Goddard violated those kids, and the small amounts of money he took from the donations were bribes to keep them quiet. You said part of bringing his house down around him was to uncover all his secrets. This one is one that definitely needs to see the light of day. Julia won't ever get the opportunity to tell her story, but the other people that man has hurt should be able to. They deserve to have a voice." Just like I'd deserved to be heard when I tried to tell people what was going on in my house up on the Hill.

I felt the warmth of his hand on my lower back as the bus rolled to a stop in front of us. The doors whooshed open and the driver gave us a considering look as we trudged up the steps. I dug my transit card out of the front pocket of my backpack and snickered as Stark had to fumble for change to pay for his ride. We made our way to a couple of empty seats. I had to put my backpack on my lap to make room for him, but even still, he took up more than his fair share of space. We were pressed together from shoulder to thigh when I realized we were getting a lot of odd looks. I realized he was the only person on the bus who knew I was a woman, and to everyone else we probably looked like the world's most mismatched gay couple. The thought turned my snicker into a full-on belly laugh, which earned me a lifted eyebrow from the man seated next to me.

I dug my elbow into his side and wiggled my eyebrows at him. "They think I'm your boyfriend."

He gave me a quizzical look then lifted his gaze to meet the curious ones watching us. I thought he would move to put some distance between us, that he would shift uncomfortably. Stark was a man who exuded masculinity and he was surrounded by men who were the same. I couldn't imagine any of them standing for having their sexuality or vitality called into question, especially by a bunch of nosey strangers, but Stark didn't seem phased by it. In fact, he moved so that his arm was behind me on the seat and lowered his head so that his lips almost touched my ear.

"I'm sorry that you felt like I was shutting you out. I get focused on a task and lose track of the real world. I didn't mean to ignore you or make you feel like you aren't a part of this, but I can't stand the idea of Goddard getting his hands on you again." I felt the tip of his tongue touch my ear and it made my entire body shiver under the layers of clothing I was wearing. "He's never going to be able to put his hands on anyone again when we're done with him. If you feel like you need to take steps to make that happen, then talk to me, smack me upside the head, stomp on my foot, or maybe pull all your clothes off and stand in front of me so I can't ignore what's happening around me. I'm here to walk with you, not force you to go around me." His fingers squeezed the back of my neck and I had to close my eyes and force myself not to lean into him.

"I was wondering if you would notice if I got naked." I meant it as a joke but there was a thread of uncertainty in my tone I couldn't hide.

He swore under his breath and leaned over so that his forehead was resting against my temple. "It might take me a minute because my mind is like a spider web, tangled and sticky. It's a trap, and once something is caught up in there, it's hard to get it free. I noticed you from the start, Noe. I see you, even when you're dressed like a boy."

His mind was like a spider web, beautiful, complex, and deadly. I couldn't stop the little thrill that raced through my veins at the thought of being caught up in those silken, delicate threads that made this man impossible to handle and hard to forget. "I appreciate you wanting me to be safe, but that's not something I've ever been." Living a life on the run was never benign. "I've learned a lot of tricks in my years on the streets. The least I can do is make sure kids like me know all my tricks, so they can learn from my mistakes." There was no Robin Hood in the Point. No one was showing up to steal from the rich and give to the poor, so those of us who were poor and were going to remain poor had to stick together.

His breath was hot and tickled the side of my neck. I had to bite back a sigh as I gave a nasty look to an older woman seated a few seats ahead of us, watching us with unblinking disgust. If I really were a gay man and Stark really were my boyfriend, I would be super annoyed at the obvious judgment and censure on her wrinkled face.

"We don't have to be what we've always been. Sometimes it's important to change, to learn how to be something better." The words were sweet, but they were also smart. He couldn't help being sharp and painfully insightful. I only wished he could apply it to himself, as well.

"And sometimes this is as good as it's going to get and that has to be enough." You took what little you had and made do.

He cocked an eyebrow and sat back in the narrow seat, something dark and hard to read floating through the hurricane that blew through his eyes. "And sometimes you find the person who makes you want more, and you have to decide how much you're willing to give."

Damnit. He always had an answer for everything and a knack for making me question what I'd always thought I'd known. This was exactly why I never asked for help or let anyone else in. Once they had a piece of you, they thought they were entitled to the whole damn pie. I didn't want to think about how hot and liquid the idea of feeding someone so clearly starving for affection and a connection made me.

Nope. I wasn't going to think about connecting with Snowden Stark at all.

CHAPTER 12

Stark

"**M**ORE BAD NEWS FOR *our currently embattled mayor.*" I looked at the TV as Booker turned up the volume. The pretty news anchor had a practiced look of concern on her face as she prattled on about Goddard.

"*After an anonymous source sent several concerning documents to the voters of this city and various members of the press, there was a resounding call for mayor Jonathan Goddard to release his financials and justify where he was spending our tax dollars. On the heels of the outrage over the misuse of government funds, an alarming look at Goddard's taxes was also released and quickly spawned an intensive investigation by the IRS. The mayor was forced to resign from his position during the ongoing investigation. He claims it's all a misunderstanding, that someone is setting him up, but the police can find no evidence of a computer hack.*"

There was no evidence. Titus had gone above and beyond his original agreement to help me get into Goddard's computer. The detective went back in after I had what I needed and wiped away any sign that I'd ever been there. He liked rattling Goddard. Liked putting the man on edge. He wanted the people playing dirty to know he was on to them. He wanted them to be afraid . . . just like the people who called the city they ruined home. He was coming for them and wasn't shy about sharing that fact. The house of cards was starting to fall, and Titus was getting a kick out of watching everyone scramble to clean up the mess.

The footage on the screen shifted to the media circus surrounding Goddard as he was escorted out of City Hall. He had his pale, thin hands over his face, but there was no missing his scowl or the stiff set to his shoulders. Flash bulbs illuminated his papery skin, making him look fragile and weak. I wanted to feel satisfied in a job well done, but I didn't. This wasn't even close to the bastard suffering enough.

"In the wake of the financial scandal, you might think things couldn't get much worse for the former, beloved mayor. However, today, in an alarming turn of events, several recordings featuring young, underage women who utilized Goddard's pet project in the Point, an after-school program designed to help at-risk youths, came forward with the shocking accusation that Goddard had inappropriate relations with them. Many of the young women are under the age of sixteen and claim the abuse started when they were barely teenagers. The recordings have not been verified at this time, but we, here at Channel 13 News, are actively looking for any accusers willing to substantiate the claims. Goddard's attorney refutes the women as vultures looking for a payday. He claims that tapes are fabricated and untrue. That the young women are just looking to capitalize on the former mayor's current legal woes. This is an ongoing investigation that we will be following until the conclusion. The police have opened an investigation and are looking for anyone to come forward and file a formal complaint against Jonathan Goddard."

Booker snagged the remote and turned the channel when the anchor went on to ramble about the weather the next day. It was going to be shitty. It was always shitty in the Point.

He leaned back on the couch and lifted his arms over his head, stretching out his big body. He'd been popping by the loft a lot the last few days. At first I was annoyed, thinking he didn't believe I could keep Noe safe on my own. I thought he was checking up on me. I quickly realized that his sudden desire to hang out had nothing to do with us and everything to do with the fact Race and his girl were back, and Booker was going out of his way to avoid the fair-haired duo. His apartment was much closer to theirs. He was hiding out.

I didn't ask him why. I figured if he wanted me to know, he would tell me, and I didn't mind his presence. It was a solid buffer between me and the tiny hurricane that was blowing my entire life apart. She'd been moody and unpredictable ever since we left that dilapidated building that held Goddard's dirtiest secrets. She told me she needed time, that listening to what Goddard did to those girls, the way he collected them, bribed them, and hurt them, forever changing them, did something to her. Some of her fight was missing. A good chunk of her defiance was gone. Instead of telling me everything that was wrong with the world, she'd gone silent and seemed buried underneath a mountain of damage. Watching others bleed had opened her old wounds and they were festering, weeping, and leaking out the kind of poison that could kill anything good. I'd been giving her space to work through it. Taking the coward's way out. Again, I figured if she wanted me to know what was working through her head and her heart, she would tell me so I could help figure it all out. She had to know I would never shut the door on her again.

She got the girls to talk to her, to tell her their stories, but she couldn't convince a single one of them to come forward and press charges against the asshole who stole their innocence and childhood. They were scared of backlash. They were terrified someone would make them pay back the measly monetary amount Goddard had forked over to keep them quiet. Now, instead of needing to stop Goddard for what he'd done to Julia Grace and to her, she felt like she needed to stop him for all those girls who would never get to have their own taste of revenge. She was consumed by it. She got up and stomped out of the room as soon as the story was over; I could tell she didn't feel like Goddard's fall from grace was far enough down, either.

Booker cracked his neck and the pop was loud enough to make me grimace and give him a look out of the corner of my eye. He ignored me and leaned forward so he could grab the beer on the coffee table in front of him. "When someone seems like they can handle anything that's thrown at them, that usually means they've been through hell and back. They've already had to handle the kind of shit that would break most people." He lifted an eyebrow at me, the scar giving him a sinister, dark look. "All this stuff is hurting that girl, boy genius. She is hurting."

He said it like I couldn't see the way her dark eyes glistened as she blinked away tears, or the way her normally pink lips were pulled tight in a pale, white line. I could see the shadows under her eyes and I felt the sharpness of her responses when she spoke to me.

"I know she is, but I don't know what to do about it." I'd been hurting for years and resigned myself to living with the pain. It was never comfortable or easy, but I'd adjusted.

He snorted and levered himself up off the couch. "Go make her feel better. Let her know she's not alone. Comfort her, boy genius.

She needs someone to lean on, and for whatever reason, the person she picked to trust is you. You already made her regret that choice once, don't do it again. For a smart guy, you can be pretty fucking stupid sometimes."

I narrowed my eyes at him as I also rose from the couch. "I'm not stupid, I'm just not good with people." I had said this same phrase so many times over the years it was starting to get old. Maybe it was time to stop using that as an excuse for shoving everyone away who got near me.

"Yeah, but she's not people, she's your girl. You don't have to be good with anyone but her. You'll figure it out eventually." He checked his phone and cracked his neck again. "I gotta go. Nassir has some bruiser from New York in the circle tonight to go up against Bax's boy. It's a good matchup and the money is big. The crowd is going to be after blood, so he pulled me out of the strip club and put me in the Pit to make sure none of the paying customers accidentally get trampled." He didn't sound like he minded the switch. I guess if you worked around beautiful, naked dancers every single night, they lost their allure. Either that, or he was as dead on the inside as I was. Our responses were broken, faulty. Blood and broken bones made more sense than undulating, glistening flesh.

Annoyed that he called me dumb, I prodded, "Is Race going to be there? If you see him tell him I said hey. I haven't seen him since they got back from visiting Karsen."

His whole body tensed when I mentioned her. The corner of his mouth tugged down in a frown and his free hand clenched in a fist so tight his knuckles turned white. We stared at each other for a long second until he visibly forced himself to relax.

"Don't got much to say to Race at the moment." The 'or ever' was left unspoken as he made his way to the door. Once there, he paused and gave me a hard look. "You have the opportunity to be exactly what that girl needs, boy genius. Do not let that pass you by, because we both know everyone else only wants the parts of us they think are useful. No one else gives a shit about the parts of us that are broken and fucked up." He flicked his fingers away from his scarred eyebrow in farewell and shut the door behind him.

I locked it and took a second to rest my forehead against the wood. I'd done it again. Overlooked someone I cared about in need of my help because they didn't ask for it. I thought Noe would tell me what she needed from me, just like I thought Savina would be honest with me about how much she was struggling. Noe told me she would give me what she wanted me to have, but I'd been blind to the invite she'd given me to ask for more. For what I needed from her.

I knocked the side of my fist against the door, hard enough that it sent a jolt up my arm and into my shoulder. I shoved off the wood and prowled toward the big bedroom at the top of the stairs that she'd claimed as her own. Once I hit the landing, I saw that she was standing at the bank of windows that acted as the outside wall of the loft. Floor to ceiling, the glass reflected the dreary night sky and the blinking, glowing lights from the struggling city down below. If this loft was anywhere else in the world, the view would be worth a million dollars. This would be a property people chose to show off and showcase. Here, it was front row to the worst the world had to offer. The view wasn't stunning; it was scary, intimidating, and threatening.

Her arms were crossed over her chest and she'd taken off the baggy, camouflage cargo pants she'd had on earlier. I'd dragged her to a store to get the essentials after her meeting with Goddard's victims. Now that she had clothes that fit, she was back to looking like a street kid. But at the moment, all she was wearing was her short, black t-shirt that stopped just below her ribs and a pair of lacy black boyshorts. They looked much better on her than Booker's sweats and were distracting enough that I forgot why I came up here in the first place. So, I just stared at her. I couldn't pull my eyes away, not even when she turned her head and looked at me over her shoulder, eyes narrowed and lips tight.

It was the sight of her black eyelashes spiky with wetness and the twin tracks of moisture on her cheeks that indicated that she'd been crying that made me move. I stalked across the space that separated us in a few long strides and had my arms around her before I could think about what I should do once I was there.

She was so tiny wrapped up in my embrace and I could feel every line of her body shudder as I hugged her hard to my chest. I pressed my cheek next to her damp one, which knocked my glasses crooked, and ran my hand up and down the smooth line of her back. Her skin was velvety smooth, soft, and supple against my fingertips. She felt like something that was expensive and coveted, like something that would snap in half if any more pressure was applied. I touched my lips to her ear and whispered, "Tell me what I can do to make this better."

I put a hand on her hip and told my body to behave because my cock was very interested in the fact that the only thing between it and her warm, sweet center was my zipper and a scrap of lace that really was no barrier at all. Blood rushed to my head and made me a little dizzy as her arms found their way around my waist as she snuggled in close to me. Her tears made the front of my t-shirt wet and I had to bite back a groan when I felt her nipples harden as she leaned her weight into me.

"That's the thing. There is no making it better. No matter what we do to Goddard, no matter how hard he falls, those girls will always have to live with what he did to them. It never goes away." She shook her head against my chest and her hands clutched at the back of my shirt. "It kills me that even after Goddard's gone, there are still going to be people out there who exploit young women that way. Being trapped in your circumstances," she shook her head and I lifted a hand to cup the back of her head as she shook against me. "There is nothing worse than that, Stark. Nothing."

I agreed. I'd been stuck, caught up in circumstances of my own making with no way out. I hated it, hated how powerless and weak it made me feel.

I twisted her hair through my fingers and let out a sigh that made her shiver against me. "Booker told me to come comfort you. I don't know how to do that, Noe. I don't know how to make you feel better, but I'm here and I'm willing to do whatever it is you need me to do." That was a lot for me. Her swirling emotions were whipping around us. I could taste them thick and heavy in the air I was breathing, but I didn't know what to do with them. Wasn't sure she wanted me to do anything. I was uncertain, and that made me clumsy. I didn't want to accidently do or say anything that would hurt more. I wanted a solution to the problem that was ripping her apart and it pissed me off there wasn't one, because she was right. This world was always going to have awful people exploiting others for their own ends. This wasn't a Point problem, it was a humanity problem.

She gave a watery laugh and rubbed her nose in the center of my chest. "He told you to comfort me?"

I nodded and lifted my head so I could set my glasses back on my face the right way. I rested my chin on the top of her head and closed my eyes as her hips shifted against the front of my jeans. My dick kicked in response and I felt something heavy and hot unfurl under my ribs. My hand tightened in her hair and on her hip.

"He told me to make you feel better and then he called me stupid." He was lucky I didn't lay him out for that insult.

She laughed again and I stiffened as I felt the featherlight touch of her fingertips on my lower spine underneath my t-shirt.

"The hug was a good start, Snow. I find this very comforting." She stepped closer and I had to suck in a breath to keep from dragging her to the floor and covering her up with my hungry body. "Honestly, you being here, letting me work through it all, is helpful. I don't need someone trying to put my thoughts in order like good little soldiers until I have a hold on them myself. Talking to those girls took me back to a place I thought I left far behind, but I guess the past is never as out of reach as we think. I wanted them to tell someone about Goddard, I wanted them to have a voice and when they didn't think anyone would listen, it sucked that I couldn't tell them they were wrong."

"He shouldn't have had to say anything. I should know what to do to comfort you. He's right, I am stupid about a lot of things." I begrudgingly admitted Booker had a point.

Her hands pushed up the wide plane of my back, shoving the fabric of my shirt up with them. I had to bend down for her to pull it off over my head. My eyebrows shot up as her palms smoothed over the black and gray ink that covered the majority of my torso. She used a finger to trace the mechanical heart that lived in the center of my chest and her palm skated over my side where the skin was inked away and all my motorized insides were revealed.

"I think you would have figured it out on your own, Stark. It took the Tin Man a while to get used to his new heart, so you get a hall pass."

I caught her wrist in my hand and gently brushed my thumb over the steady thump of her pulse. "Those girls, you listened to them, Noe. You heard them and believed them. You made sure their stories were heard. You gave them more than you had."

She blinked at me and then gave a little nod. When her chin was dipped down, her gaze stayed focused on the straining front of my jeans and the way my abs were locked tight. Her hand trailed over my side, her thumb tracing the indent on the side of my abs that cut a hard V into my waistline. Her small fingers tapped against my belt buckle and I felt the tiny vibration all the way down to my toes.

"You really want to comfort me, Stark?" There was mischief under the pain in her dark eyes. This was a trap I could spot from a mile away, but fuck me if I wasn't going to walk right into the center of it anyway, eyes wide open.

"Yeah. Tell me what I can do to make you feel better." My voice was gruff and slightly unsteady.

She tapped my belt buckle again. "Well, you've seen me naked, I think it's only fair I get the same opportunity."

I balked at her and my hands spasmed where they were holding onto her. "You want me to strip for you?" It came out slightly strangled, more from surprise.

She laughed, her breath light and warm against that iron heart on my chest. "Well, you've seen me at my most vulnerable. Stripped down, bare, nowhere to hide. Return the favor, Stark. I think I would find that very comforting. It would make me feel *way* better." She was teasing and she was taunting, but her fingers were insistent on my belt so I took a step back and replaced them with my own.

"You're fucking with me." I knew it and she knew it, too, but I still took my belt off and started to pry open my jeans. Her dark eyes were fixed on each and every movement, her dark, feather eyebrows arched with interest. She shrugged and gave me a slight smile that made my stomach flip.

I bent down and tugged my boots off, and when I lifted back up, there was no more humor in her eyes. They were glossy black, shining with something that made my heart beat faster and my skin feel too tight. I pulled my zipper down, carefully. The flesh behind it was rock hard, aching and pulsing in time to my heart beat. I grunted when the pressure was off of my dick and swiftly yanked the denim down my long legs so that I was standing in front of her in nothing more than a pair of black boxer briefs. The tip of my cock was bulging behind the elastic, eager and ready for whatever she had in mind.

I put my hands on my hips and spread my legs so she could look her fill. Her eyes were caught on the ridge behind the black cotton but they moved over the rest of me, hungry and curious. Her hand darted out and touched the front of my thigh. I almost moaned at the contact.

"Tesla." It skipped over to the side where my muscles were locked so tight they were quivering. "Edison." Down by my knee. "da Vinci." The other side of my knee. "Einstein." Up higher on the inside of my thigh, so close that if she moved her hand at all, her knuckles would touch my balls. "Curie." Around to the back of my thigh. "Newton." She let out a breath and I wished to God I'd managed to pull the cotton down already so I could feel that wet heat on the tip of my cock which was already damp and leaking pearly pleasure.

She circled back around to the front of me, her fingers trailing around my waist as she went. "You are a beautiful, interesting man, Snowden Stark. I've never met anyone like you."

Usually when someone said I was interesting, they meant I was weird and they had no idea what to do with me. With Noe, it was clear on every line of her pretty, expressive face that she meant what she said. She was fascinated by me, intrigued and confused. She wasn't alone, because I felt the same way about her.

She put her finger in the waistband of my underwear and tugged. "Off. Fair is fair."

I sucked in a breath because her hand was so close to my dick. All she had to do was move a millimeter to the right and she could hold, touch, stroke it. I felt my pulse pound at the thought. Throwing my head back so I was looking at the ceiling and not at her, I did as she asked, tugging the black material free around the throbbing, thick flesh that immediately jerked and bounced against my lower stomach. I heard her suck in a sharp breath and all that emotion filling up the space between us shifted, turning from something thick and oppressive into something that fluttered and danced over my skin.

Anticipation.

Neither one of us moved or said a word. Visions of me standing in the room as she came out of the shower were like flashpoints in my brain at this moment. Both of us wanting, neither of us sure, forced to make a move but unyielding in our actions. My cock swayed between us, huge, heavy, hard, and wanting. I couldn't remember a time in my admittedly scarce and limited sexual history where my body reacted so strongly to another person. I was usually vaguely interested, but with Noe, I was more than that. I was invested. It was like every single part of me was attuned to every single part of her. I breathed when she breathed. I blinked when she blinked. My heart beat when hers did, and my dick, well, it grew, preened, practically screamed at her for attention. I'd never been so needy, so desperate for contact with another person. I was used to craving distance and space. With her, there was only one way she would ever be close enough.

She exhaled and looked up at me as she lifted her hands and slid her tiny t-shirt up over her head. I couldn't hold back a groan at the sight of her pert, pointed nipples. She was built sleek and lean. I loved it. She was built for performance and speed, like all of my favorite machines.

"I heard a lot about you before you came looking for me, Stark. Rumors, whispers, speculation. I had this idea of who you were, this dream of the kind of guy I wanted you to be. I put you up on this fantasy pedestal, up so high no one, including me could touch you." I watched wide eyed as she pulled the lace of her panties down her legs so that she was suddenly as naked and exposed as I was. Most of her bruises had healed, but she was still just as marked up as I was. Hers were far harder to see since they lined her insides and slashed across her soul. She was the prettiest thing I'd ever seen. "When you shut the door in my face, when you told me not to pick fights I couldn't win, you tumbled off that pedestal so fast I didn't even see you hit the ground."

I swore under my breath. "I'm sorry." I wanted to touch her, to taste her. I wanted inside of her, and for the first time in my life, I ached to let someone inside of me.

She gave her head a quick shake, the red strands whipping out. "I'm not. No one could touch you up there, no one could reach you on that pedestal. Down here with the rest of us, I have no problem getting my hands on you." Her eyes lifted to mine, darker than the night outside the window behind us. "You want to make me feel better, Snowden, then do it. Make me feel better."

I'd been compared to a lot of different things in my life. A robot. A machine. An automaton and she just called me the Tin Man. I didn't feel like any of those cold, metallic things at the moment.

No, now I was something else. Something animalistic. Something primitive. Something raw and unleashed.

A growl ripped out of my chest and I moved on her like she was prey that was going to turn and flee, leaving me hungry and empty. My mouth was on hers, my hands spanned her narrow waist, lifting her up so she could twine her legs around my hips. My cock hit her warm, wet center and leapt with undisguised excitement. Our chests pressed together as I moved her toward the giant bed in the middle of the room. My heart thundered as hers raced. Her nipples were tight and poked impatiently against the ink on my skin. I wanted them in my mouth. I wanted them against my teeth. I wanted them covered in the thick, sticky liquid that was already seeping out of the slit at the tip of my dick. The lights from the window outside painted her skin various shades of blue and red. She was Technicolor, brighter than anything I'd ever had my hands on, and far more precious.

I devoured her. My teeth and tongue eating up every surprised sound she made. I kissed her harder, teeth clicking, tongues dueling, sighs mingling, as I tried to get in as deep as I could go. It wasn't a skilled kiss. It was sloppy, messy, desperate. I kissed her like I was trying to eat her whole, which I was. I wanted to inhale her, consume her. I wanted to take everything she was offering and never give it back. I was greedy, trying to get my hands on everything she was and refusing to let go, even as she wiggled against me impatiently.

That little shimmy had my hips involuntarily grinding into her soft, sweet spot. The tip of my cock hit her damp fold, felt her body flutter around the pressure, and I almost dropped her because it felt so good. I hit the side of the bed and bent my knees so I could sit her down on the edge. When I was done, I was on my knees between her spread legs. I stopped breathing for a second at the sight of all her shiny, pink skin. She twitched like she was getting ready to close her legs against my intense scrutiny, but I used the width of my shoulders to stop her. I was so close to knowing how she tasted, how she felt spread across my tongue. I put a hand on the inside of her knee and trailed it up the inside of her thigh.

She quaked and quivered against my fingertips and when I looked up at her, I was surprised to find her reaching for me. She tagged my glasses and tugged them off my face. I felt my eyebrows furrow as I told her, "I can't see without those."

She tossed the expensive frames on the bed next to her and flopped on her back with her forearm over her eyes. "I don't think you need to see what you're doing down there. You can go by touch." She sounded slightly amused and a little embarrassed.

I huffed out a little laugh and leaned forward so I could give her one long, thorough lick. It brought her hips up off the bed and had her heels digging into the side of the mattress. I grinned against the sensitive flesh under my lips and let my tongue dart out to tap against that sensitive bud hidden within those slick folds. "Yeah. I think I can feel my way along with no problem. If I get too far off track, just let me know."

She moaned as I locked her clit between the blunt edge of my teeth and pulled, swirling my tongue over the trapped bundle of nerves. Her hand found the back of my head and her nails dug into my scalp. Her back arched and I felt her whole-body shudder in my hands. She was small, but every response was huge. She wasn't shy about letting me know what she liked, and her body couldn't hide the way it reacted to mine. She was hot, quivering against my face, liquid and molten where I tasted her. She rocked against my tongue, hips lifting and grinding as I fucked her with my mouth. She moaned and moved the arm that she had crossed over her eyes to her chest.

I wished I had my glasses on so I could watch her touch herself. She was all a blur of creamy skin and dark hair. If I narrowed my eyes just a tiny bit, her features came into stark relief and so did the pleasure that was etched in every line. Her fingers plucked at one straining nipple and moved to slowly roll over the opposite one. It was hot. She tasted good, too. Bright and warm on my tongue, she wasn't someone I was going to be able to forget. I liked everything about her, including the way she mumbled my name and pulled me closer with her hold on my head.

I was only too happy to oblige. I moved farther into the V between her splayed legs. No more being shy or trying to cover up, she was open, exposed. She was inviting me in, and once I was there, I planned on making a place for myself. I flicked my tongue over her clit and moved the hand that was holding her leg to the bed down to her soaked opening. My fingers found her entrance with a slick sound. It was loud in the quiet room, sexy and unmistakable. She was turned on, she wanted me, and I could feel it as she pulsed around my fingers. All of her was small and compact, this part of her was no different. It took a second for her body to soften, to loosen enough around the thick digits that were stroking her. I spread them apart, twisted my wrist and pumped them in and out of her. Her breath caught and she went still as I curved my fingertips, searching for that tender, elusive place that would break her into a million pieces.

Technically, I knew what women liked. I was an observer by nature, a student, and a studier. Whenever I was with someone, I paid attention to what worked and what didn't. There were things that all of them seemed to enjoy the most, so those were the things I tended to focus on. Because of my attention to detail, I felt I was a skilled lover. I knew all the tricks of the trade, but I'd never, not once, felt a personal investment in getting my partner off. I knew they would, I made sure of it. At least not until this woman who was currently writhing and moaning under me. I didn't want her to come in my mouth because I *knew* what I was doing. I wanted her to come in my mouth because I was the one doing the touching and tasting. I wanted her to get off because of me and all over me. I was invested as hell in Noe's pleasure and bringing her as much of it as I possibly could.

Lick, suck, swirl. I was relentless against her clit as she bucked against my invading fingers and ground herself down on my hand over and over again.

"Snowden." My name was breathless and pleading. No one called me that but her, and it felt significant. To her, I was more than Stark.

"You're so tight. I can feel you squeezing my fingers. I can't wait until it's my cock you're strangling." She gasped and I saw her eyes fly open as her head lifted so she could look at me. "You're fucking hot, too. It feels like I'm sliding my fingers through liquid fire. Can you feel how wet you are?" She twisted up and scratched at the back of my head. I nudged her slippery folds with the end of my nose and breathed out the warning, "You're gonna have to get a whole lot wetter than that when I fuck you, Noe. My dick is a hell of a lot bigger than my fingers." I inserted another one and twisted my wrist at the same time as I dragged my teeth over her straining little clit.

She gave a muffled scream as her entire body tightened and locked around me. I felt the heated flood of her release circle my still gliding fingers as her silken walls fluttered around them. I lifted my head so I could kiss her right below her belly button and grinned as her stomach hollowed out. She shifted so that she could put her hands on my cheeks as I levered myself up and over her, blocking out the less-than-stellar view outside the big windows.

"I take your glasses off and you become some kind of dirty talking lothario. Who would've thought?" She was breathless and pliant beneath me. I loved that she looked a little dazed and bewildered.

"Like a kinky version of Superman." I kissed the side of her neck and braced myself above her with the bar of my forearm over the top of her head. The bulk of my body covered her delicate frame from head to toe.

She lifted her legs and wrapped them around my waist as I slowly dragged my cock through the moisture that was left between her legs. She dug her heels into the curve of my ass and told me, "You're your own kind of hero, Stark. You don't need to be a knock off of one that doesn't exist." I closed my eyes against the way her words made that vacant place in my chest, where my heart should be, ache. I wasn't any kind of hero.

"I need to get a condom." She twisted my head all around, but I could never quite shake that logical reasoning that always had me in its stranglehold. If I got inside of her uncovered, skin to skin, it was going to be all over. There would be no thinking clearly and doing the right thing.

She stared up at me with wide, honest eyes and I almost said 'fuck it' and sank into her bare without asking her if it was okay.

"I've got an IUD. I'm good, clean." She lifted an eyebrow. "Hard to date when you're homeless."

I gritted my teeth and closed my eyes against the reminder that she had nothing and wanted to keep it that way, that she was going back to nothing, disappearing once it was safe enough to do so.

"I'm clean. I'm picky and I'm careful. It's hard to date when you don't have a heart." Even though the once absentee organ was now pounding furiously and erratically in the center of my chest.

She scowled but her quick nod gave me the go ahead to take her bare and raw, but her scowl quickly melted when I rocked forward, opening her up and making room for myself inside of her.

We both groaned. We both moved closer. We both closed our eyes. It was intense and it was electric. I felt every quiver and shiver along my bones.

"You feel better yet, Noe?" The words came out on a rasp as I worked to get a few more inches of my throbbing, aching cock into her snug channel. I was right. She was tight enough to strangle my dick, her body holding onto mine like she never wanted to let me go. God, I hoped the rest of her felt the same way because after this taste of her, after pounding into her, riding her, owning her, I wasn't sure that I was going to be able to let her walk away from me.

"Getting there, Snowden. I'm getting there." There was humor as well as passion in her voice and when she came the second time, she took me with her, and I was pretty sure neither one of us could feel anything but good.

I'd been born to be one of the best, but I was broken. With her, I was something in between those two things, and for the first time in my life, I wondered if I had found what 'normal' looked like. If I had found the place where I could just be . . . be what this woman needed and whom I needed to be in order to find happiness.

CHAPTER 13

Noe

I WAS BACK TO being impressed by him.

It was hard not to be when all that muscle and strength was moving over me and inside of me. It was also impossible to keep my head clear when those stormy eyes watched every response, picked up on every reaction, and dissected my every shiver and shake. He was studying me, learning me, observing me, and there was something undeniably erotic about having all that intensity and focus directed at me and nothing else. It was like I was the only thing in his entire world that existed. There wasn't a crumbling city outside the windows. There wasn't a looming plan for revenge eating away at him. There was no axe hanging over his head, no worry that he had to pretend to be something he wasn't to keep himself out of the government's hands. There was just me, and only me, and there were the things he did that made me scream his name and fall apart in his big, skilled hands. It was a powerful feeling, intoxicating and heady.

Having Snowden Stark's entire attention did more to make me feel like I was in control of my life and my choices far more than any of the years I spent sleeping around. He knew the only reason he had access to my body was because I let him. In turn, he let me know that he was appreciative of the gift and planned on taking really, really good care of it. I wasn't going to be able to sit down without cringing tomorrow, but the multiple orgasms and mind-numbing pleasure made any discomfort worth it. The man kept saying he wasn't any good with people, and I wanted to tell him it didn't matter because he was far better with his hands and his mouth than anyone else I'd ever encountered, not to mention that glorious, gigantic cock of his. With that face and body, he shouldn't be allowed to pack such an impressive piece of anatomy between his legs. It wasn't fair to the female population. On second thought, I was going to let him go on being bad with other people. His standoffish and chilly personality was more than likely the only thing saving him from having to beat off interested parties with a stick. He was as close to irresistible as any man could be.

Then there was his dirty mouth. A shocking surprise, one that made my pussy clench and my nerves shiver in pure delight. A man who could talk about code and processing speeds in his sleep shouldn't be able to make me come with nothing more than his words, but then again, nothing about Stark was what I expected.

"You look so good on my cock, Noe." Deep and raspy, the words pricked at my skin and had my eyes popping open to look at him.

His broad back was propped up against the headboard. His gray-blue eyes were heavy lidded and intent on where we were joined. His skin had a red flush to it and his dark eyebrows were lowered in a V over the top of his nose. His glasses were long gone, landing somewhere on the floor after the first bout of fucking. He looked less severe without them, a little younger, and more approachable. It turned me on that the only time I'd seen him without them, the only time I got those pretty eyes uncovered, was when he was inside of me or had his face between my legs. It was like a secret version of him that only I got to experience, and that did something to my insides I was too afraid to examine.

One of his hands was cupping my breast. His thumb was rolling lazy circles around my tender nipple. I had marks all over my collar bone from his voracious mouth and I was surprised the touch felt good rather than stung considering the amount of time those stiff little peaks had spent in his mouth. My entire body felt like it was hovering on the edge of too much sensation. If I tipped a little either way, I was going to explode with too much pleasure or too much pain. It was one of the most erotic, most intense feelings I'd ever experienced.

His other hand was between my legs where I was riding him at a steady, slow pace. It took some work to get my body ready to accommodate his. For one, I'd never been with anyone who was as big as Stark on any level. I liked to maintain control, to be in charge, to feel like I was the one taking what I needed and not the other way around. That was impossible with him. There was too much of him, everywhere, to pretend like I was in charge. He blocked out the rest of the world when he was on top of me, he became the only thing I could see. The only thing I could feel. The only thing I could think about.

He was careful, deliberate. He moved with purpose and finesse. He was thoughtful with my body and the way he took it over, but he was determined. He was the guy who was going to make it work, no matter what it took. And, boy, did he make it work . . . several times. Now, it was my turn, and I didn't care that my insides twinged with a sharp mix of pleasure and pain each time I sank back down on that unbending shaft between his tattooed thighs. It was like I was being opened up, split wide, and revealed to him in a whole new way. There wasn't a single place inside of me he wasn't touching, and for someone who was used to being mostly empty and hollow, it was slightly overwhelming being this full, this complete.

I had my hands on his solid shoulders and was rocking into him with each lift and drop. The pressure he had on my clit was featherlight, taunting, and teasing. He knew I was hovering on the edge of something terrifying and I knew he would catch me either way I fell.

I arched my eyebrows at him and shot a look down where that swollen, slick flesh was slipping in and out of my welcoming body. We looked pretty together, all his illustrated, colorful skin spread out under my pale golden thighs.

"Your cock looks good inside of me." And in my mouth, and clutched in my hands, and when he had it in his fist pumping it up and down while he watched me get myself off. It just looked good . . . period.

"Feels good inside of you, too. Every time I do something you like, you tighten like a vise. It's better than my own hand has ever been. And when you come," his eyes darkened so the blue was almost crowded out by the gray. "It feels like silk and honey. One of these days you'll lick yourself off my fingers and you can see that you taste just as good as you feel."

I swore as his words and my body did exactly what he wanted them to do. My muscles clamped down on him and fluttered around his rigid shaft. He grunted in approval and the next time I lifted up, his fingers dove in and attacked my oversensitive clit. He gave the little nub a tug that had my eyes rolling into the back of my head as his mouth hit mine with a force that stole my breath. His tongue tapped mine and his teeth scraped over the inside of my bottom lip. It made me mewl against him. I sighed when his hand left my breast and skated down over my ribs to land on the curve of my hip. He pressed me down and guided me back up, grinding our pelvises together in a way that made me moan into his mouth.

He was apparently done with slow and steady. The pace he set was far more frantic and frenzied than the one I'd been torturing us both with. His cock speared up into me, hitting so deep that I didn't even know anything existed before him. The pleasure made my body lock and caused any semblance of control I might have had to spiral unnoticed out of my hands. His mouth stayed on mine, sometimes kissing, sometimes doing nothing more than catching the noises I made as I bounced wantonly on top of him.

"Noe." My name whispered out between his lips and I felt those thick, massive thighs I was straddling tense up.

"Yes." I whispered the word out and watched him catch it with his tongue.

"Noe." He said it again more insistent and warning. He never came first, never let go until I was a wilted, boneless mess beneath him. He was close, also hovering on the edge and he was desperate to have me drag us both over in free fall.

He pulled on that tender, sensitive spot between my legs again and I ground down on his cock determined to send him over first.

"So fucking wet." He bit the words out and I knew without looking that he was staring at the moisture that was slicked across my inner thighs and all around the base of his cock. It made the way he was taking me, thrusting into me below, audible and distinct. I'd never been one for messy sex, but with him, I didn't really have a choice in the matter.

Since he had taken over most of the heavy lifting, I let go of his shoulder with one hand and arched my back. His eyes watched me closely as I slid a hand between his spread legs and tickled the inside of his knee. His eyebrows lifted so high they almost touched his hairline, but they snapped back down and a groan rumbled out of his chest the second my fingers touched the heavy sac pulled up tight between his legs. His whole body shuddered and his legs shifted restlessly underneath me. All it took was a gentle stroke, the brush of my fingers over that sensitive, thin skin and he lost it.

He barked my name and clamped his hands down on my waist to hold me still as he emptied himself inside of me. The warm rush of his pleasure, and the pulse of his heavy cock as it kicked inside of me, was enough to drag me over the edge with him. I folded over on top of him and panted into the side of his neck as my body shook with an orgasm that stole all my thought and energy. I smoothed a hand over that mechanical heart on his chest and listened as he breathed heavily into the crown of my head. He was always alert, always intense, and seemingly distracted by whatever complicated mess he had tangled up in his head. Right now, he appeared to be completely at ease. Relaxed and sated in a way he never was.

One of his hands moved up and cupped my cheek. His thumb brushed over the high arch of my bone.

It was quiet except for the sound of our breathing. I couldn't even hear the silent wheels in his head turning like they always seemed to be. I enjoyed that he didn't feel the need to fill the space up with sound and questions neither one of us were ready to answer. Just like I appreciated he hadn't hounded me to spill everything I was working through after I spent an afternoon with those girls getting them to talk. I was stuck in the past, remembering when I was one of them and needed someone to help me but didn't have anyone. He didn't try to drag me back to the present, didn't offer useless platitudes and promises. He let me know he was there, that he wasn't running, even though I wasn't any kind of picnic to be around, and that did more for me than he would know. No one had ever simply *been there* for me before.

"Need to clean up." We were both covered in sex and sweat, and while that was fun during, afterward it lost its appeal pretty damn quick. He grunted his agreement and let me go so I could climb off of him. We both let out a little gasp when our bodies separated and I had to grab the side of the bed when I went to stand because my legs felt like wet noodles and my thighs were jelly.

I wasn't going to be able to sit down or walk right, and by the smirk on Stark's face, he had no sympathy for my current condition.

I flipped him off and made my way to the bathroom. I heard him rustling around in the other room and decided I needed to take a hot shower to get some feeling back in my lower extremities. When the water was running over me, chasing off the bubbles from the body wash I had slathered all over me, I noticed I had marks from him all over my body. Ones I hadn't noticed him leaving. Marks I'd been too caught up in him and how he made me feel to protest.

Fingerprints in tiny blue bruises on the outside of my breasts and across my hips. Red marks from either his stubble or his teeth on the inside of my thighs. White half-moons in my palm where I had dug my fingers in so hard, I broke the skin. Pink lines along the inside of my thighs where his diamonds had dug into my skin. Even if I couldn't still feel him between my legs and deep within my body, there would be no forgetting him because he'd left his signature all over my skin. I got to him. I made him react and I wore the proof of his humanity all over my skin. There was something addictive and alluring about that.

We both lost control, yet kept each other in check in our own way simply by being together, both physically and emotionally in the moment.

I was finishing drying off and wrapping myself up in a towel when the bathroom door opened and Stark walked in with my laptop in his hands. He'd found his glasses somewhere and had donned a pair of white boxer briefs. He looked like he should be selling expensive sports drinks or designer underwear, not tapping on a computer and frowning at whatever he was seeing on the screen.

"Your email pinged when you were in the shower. I wouldn't have paid any attention to it but it seems to be in some kind of code and I . . ." he trailed off and gave me a sheepish look.

"And you couldn't resist trying to figure it out." I shook my head. The man was incorrigible. His brain never stopped.

I took the laptop from him and almost dropped it when I saw it was sent from *Lisbeth Salander*. I shifted my eyes up to Stark who was watching me with open curiosity. *"The Girl with the Dragon Tattoo.* She's one of the most famous fictional hackers in all of modern culture. This has to be from someone who knows who I am."

I clicked to open the email hoping to God it wasn't a virus or a Trojan Horse that would attach spyware to my computer. I would have to run a scan just to be sure, but I needed to see who was reaching out to me in such a cagey fashion.

The body of the email was nothing but a series of numbers in sets of two. Rows of them that went on and on. It wasn't signed and when Stark went and got his own laptop to trace the IP address, neither one of us was surprised when it traced back to a proxy server that bounced the signal around a thousand times making it untraceable. He took the computer from me so I could get dressed and told me to meet him in the kitchen. Now, I could see those wheels in his head turning and practically hear the gears grinding as he poked at the keyboard and ran his eyes over the numbers. It was obviously a code of some kind, but I was at a loss as to what the key was.

When I made it to the kitchen, he had both his computer and my computer open next to each other and his was running some kind of program. There were thousands of numbers flashing across the screen, blinking as they rolled by.

"What are you doing?" I propped myself up on a stool next to him and watched as he tapped his fingers on the counter. He should look ridiculous, a giant beast of a man covered in ink and heavy muscles, standing in nothing more than his underwear and glasses holding a computer. He didn't. He looked smart and sexy. He looked completely comfortable in his decorated skin. There was nothing cold about Snowden Stark at the moment. I could feel heat radiating off every inch of his naked skin and it made me lean in closer.

"Running an algorithm that traces any instances of those numbers located together anywhere. It'll place them in addresses, phone numbers, location coordinates, and if anything hits, it'll tell us."

I shot him a look out of the corner of my eye. Yeah, I was definitely back to being impressed.

"How long will that take?"

He shrugged and frowned at the screen. "Depends on if it hits on anything. Did you say the sender is a character from a book?"

I nodded. "Yeah."

His eyes narrowed and a muscle ticked in his jaw as he cut a look to me. "What if it's a book cipher? The numbers could be chapters or page numbers. The second number could be the word on the page you need to decipher the message."

I blinked and looked at the numbers. It was simple but complicated at the same time. "You think?"

"Only one way to find out." He picked up his cell and opened his Kindle app. After a few minutes, wherein he bought the book and downloaded it, he told me to read off the numbers and then rattled off words that corresponded with the numbers. We figured out quickly that it alternated between chapter number and page number depending on how big the number was, but the second number in the row was always the word we were looking for. I watched his lips move as he silently counted the spaces out on the page and marveled at how quickly he had put it all together. I liked to think I would have figured it out on my own, but could begrudgingly admit I wouldn't have seen the connection as quickly as he did.

When he was done dictating, I gaped wordlessly at the message in front of me.

She found a hacker the same way she found me when she wanted out of the Point. The girl was fearless when she wanted something. She wasn't scared of the dark or the monsters that hid inside of it. The guy she found coded the message for her and figured out a way to send it to me so that it couldn't be traced.

Julia Grace had seen the stories about her stepfather on the news. She knew the girls from the streets, the ones from the kind of homes that had driven them into Goddard's clutches in the first place, weren't going to talk. She knew no one would believe them, but they would believe her. She wanted to tell her story. She wanted to press charges. She wanted to see the man rot behind bars. She wanted to come back home, but she needed to know that she would be safe. That someone could protect her until Goddard stood trial.

"If she comes back, I can put Nassir or the cop on it. Either one of them would go out of their way to see that man go down, and both have a soft spot for girls on the run." I felt his presence steady and strong behind me.

"If she presses charges, our plans get derailed. He needs to be alive, both physically and digitally, in order to stand trial, Stark." The idea of letting go of my revenge, my payback, was a hard pill to swallow.

"He does, but we already took his money and he doesn't have a friend left in the community. He's not going to be able to afford any kind of defense. And chances are once he's in lock up, he won't last very long, so that life insurance policy will go to Julia anyway. Cons don't like child molesters. They like them even less when they spent most of their tenure being tough on crime. Who knows how many of them are there because of Goddard? This is for the best, Noe. Julia needs this. She wants to tell her story because she knows people will listen. She wants to speak for all those girls who can't."

I knew he was right, this was what was supposed to happen, but then I remembered the dirty cop touching me and Goddard watching me with those cold eyes as I was tied to a chair. He was going to kill me and had no remorse about it. He treated me like I was disposable. I curled my hands into fists on the counter and lowered my head so he couldn't see the conflict in my eyes.

"Make sure your people can keep her safe and I'll reach out to her." I figured she would be checking the email address she'd reached out to me with. I would send her an email and see if she responded. After everything that had happened, it felt so anticlimactic and easy. A little girl was going to take him down with nothing more than her appearance and a few words. I was back to wondering if I was nearly as in control as I told myself I was.

Stark ran his hand down the length of my spine and gave my ass a little tap. He told me he was going to make a few calls and left me stewing in my own thoughts.

Once Goddard was locked up, once he went down, I had no reason to hang around Snowden Stark anymore. I wouldn't need him and he would have no use for me. I was going to have to get back to my life, back to being unfettered and free to jump from place to place. Suddenly, the idea of not being weighed down, not being pinned by something heavy, wasn't as appealing as it always had been before.

Even when things were easy, they were still incredibly hard. I guess it was a good thing I was used to sleeping on the ground because I was going to be back there before I knew it.

CHAPTER 14

Stark

S HE WAS YOUNG . . . SO young.

She was also small, except for her baby bump. It was hard to look at. She was hard to look at, but luckily Nassir's knock-out wife was great with skittish young women who had everything on the line. She was leaps and bounds ahead of the rest of us when it came to assuring the frightened teenager that nothing would happen to her. She soothed her, calmed her, and generally made the girl believe that she was making the right choice. Keelyn Gates cut her imposing, quiet husband a look, practically demanding that he make sure her words to Julia Grace were true. In the end, it was decided that Nassir was the better bet to keep the teenager safe after she filed a formal complaint with Titus against her stepfather. The cop told us that the police department was in disarray with the sudden loss of not only the assistant commissioner, but also several beat cops and a couple of higher ranking officers who had all been on Goddard's payroll. Titus was currently running the station and trying to do the job of twenty men. He grudgingly admitted that the girl was better off under Nassir's protection. His name carried more weight than a police badge; no one could deny it.

The girl seemed skeptical, but when Noe promised her that no one would touch her, she appeared to relax. She had a lot of faith in my little thief and Noe was just as impressed by the teen. The fragile looking young woman was smart, far smarter than someone with her privileged background needed to be. When she caught wind of what was going on back in the city, she tracked down another kid who was good with computers and asked him for help getting her message to Noe. She didn't want to be able to be tracked if Noe had been compromised, so he came up with the book cipher. He was also standing in Nassir's opulent, extravagant office looking a lot lost and a little like he was going to get sick. He wanted to help Julia, which was admirable, but he had no idea what kind of shark-infested waters he offered to dive into by being a helping hand. They were both just kids; I couldn't blame either of them for being overwhelmed by everything that was going on.

In fact, watching him rub her back and protectively hover over her while she listened to Key softly tell Julia Grace that there were lots of options when she was ready to decide what she wanted to do with the baby, I realized he was more of a man, more of a standup guy than I had ever been. My dad was still behind bars because of the choices I made, and no matter what I did, neither my mother nor my sister were coming back. The last member of my family was on the hook because of me, and it was about time I did something to rectify the situation.

"Do you need me for anything else?" I'd paid for the kids to get back to the Point, and even with Keelyn taking care of Julia, I was still going to owe Nassir a thousand more favors for taking the girl under his wing. The man didn't do anything out of the kindness of his heart. Mostly because he didn't have one. That was probably why we got along as well as we did.

Noe gave me a questioning look that I wasn't ready to give her answers for. "I have something I need to take care of, and I'd rather do it knowing you're safe and sound with Nassir."

That sent her eyebrows shooting up, but she didn't question me further. She'd been doing that a lot the last couple of days, looking at me like she wanted to say something, but staying silent. We were as close physically as two people could be. I was all over her every chance I got and she was all over me. We were like two people who were starving, ravenous, and greedy. We couldn't get enough, and I hated that it felt like we had to have our fill of each other because we both knew it was only a matter of time before the food ran out. I could touch her however I wanted, take her without complaint, but ever since we agreed that revenge against Goddard belonged to his stepdaughter, she had been drifting away. She wasn't challenging me, pushing me, and fighting me every second of every day. She wasn't poking and prying at all my soft spots she'd uncovered over the last few weeks. Her hands always found their way to the mechanical heart on my chest, but I didn't miss that she no longer seemed interested in fixing it.

"How long are you going to be gone?" She sounded carefully curious instead of concerned.

"Just a couple of hours."

Nassir grunted and leaned back in his fancy leather chair. It was black. All it needed was a couple of skulls and some flames and he would look like Lucifer sitting on his throne of fire and lost souls.

"My lawyer is on the way over. He's going to represent the girl. When we're done here, Key is going to take her and her little friend to one of her safe houses. We'll keep them stashed there with a security detail until Goddard is behind bars. The cop agreed to keep us updated on Goddard's status. We're all lucky his lady likes me as much as she does." He sounded amused and I didn't miss the way his wife rolled her eyes. "Not much you can do here until the legal ball gets rolling."

Nassir's wife had made it her mission upon coming back to the Point and going into business with the dark, dangerous man she slept with at night, to make sure that anyone who felt trapped here had a way out. She was the only person who could get you out of the Point alive and intact with very little effort. She was the downtrodden and destitutes' only savior. She was the only one who could cut the ties this place wrapped around its citizens. It was an odd combination, she and him. She was like an avenging angel dressed in very little wearing sky-high heels. He was the devil incarnate, dressed better than any A-list actor on Oscar night. No one questioned their connection because it was impossible to miss. She didn't move without his eyes tracking her, and he didn't breathe without her watching the steady rise and fall of his chest. It had been blown wide open by a bullet not too long ago, so there was no surprise that she appreciated the fact Nassir was still around to give everyone hell.

The teenager looked at Noe with wide eyes and her small hand clamped down on her forearm. "You're not leaving me, right?"

Noe looked at Julia almost the same way I looked at her when she asked me for help, uncertain and unsure. She'd already put her neck on the line for this girl and it had gotten her kidnapped and tortured. But once again proving she was so much better than me, she patted Julia's hand and told her, "Of course, I'll stay with you. I'll even go with you to the safe house."

Nassir gave me a knowing look. "I'll keep an eye on your girl. If you're not back by the time she's ready to go, I'll pull Booker from the club and have him escort her. He seems fond of her."

The taunt hit its target as I narrowed my eyes at him. "I owe you. Both."

Nassir lifted a midnight eyebrow and smirked at me. "You do."

It was my turn to smirk when Key shifted from where she was standing and leaned over so that her hands were flat on her husband's desk. She shook her head and told me, "We're happy to help, aren't we, honey?" She didn't give Nassir a chance to answer before she stated, "This one is on us, Stark. We need all the good karma we can get. The lawyer is on retainer and he'll be excited to represent a client who's easier to deal with than my husband, for once. Go, do what you have to do."

I turned to say something, anything, to Noe but she wouldn't look at me. Her head was bent close to the teenager's, but it was clear she was actively avoiding looking at me. I couldn't tell where her head was at, but it wasn't on how things were going to play out between us when all of this was over. Revenge had gone cold, and so had whatever was building between the two of us.

Leaning forward so I could tap knuckles with Nassir, I paused when he muttered quietly, "You've never been one I've had to worry about, Stark. Don't become more trouble than you're worth."

It was a warning, one I wanted to heed, but with the way things were going it felt like trouble was endless.

"We need each other, boss. Best not forget that." I wouldn't have challenged him before Noe. She reminded me that I was one of a kind and irreplaceable. Not many men could stand in Hell next to the Devil himself and not get burned. I was one of them.

Those black eyebrows shot up and the smirk was back. "I don't know if I like you when you're firing on all cylinders."

I shrugged and made my way over to the elevator that was the only way up into the office. I wasn't too concerned with what anyone liked or didn't like about me. Well, anyone besides the little thief who still wouldn't look at me. I cared a whole hell of a lot what she thought about me, I just wished she would pick an emotion and stick with it. I was having a tough time following the swings of being her favorite person to being one she could hardly stand to be in the same room with.

There was one other person's opinion I cared about and I needed to go see him. It had been too long, and there were questions I needed to ask that I was done letting him avoid.

I needed to see my father.

My truck ate up the distance between the city and the outskirts where the prison was located. I'd made the trip more times than I could count when I was finally free of the iron grip of the DoD. It was always hard to see my dad. The way he'd aged, the way he'd changed. He was haggard and hateful in the way only a man who had lost everything—his family, his career, his patriotism, his sanity, and his freedom—could be. He was never happy to see me when I came for a visit, and I had a feeling that after today he would ask me to stop coming altogether. If a teenaged girl could face the man who had taken everything from her, if a teenaged boy could walk into the unknown by her side because he thought it was the right thing to do, then the least I could do was tell my dad the truth.

The reason he was still behind bars was because of me. Because I couldn't be who he wanted me to be. I couldn't be who my mother wanted me to be. And I sure as shit was never going to be what the government wanted me to be.

Getting through security sucked. I hated being searched and

poked and prodded. I hated answering their stupid questions. I hated that I was forced to go through all of this to spend thirty measly minutes with my father. It always left me feeling violated and dirty. If it was that unsettling for me, I couldn't imagine what endless hours under that kind of observation and scrutiny had done to my remaining parent.

I sat stiffly at the metal table trying to ignore the other people around me meeting with inmates. The crying and fevered whispers made my skin itchy and had tension coiling tightly around the base of my neck. There was no happiness in this place, no light. It was no wonder Benny had been willing to do *anything* in order to make sure he never walked inside these walls again. And I totally understood why Bax had gravitated toward someone as bright and clean as Dovie. She was the opposite of everything that made this place what it was.

It took a while for my dad to show. The look on his face as he was led toward me, hands cuffed together at his waist and ankles shackled, made it clear he wasn't exactly thrilled with my surprise stop in. His hair was longer than the last time I visited him and the lines around his eyes and mouth appeared deeper. He was turning into a stranger who used to look exactly like me, but every day those similarities seemed to slip away, both physically and emotionally.

He lifted his chin at someone across the room and waited impatiently while the prison guard situated him on the opposite side of the table. There was no missing the click as his feet were locked in place to the ground. There was no running from your fate in the Point, and if your fate led you here, it felt like all hope was lost.

"What are you doing here, Snowden? You didn't mention in your last message that you were coming for a visit." His voice was flat and empty. The same way my insides had felt until Noe brought an earthquake with her into my life. All of my fault lines were rubbing up against each other now, breaking off the brittle, breakable parts and shaking them loose.

"I wasn't planning on coming to see you but there's been a lot of stuff happening in my life lately, and I realized I needed to have an honest conversation with you, Dad." I folded my hands on the table in front of me and willed him to look me in the eye.

His graying eyebrows pitched low over the top of his nose, and his mouth settled into a hard line. "Can't do much with honesty or conversation in this place, Son."

He was resigned to a life spent behind bars and didn't realize the key to his freedom was sitting right in front of him.

"Dad," I blew out a breath and lowered my head so I was staring at the top of the table. "You don't belong in here. You lost so much and I . . ." I trailed off when he suddenly leaned forward on the table, hands curled into fists so hard his knuckles turned white.

"Snowden." My name was sharp and hard, the same way he said it when I was growing up and not performing up to his high standards. It wasn't enough to be advanced and special, no, I had to be superhuman and remarkable. "I had a family, a wife I loved more than anything. I had a nice house and a good job. You and your sister were good kids, better than I ever deserved." His voice dropped lower and one of his fists hit the table with a thump. "I wanted something more than I wanted any of that. I gave it all up for revenge."

I blinked at him and leaned back a little on the very uncomfortable bench. People called him crazy, said he was off and not all there. I always thought he was eccentric, the product of a mind that other people didn't understand. I was the same way. But staring at him now, looking at his wild eyes and flushed face, I wondered if maybe there was more truth to the claims than I wanted to admit.

"Dad, I wanted revenge, too. That's how I ended up in the wrong hands." They exploited my weakness, my love for my family.

My dad shook his shaggy head and scowled at me. "No, Son, you wanted answers. You wanted proof and a reason why. I wanted everyone to pay. I wanted them to suffer and burn, the way they caused your mother to suffer in that explosion."

I bit back a gasp and leaned even farther back from the stranger who was once my father. "Dad?" His other fist hit the table and I caught one of the guard's moving closer out of the corner of my eye. My dad was getting all worked up and it hadn't gone unnoticed. "What are you saying?"

He shook his head at me and sat back on his side of the table. "I loved your mother, Snowden. Loved her more than anything. She deserved better than what happened to her. I don't regret anything. I'm exactly where I'm supposed to be."

Was my dad admitting to selling government secrets to the enemy? Was he really a traitor? Did he really not care about what kind of damage he might have done to millions of innocent people?

"The DoD offered to get you out, Dad. They told me if I stayed, if I got my shit together after Savina's death, they would spring you. They said they would clear your name." I sounded as bewildered as I felt.

"They lied. They always lie." He sounded so certain and I couldn't disagree with him. They promised to keep my sister alive, and here I was, alone and lost without her.

"I could go back. Push them to let you out." It's what I should have done when they first put the offer on the table but I was too scared, too turned around, to do the right thing.

"If you go back, they'll use you to kill, Son. They'll take whatever is in that brain of yours and make it into something deadly. They won't care what the cost is to you. They'll bleed you dry and dump the empty husk like trash. They killed your mother to get to you, Son."

Did they? I wasn't so sure anymore. It was all cloudy and convoluted in my mind. The silken strands of that intricately woven web were twisting around reality and this broken man's beliefs. I had lost my sister, but he had lost everything. It was enough to send anyone over the edge of sanity.

"They might come for me anyway." Goddard was all over the news, and so was the fact that someone had hacked into the city's database and his computer. The black suits that came for me once would be back if they knew I was doing more than running background checks on Nassir's clients and working girls. Like the man said, I was firing on all cylinders again and that was hard to hide.

"Let them come. You're older, wiser, and a hell of a lot harder than you were as a teenager. They taught you to fight, so fight. They knew your weakness, Snowden. They exploited it. Don't let them do that again." His voice was hard and there was no getting around the warning.

Immediately, I thought about Noe. Was she a weakness? I didn't think straight around her. She confused me and distracted me, but she also woke me up. I was sleepwalking through my days, going through the motions of living my life, but then she crashed into it and sent everything spinning. She kickstarted something inside of me and I couldn't imagine going back to being numb. She had me feeling things I'd never felt before. Things I couldn't name because they were so foreign. She forced me to be strong.

"I don't want this to be where you spend the rest of your life, Dad. You're all I have left." He shook his head before I was done with the sentence.

"No. You don't have me. You have a life out there, time to make something work for yourself, time to make a difference. I got what I wanted, Snowden. I got my revenge. I made the enemy just as strong as those bastards are. Knowledge is power and I armed the other side with as much as I could. I made the fight fair." He banged his hands at the table and motioned to the guard who came over to tell him to keep it down. We both got to our feet, him watching me with cold eyes, me watching him with a new realization. "The only thing I know how to do is punish. If you need me to hurt someone, to make them pay, that's all I got for you, Son. Next time you come for a visit, you let me know ahead of time." It was like a knife in the center of my chest. He needed to prepare himself to see me, because while I was still holding onto him, he had let me go long before.

"I'll see you soon, Dad."

He didn't even turn around to look at me as he was guided out of the common room.

My dad was a bad man, a sociopath, and a betrayer. The good guys wanted to turn me into a killer. The heroes hardly ever won. The only people in my life who had bothered to try and make it better were the criminals and the felons. I owed the villains everything. They took me the way I was with no questions asked.

He was right. I knew how to fight and I finally had something . . . someone I was willing to fight for.

CHAPTER 15

Noe

NASSIR'S ATTORNEY WAS YOUNG and looked just as good in his expensive suit as the man footing the bill did. He was blond, stylish, incredibly fit, and very focused. He actually reminded me a little bit of Race. He was how the other man might have turned out if he hadn't run across Shane Baxter all those years ago, if his life on the Hill had never been exposed for the sham and lie that it was. It was clear Nassir was his most recognizable client and his biggest meal ticket. It was also obvious that he couldn't afford to lose when he was representing a man who was as ruthless and brutal as Nassir was. The lawyer took one look at Julia's protruding belly and declared that she needed to get a paternity test done ASAP. The irrefutable proof of what Goddard had done to her was growing inside of her, the key to putting the man away for the rest of his life. He told her the District Attorney's office would ultimately be the one prosecuting the case, but he would represent her and make sure they didn't screw anything up, considering it was still unknown how far Goddard's reach extended.

Julia was understandably upset at the idea of going through such an invasive procedure. It was far easier to determine paternity when the baby was born, but Julia still had a few months left of her pregnancy. However, he explained that Goddard had reached out to an attorney from the Valley, a neighboring city on the other side of the interstate. His lawyer was a man who would twist her words and try to convince the jury she asked for it, that she was a consenting participant in her abuse, so she begrudgingly relented to the paternity test. It didn't matter that she was underage and legally incapable of giving consent, they would crucify her in the media and make the last months of her pregnancy a nightmare.

"Who's the attorney?" Nassir asked, sounding bored rather than curious. It was such a simple question, one that I would have asked myself if I was at all familiar with the legal system. I wasn't prepared for the answer to send my world careening off its axis.

"Aaron Cartwright. He's made a name for himself over the last few years taking on some big cases. He got a cop killer acquitted and that guy who kept those girls chained up in his basement for three years off on a technicality. He's salivating over this one. Offered to do it pro-bono when Goddard got in touch." I thought I was going to pass out. My past nightmare was now colliding full force with my current one.

I was having trouble breathing through the panic that was clawing at my throat. The room around me started to spin and I barely heard Keelyn ask me if I was okay. "Do you need to sit down, Noe? You look a little pale."

I felt like I was going to hurl. I put a hand over my churning stomach and looked everywhere but at the prying eyes coming from everyone in the room. "It's been a long few days. I'm tired."

Horrified was more like it. Of course, Aaron had gone off to law school and was getting people off the hook who were just as awful and demented as he was. He probably sympathized with the monsters he represented. I knew firsthand that he understood them, that he came from the same kind of tattered and torn fabric that made them. I never thought I would see him again, or hear his name, unless it was ripped out of me in the middle of the night when I couldn't escape the things he'd done. I couldn't believe he was smack dab in the middle of everything that was going on now.

Goddard. The man had gotten away with more than murder for a long time, so clearly, he wasn't stupid. We were so busy keeping track of him, we never stopped to wonder if he was doing the same kind of research on us. He could have easily found a low-rent attorney in the Point or one from the Hill who might be attention hungry and looking for glory, but he hadn't. He'd deliberately found the one person who would make me run. The only person I feared enough to turn my back on the young girl who needed me and the man I was growing more reliant on every single day. He'd played his hand well, and when I wasn't terrified and choking on panic, I would take a minute to be impressed by how well the old man played the game. But right now, I had to *go*.

I had to vanish, disappear, dissolve into nothing. I needed to get my ass on the first train or bus out of town and never look back at this fucking city again. I needed to escape. I needed to be where no one relied on me. I needed to get somewhere that stormy gray eyes didn't follow my every move and catalogue my every thought and feeling like I was some kind of newly discovered creature. One that he was determined to figure out and tame. I needed space to get my head around how easy it had been for him to get through my walls. Until I heard Aaron's name, I didn't even realize I was standing on the ruins of everything impenetrable I'd built up over the years. I hadn't noticed the bricks crumbling to ash every time Snowden Stark touched me, or pushed me to do more, or caused me to think harder and be better. He wanted me to want things and he'd managed to make that happen. I wanted him, but not nearly as bad as I wanted to get someplace where Aaron Cartwright couldn't find me. A place he would never, ever think to look.

"I just need . . . ," I cleared my throat as the words squeaked out too high and shaky. "I'm going to go to the bathroom. I'll be back in a minute."

I grabbed my backpack from the floor, clutching it like it was a lifeline and not an anchor that weighed me down. I started for the elevator, intent on getting out of the club and hitting the streets when Nassir's smooth as silk voice stopped my hasty retreat.

"You can use the private bathroom up here. You don't have to go all the way back down to the club." He was watching me carefully, eyes dissecting my every twitch. He might pretend to be a heartless bastard, but I knew he cared about Stark and he made it clear he knew that Stark cared about me. He wasn't going to let me evaporate into thin air because it was going to piss his boy off, and he wasn't having any of that.

Too bad. I was beyond caring what either he or Stark thought about my need to flee. All I could think about was getting somewhere I felt safe, somewhere nobody knew me and wouldn't look for me.

"No. I think it's better if I head downstairs. When I say I have to go to the bathroom, I mean I have to *go*." I left no question about what I meant. The handsome lawyer looked properly disgusted and the teenaged boy who trotted into town with Julia snickered in the way all teenaged boys tended to at toilet humor.

I jabbed at the elevator button like my life depended on the car showing up in the next couple of seconds, because it felt like it did. Once the metal doors swished open, I practically jumped into the interior, turning to push the button for the ground floor only to catch Julia's questioning, terrified eyes. I told her I would protect her, that I wouldn't leave her. I was a goddamn liar.

"I'm so sorry." It sounded just as pitiful as Stark's apology had the night he got me back from Goddard's men. It sounded just as useless, as well.

The doors closed and I pressed a button for the floor that had the private rooms. I didn't trust Nassir to let me go. If he put one of his guys on the front door, there was no way I was getting past them, but I knew from pictures all over Instagram that the club had a private terrace used for the high rollers and big spenders. They were also the people who paid for sex and debauchery, the likes of which Goddard could provide, but that was neither here nor there. The private patio was just high enough that jumping over the edge and down into the alley below was risky, at best. Flat out stupid and irresponsible was closer to what I was doing, so I couldn't stop and think too much about it. Sure, running away with a broken ankle was going to be a hell of a lot harder than skipping town with two working legs, but there wasn't a chance Stark was going to let me go when he found out Aaron was back in the picture. He would make a broken bone seem like nothing more than a minor inconvenience.

The bar in the VIP area was closed since the club didn't open until late into the night. I sent a quick prayer up to whomever might be listening and feeling generous with their miracles that the doors leading outside wouldn't be locked. I heard something that sounded like an electronic *click* but I refused to stop and think about what it was as the heavy, glass door swung open under my hands. I bolted to the railing and gulped when I looked down. It seemed a lot higher up in person than it appeared on the Internet. There was no question that going over the side and landing on the asphalt below was going to hurt, bad.

I couldn't see another way around it, though. I was like an animal caught in a trap. I was willing to chew my own leg off in order to get free. I had to get away. There was no other choice. I could feel my past breathing down my neck with hot, acrid puffs of air and it was suffocating me. I tossed a leg over the metal railing and briefly closed my eyes. I deserved a break. Maybe I would land on some trash or hybrid car. Something soft or something that would crumple easily and break my fall.

I pried my eyes open, preparing to hurl myself into oblivion, when I caught sight of the shiny, sparkly, perfectly maintained fire escape leading off the far side of the terrace. I couldn't believe a guy like Nassir Gates bothered with something as mundane as keeping his club up to code. I decided next time I saw him, which would be never, I was going to give him a kiss of gratitude. I didn't even care that Keelyn would kick my ass over it.

I ran to the ladder, used my foot to kick the latch that held it in place, and sighed in relief as the separate parts started to roll toward the ground below. I was scampering down the side of the building before the last rung hit the cement. When my feet were back on solid ground, I shot a look up to where I had come from and noticed that there were surveillance cameras on every corner and along every outside wall of the massive warehouse. My escape wasn't going unnoticed and I didn't have to wonder if I really was breaking free or if Nassir was letting me go. If I gave it too much thought, I would stop moving and I couldn't afford that.

I darted out of the alley, pulling my beanie down over my head and tugging a hoodie on over my thin t-shirt. I kept my head down as I melted into the shadow and shade that was always present in the Point. The darkness used to be my friend, used to be the place I knew I could hide. The gloom and the gutters was where I always felt safe, but now Stark knew where to look for me. And I knew he would. Even though I'd been working at putting space between us, driving a wedge at the same time I pulled him closer, he would look. He wasn't going to let me go without a fight, because I knew him. I understood him. I appreciated all of him, and I told him that over and over again when I let him take my body and challenge my mind. My heart was starting to get jealous of all the other parts of me that were full of Snowden Stark, which was another reason I needed to hit the bricks. I didn't want to fall for a man who claimed to be heartless, but was anything but. I had too much on my own plate to take on his search for his lost ability to love. If he found it, I was a goner. As it was, I was barely hanging onto my resolve to protect my heart from him and his awkward, untried affection.

I stopped at a bus stop, but remembering Stark's warning that all buses had cameras nowadays, I quickly changed my mind and slipped into the shadow of a nearby convenience store while I tried to figure out the best way to get out of town without being tracked. Stark could hack into any of the city's surveillance systems so public transport was out. He could hack into Uber to see if I ordered a ride, even if I used a fake name. If I stole a car, as soon as it was reported, he would have the description and plate number. Getting away from a genius was a lot harder than running away from my family had been . . . in more ways than one.

I decided my best course of action was to hop one of the freighter trains that rolled in and out of the city on a regular basis. The security was lax because everyone knew the good stuff came into town through the docks. Plus, I'd run across many a gutter punk who had made their way from one coast to the other hopping trains. I figured if they could do it, so could I.

It was a long walk to the freight yard, one I spent looking over my shoulder every two seconds. I was breathing hard and was so tired when I slipped through a hole in the chain link fence that surrounded the noisy, dirty trainyard. It sucked that I had no idea where any of the trains were going, that I didn't get to pick where I was running to, but as long as it was away from the threat of Aaron and the promise of Stark, I wouldn't complain. It took a minute to find an open boxcar, one that I could toss my backpack into and hoist my body upon. The train started rolling just as my boots left the ground. I threw myself on my back and stared up at the top of the boxcar, telling myself I wasn't going to cry.

I left. That's what I did. That's how I kept myself safe. It was for the best, even if I couldn't convince myself that was the truth. Goddamn liar.

The train rolled through the Point and out of the city into the Valley. I freaked out when I thought it was going to stop in the place that harbored my biggest fear. Luckily, it kept on rolling, eventually chugging through the foothills and over the slight incline of the mountains. It slowed that night through a quaint, small town that was only a handful of hours away from the Point, but eons away from my home in terms of infrastructure and morality. There were legitimate white picket fences lining the streets and nothing was open after dark.

I worried I was going to stick out like a sore thumb, that the local police would show up and run me out of town before I found a place to sleep for the night, but this town was a throwback to when people cared for their neighbors and watched out for their community. I wasn't on the street searching for an alcove or alley to camp out in for more than a half an hour when I was approached by a middle-aged woman. Her face was clouded with concern when she asked me if I had anywhere to go or anything to eat.

I opened my mouth to tell her I was fine, that I was just passing through, on my way to somewhere, anywhere, but what came out was a wailing sob that made my entire body shake. I was crying for who I was and where I had come from. I was confused, and for the first time in my life, not sure if I should be moving forward or running backwards.

She took a step toward me, putting her hands on my trembling shoulders and told me, "We see a lot of young kids like you passing through here. They come from the city. It must be an awful, awful place to not notice its young people fleeing. The church has a place you can spend the night and shower. It might be too late to get you something to eat, but if it is, you let me know and I'll bring you something from home. Let's get you somewhere warm and safe." She thought I was pathetic, weak, and pitiful. All the things I'd fought so hard not to be after the first time Aaron ruined my life. She didn't look any deeper, couldn't see how much more there was underneath the surface, because she didn't come from where I was from. Everyone was so much more than they appeared to be, they had to be to survive.

That was all I ever wanted . . . somewhere safe. I was starting to wonder if it was somewhere or someone that held the security and safety I craved.

I wiped the back of my hand over my wet cheeks and took a shuddering breath. "It is an awful place, but the people . . ." Well, some of them were awful, but more often than not, they were special because they survived and sometimes even thrived in a place that was hell on Earth. "The people make it home."

She lifted her eyebrows as she guided me toward a white clap-board and brick building with stained-glass windows and a steeple holding a bronze bell. It looked like a scene off of a postcard you sent back home. I'd never seen anything so . . . clean and pure. It made me feel a little uneasy and completely out of place. I shouldn't have been running away, I should have run toward the one person who actually made me feel invincible. Hindsight was always so crystal clear.

"A home you ran away from, so it must not be that great." She sounded so sure, so judgmental of the place that had protected me when I really did run away from home. I didn't like an outsider, someone with no idea of the miles I'd travelled, disparaging the city that had made me.

I rubbed my face with my sleeves and told myself to settle down. I'd been frantic to get away but now it was clear there was nowhere else I belonged. I had space, I had air, I had freedom, and it was absolutely not what I wanted. "I didn't run away. I just got a little lost." I could have used some of Stark's robotic reasoning. It would have stopped me from overreacting and jumping the gun.

The woman opened the doors to the church and I followed silent-ly. I had no choice but to accept the town's hospitality for the night. In the morning, I was going back to face my double nightmare, knowing I wouldn't have to do it alone. I was too old, too smart, and too strong to keep running from the things that scared me.

"Well, you have a place here until you figure out what you want." The woman offered me a smile that I returned.

"I don't need to figure it out. I know exactly what I want." And I would bet all of my meager belongings and my foolish, fragile heart that he was already on his way to find me. "He'll be here in the morning." I believed that as reverently as I believed he would never, ever let Aaron get anywhere near me.

I needed to go so he could bring me back. Show me my place in life. In this big, bad world. And once he had me, I was going to help him find his heart . . . because that elusive, tricky thing was mine.

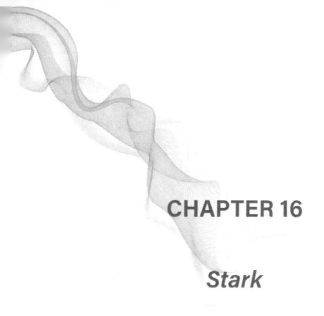

CHAPTER 16

Stark

I WAS SURE I would never be cold again.

I was so hot, the fury boiled under my skin melting any part of me that wasn't blood and bone, leaving behind an uncomplicated, primal, uncaged animal. I wanted to tear my prey limb from limb. I wanted to feel their blood on my hands, smell their fear, and watch as they cowered before me. There was nothing logical or reasonable about my reaction and I was as far from numb as I had ever been.

I felt everything.

There were no more sticky webs wrapped around my thoughts. I was seeing more clearly than I ever had. The spider finally caught the fly and there was no way it was getting free.

Titus gave me a warning look as we watched Goddard and his lawyer speak, their heads bent close together. They were in an interrogation room and I was on the other side of the two-way observation panel, meaning I could see the assholes who ruined

Noe's life, but they couldn't see me. Titus hadn't seemed surprised when I called and told him he was getting me in with both men as soon as they hauled Goddard's ass in for questioning. What he didn't know was that I was just as interested in the lawyer as I was in the former mayor. He was a good cop so he didn't bother to ask why I was so insistent. We both knew I was the reason his department was now on its way to being above board and cleansed of all the bad seeds. He owed me.

Nassir called me the second Noe bolted. He wanted to know if he should stop her or have his guys tail her. When he told me she was ready to jump off his building to get away, I knew the best thing to do was let her go. She was panicked, freaking out, and scared. There was no telling what she would do in order to put distance between her and the man who terrified her. I didn't want her to hurt herself or anyone else. I assured him I would track her down and bring her back. Julia Grace was bewildered and more frightened than she already was. She looked up to Noe, viewed her as a savior. It was hard for her to see that my little thief was nothing more than flesh and bone. A young woman with secrets and scandals that she didn't know how to fight.

Which is why I was at the police station, teeth grinding together, hands clenched into fists as Titus warned me if I killed anyone, he was going to have to arrest me. He didn't really seem too concerned about protocol or losing his badge. With the entire police force in disarray, everyone was relying on him to call the shots and pull it all together. He was the last good guy left, the last man anyone trusted. No one was going to report what went on in that interrogation room . . . unless I lost control and someone died. The rage I was feeling was as close to murderous as it had ever been, so I made no promises. If I lost control, if I pictured all the ways those men in that room had abused and manipulated Noe, there was a good chance someone was going to stop breathing.

The only thing keeping me in check was knowing I had to go after her. I needed to find her and bring her back. She needed to know I would always come for her and it didn't matter where she hid, I would track her down. She was the only thing that made sense to me. She was the only one who understood me. She was the only person who wanted *all* of me, and I wasn't going to fight the fact that I wanted all of her. Everything inside of me had been in disarray and out of order until she broke into my house and into my heart. She was the thing that reset everything, the person who knocked the rust off and started the machine back up. I purred steady and loud now, all because of her.

"I will come in there and pull you off if I think you're going too far." It wasn't a threat. Titus was simply stating the way it was going to be. He was big enough that he might have a shot at reigning me in, but he had no idea there was an unholy fire burning in my belly when I imagined Noe being under the smarmy lawyer's thumb, too young to fight the monsters herself.

He was an average looking guy. Not too big, not too small, but definitely a lot larger than Noe. He had a soft face, a cleft in his chin, and his hair was done in an artfully messy way. He looked media ready and unnaturally confident. He even had the gall to slap Goddard on the back and throw his head back and laugh at something the older man said. There wasn't anything funny about why they were in that room. I wanted to make him stop laughing. I wanted to break his teeth out and snap his jaw in half. It would be impossible to laugh through a face full of metal. It would be hard to represent anyone that way, as well.

The lawyer laughed again and I couldn't handle it anymore. I reached out and touched the button that blacked the glass out and turned to look at Titus. "Five minutes. Don't give me any longer than that." I pointed to the video feed and told him to turn it off. I wasn't sure he was going to comply, but even if he didn't, I planned on going into the system and erasing any evidence of my visit. Nothing needed to tie me to this visit. I breathed a sigh of relief when the cop did as I asked.

Titus finally started to look slightly uneasy. His sharp gaze rolled over the set of my shoulders, my clenched hands, and the fury I was sure was stamped all over my face. "A lot can happen in five minutes, Stark."

I dipped my chin in a nod. It took both men in that room less than five minutes to change my girl's life forever. "I know." I planned on keeping up the tradition.

I stepped around him and pulled open the door to the interrogation room. I was immediately hit with the smell of expensive cologne. Noe had to fight for her freedom, her body, and her mind, and this piece of garbage was all gussied up like he was going somewhere fancy. He'd donned his best to represent a monster.

"Who are you? You're not with the prosecution." The lawyer started to get up, but I was on him before he could rise to his full height.

I grabbed the back of his head and slammed it forward, shoving it into the unforgiving edge of the metal table. There was a satisfying sound of bone crunching as his nose took the brunt of the contact. Immediately, the coppery scent of blood overlapped the cologne. It was deeply gratifying. I used my hold on the back of his head to ram his face into the edge of the table a couple of more times, ignoring his shouts of surprise and Goddard's wails for the police.

I kicked the lawyer's chair out from under him, landing him and his ass in that fancy suit on the dirty floor at my feet. I glared down at him as he put his hands over his gushing nose. He was clearly bewildered and frightened.

Good.

"Consider me the judge, jury, and executioner all in one. Your sister is someone who is very important to me, so you've already been found guilty beyond belief."

"I don't have a sister. I'm an only child." The words were garbled and wet as he spoke them through the blood covering his face.

The fact that he never looked at Noe like family, that he was denying who she was, made me see red that was brighter than his blood. I put my boot into his ribs and while he was curled on his side, whimpering on the floor, I put the heavy tread on his neck and pressed down. He couldn't breathe. He was clawing at the leather and laces desperately. His watery eyes were bugging out of his head. He looked as frightened as my girl must have been when he caused her to run.

"That was the problem all along. You never considered her your sister. You treated her like property, like she belonged to you. You never thought she was family." I lifted my foot as he groaned and wiggled under my weight. I bent and picked up his heavy briefcase, pressing the stiff bottom into the center of his chest, pinning him back to the floor. "If you stay on this case, I will find you, and I will end this. I'll make it so you can't represent anyone ever again. I'll rip your life apart from the inside out. Ask your client how good I am at taking away everything that matters."

My gaze lifted to Goddard who was pounding his fists on the two-way glass. He was screaming that he was going to sue the police department, that he was going to have Titus fired. All that noise and the door remained shut. That meant I had a few minutes left. I grabbed the handle of the briefcase and swung it as hard as I could into Aaron Cartwright's face. The thud it made pleased me all the way down to my bones. So did the way he slumped to the floor, bloodied and unconscious. I let the briefcase fall and watched Goddard through narrowed eyes.

"That's how you win a fight? A sneak attack on an unsuspecting man and threatening a helpless old man? Who are you and what do you want?" It was all bluster and bravado. I could see the fear in his eyes and the way he was sweating. His voice was a few octaves too high; my presence was the cause.

I stalked toward him, forcing him to retreat into a corner of the room. "He doesn't deserve a fair fight. He never gave his sister a chance at one." And even if the lawyer had a warning, I still would have pounded him into the ground. When we were chest to chest, I wrapped my hands around the lapels of Goddard's suit jacket and lifted him up so that only his toes were touching the ground and we were almost nose to nose. He wiggled like a caught fish in my hands. I gave him a shake so that his head thudded heavily against the brick wall behind him.

"They call you God, don't they? The man with all the power? The man who calls all the shots and decides who's worthy and who isn't? Why don't you tell me what happens next?" I got really close to his face so he could see the white-hot rage. "Why don't you tell me how helpless you were when you raped your stepdaughter and all those girls from the after-school program you set up? Explain to me how weak you were when you kidnapped my girl and locked her up for two weeks while your men touched her, fondled her, scared her?" I shook him again and let him go once he started screaming for the police. "Who do you think told me you were here for questioning, old man? The police who actually give a shit about their jobs and this city aren't on your side. No one is. I could snap your neck right now and no one would care." I pointed a finger at the center of his face and growled, "Your life, or what's left of it, is in my hands. I own you, you sick fuck." I had all the power and he was nothing but a bug I was about to squash.

Goddard smoothed a hand over his wrinkled suit jacket and shirt. His beady eyes narrowed on me. "What do you want then? Why are you here?"

I put my hands on my hips and looked down at the crumpled form of Noe's tormentor. "I want to go back in time and give those girls a fresh start. I want them to have their youth and their innocence back. Since that's impossible, I want you to make all of this going forward as easy on them as possible. Fire this asshole." I nudged Aaron with my foot, eliciting a groan of protest. "Plead guilty when you're charged so Julia Grace doesn't have to look at your wrinkly old ass ever again. Go quietly away, Goddard."

He huffed out a breath. "Why would I do that? It's my word against that little tramp's. I'll explain that she seduced me, that she was desperate for a father figure. She was the one who instigated it. I'll find another lawyer." His confidence was unbelievable.

I shook my head at him. "I already took your money, old man. I took your title away. I dug up each and every single one of your secrets. I'm so deep inside your life, you can't see me. I know what you've done. I know where the bodies are buried. If you don't go to jail for rape, I'll send you away for fraud and tax evasion. I have more tricks up my sleeve than you can imagine." I pointed at him and narrowed my eyes. "And if you think I'll let anyone take your case, you're an idiot. He," I inclined my head toward Aaron, "Was personal. He needed to know what it's like to have someone bigger than you, stronger than you, someone more determined to get what he wants. I'll go after any other attorney you hire without stepping foot inside this room. I'll fuck with their law license. I'll erase their credentials. I'll freeze their assets. I'll have warrants issued for them. I'll put their houses in foreclosure. There is no limit to what I'm willing to do in order to see you rot behind bars, Goddard." I narrowed my eyes at him. "I'll go after everyone you care about. Your wife. Your siblings, their kids. Anyone who's still taking your fucking calls. Anyone who visits you in lock up, I'll check off their names one by fucking one. I'll ruin anyone and everyone who tries to help you."

We stared each other down for a long moment. Aaron groaned from the floor again and I heard the door to the small room open. Titus let out a string of expletives and barked that it was time for me to go.

"You think you're smart, don't you?" Goddard sounded frustrated and furious. "You think you have all the answers."

"I know I'm smart." The only answer was him paying for what he had done.

Titus grabbed my elbow and I let him haul me out of the room. Goddard didn't say anything else and the cop purposely ignored the bleeding man on the floor. Once the door was shut behind us, I took my glasses off and dragged a hand over my face. Titus lifted a black eyebrow in my direction and looked at the closed door over my shoulder. "What would have happened if I gave you another five minutes, kid?"

I shook my head and put my glasses back on. "If Goddard asks for another lawyer, let me know."

"He's facing some pretty ugly charges. He's not going to walk away from this no matter who his lawyer is."

I grunted in response and pulled out my cell phone to look at the app that was tracking my laptop that Noe still had with her. I'd installed the software a couple of days ago when she started pulling away from me. I knew she was going to run and I was going to chase after her like a desperate, needy fool. She'd finally stopped moving. She was in a small town up north. I would have to drive all through the night to get to her by morning.

"He can sit in front of a judge with a public defender. If he's smart, he'll plead guilty and just go away." I tapped my phone and looked up at the man I admired and respected. He was looking at me like he finally realized there was more to me than quick fingers on a keyboard.

"What happens if he doesn't go down quietly?" That was the cop asking, not the guy who let me in the room to kick the shit out of my girl's adoptive brother.

"You don't want me to answer that. The less you know, the better. I gotta go get my girl. I appreciated what you did for me today, Titus." I stuck out my hand and tried not to wince when his shake squeezed my fingers together in a crushing grip. It was a warning that I couldn't miss.

"I like you, kid. You think before you act and you weigh the odds of things going south before jumping in with both feet. You helped me get my department in order, which means you care about this city and the people in it the same way I do. Don't do anything that forces me to consider you an enemy. I got enough of those as it is."

I rubbed my hand when he let it go and started for the front doors and my truck that would take me to her. I was floored that he liked me. Most people didn't, but since Noe, it seemed to be happening more and more. She humanized me, softened me. She made me likeable. "I can't promise anything, King. Sometimes the ends justify the means." If it wasn't already, it should be the slogan for the Point. Sometimes bad things had to happen in order for the good to have a shot.

After Goddard was sentenced, I was going to do my thing and make sure he was locked up in the same prison as my old man. My father might not have any warm, fuzzy feelings for what was left of his family, but he was fueled by justice. I had a feeling if I let it slip that Goddard was in the same cell-block as he was, even if it was solitary, my dad would find a way to get to him. The man sold out his country to avenge my mom. He wouldn't blink at giving Goddard a proper welcome if I passed on all the dirty shit the former mayor had brought into my life. He promised he knew punishment, and no one needed punishing more than Goddard. It would give my dad a way to show he still cared in his own, twisted, vengeful way that didn't involve any more heart to hearts or uncomfortable truths. He wouldn't even have to see me in order to prove I still mattered to him.

He swore again and flipped me off before the doors closed behind me. I jogged to my truck, hoping against hope that Noe didn't realize I'd put a tracker on the computer. I didn't know what I was going to do if she ditched the damn thing. I was betting on the fact that she was like me, unable to be unplugged for any length of time. I was also holding out hope that she wanted to hold onto the damn thing because it was mine, something she took from me when we first met. I wanted her to have the same connection to me that I had to her.

I'd lost one person who meant everything to me . . . I wasn't about to lose the one who meant even more than that.

CHAPTER 17

Noe

I WASN'T ALONE IN the basement of the charming little church. As it turned out, even picturesque small towns had their fair share of victims and castoffs. When you were stuck in the Point, it often felt like the rest of the world had it so much better, anyplace else would be an improvement. Sitting in the basement of this building, in a town that shouldn't remind me of home, I couldn't help but notice the similarities, and I realized anywhere I ran wouldn't be perfect. There was a teenage boy who had the same kind of bruises and fear in his eyes that Julia Grace had when she first found me. There was a young mother with two young children. All three of them were too thin and jumped at every noise and shadow. There was another young woman who was around my age; she was twitchy, nervous, and unable to sit down. She kept looking at my backpack with unnatural interest, forcing me to keep the tattered material close at hand. She was no different than the junkies who ran the streets. All she wanted was a way to score another fix, she didn't care about the roof over her head, the small bathroom we could shower and freshen up in, the stale peanut butter and jelly sandwiches a kind volunteer scrounged up for us, or the fact we all had a somewhat comfortable bed for the night.

Her frantic pacing and incoherent mumbling made for a restless night, not that I would have slept anyway. I was pissed at myself for letting old fear and panic rule me. I was angry that I reverted to the helpless, trapped teenager who felt as if she didn't have any options. I was beating myself up, which kept my eyes pried open and regret flowing through my blood well into the early hours of the morning. I should have stood my ground, faced Aaron down, and showed him he was no longer calling the shots. It didn't matter that he'd gone on to live a productive, prominent life like he'd done nothing wrong, as if he hadn't taken everything from me. He'd moved on. I was the one running, the one refusing to let myself get attached to anything or anyone. I was the one who hadn't let myself live a normal life. I told myself it was best that I relied on no one, that I trusted only myself, but running from Stark and leaving the city behind forced me to realize how entirely alone I was. And I was lonely. I wanted someone to tell me it was going to be all right. I needed someone to lean on and remind me that I was no longer the young woman who didn't have a voice. I'd not only found mine, I used it to speak out, I used it to scream for others, to beat the drums of justice so loud that the violators were forced to cower, yet I couldn't beat those same drums for myself. I was done running; this was stopping right here, right now.

My strength and dignity wouldn't be compromised by the memory of the man who had taken it away in the past. I was so much better than the likes of Aaron Cartwright and Jonathan Goddard. I had nothing and it was more than either of them would ever have.

Well, that wasn't entirely accurate. I had faith that Snowden Stark wasn't ready to let me go quite yet. We had unfinished business between the two of us, things that needed to be said, promises that needed to be made. I wasn't worried when he didn't show by the time the sun came up. I wasn't fazed when another church volunteer showed sometime in the morning with a box of cereal and fresh fruit. I wasn't concerned there was no sight of him when the pastor of the church came down and offered to speak with the mother, the teenaged boy, and the junkie. He took one look at me and determined I had somewhere else to be. I didn't need to talk to him, I needed to talk to the giant, tattooed behemoth stomping down the stairs, boots making his approach echo through the building.

His eyes looked tired but they were only for me. His scruff had taken over the lower half of his handsome face, highlighting his fierce frown. His eyebrows were knitted in a scowl that would scare the bravest of men, and when he said my name it made the junkie jolt, the battered mom jump, the teenaged boy cower, and the pastor stiffen. That low rumble had me melting, and once again, I couldn't hold back tears. Before a choking sob could find its way out, his strong arms were wrapped around me not feeling anything like the old, mechanical parts that were inked across the surface. He was all man . . . my man. I was never running from him or the haven of those heavy arms again.

He tucked my head under his chin and squeezed me tight enough that I squeaked in protest.

"I know I fucked up the first time you gave me your trust, but I've done everything I can think of to prove you that I won't let anything happen to you, Noe. I will keep you safe. Trust me."

I wrapped my arms around his waist and snuggled into his chest. I buried my nose into the spot where that hard heart lived.

It wasn't nearly as impenetrable as he wanted me to believe. "I do know that . . . I just forgot for a second. I wasn't thinking clearly." I leaned back so I could look into those storm-colored eyes. "The truth is I might forget again. It was a knee-jerk reaction. I regretted it as soon as I had room to breathe. I've been running a long time, Snowden. It's all I know."

He lifted a hand so he could tuck a loose piece of hair that escaped my hat behind my ear. "You slowed down so I could catch you, though, and that tells me something."

I let out a sloppy laugh and nodded weakly. "I guess I did. Ummm . . . how exactly did you know where to catch me?"

He took a step back, but kept one of my hands clasped in his. He bent and picked up my backpack and held it out in front of me. "You left your computer unattended more than once. I figured you knew I would install tracking software."

Of course he had. If I could think beyond the terror that had me in a stranglehold at the mention of Aaron's name, I would have taken inventory of everything he'd been around and could use to track me. It would have killed me to let go of the only thing I had to remember him by, but I would have ditched the laptop in the heat of the moment if I'd been thinking clearly. I was glad I hadn't been. I was weak-kneed with relief that he hadn't let me go without a fight.

His pointed gaze flicked around our audience and his lips started to quirk upwards. "You wanna get out of here?"

I nodded quickly. "Yeah. Take me home, Stark."

He tugged on the hand he was holding and led me up the stairs he'd just stomped down. It was a cloudy, overcast day making the scenic little town look just as dreary and unwelcoming as the Point. I guess it was all about perspective. Yesterday, when I'd been motivated by the need to escape, this place seemed perfect. Today, now that my eyes were wide open, I couldn't see a single thing that appealed to me. There was only one place that would ever be home, and only one man who would ever feel like he belonged to me.

He had to give me a hand climbing into his huge truck. The vehicle was black on black on black and lifted up to the sky. It was slightly ridiculous for a guy who lived in the middle of a city but the big machine fit him, nonetheless. It would dwarf a smaller man, make me question his virility, but Stark took up a lot of space. It only made sense what he drove did as well.

The rumble of the engine and the adrenaline crash from the day before had my head dropping and sleep pulling at me as we backtracked through the landscape that the train had traveled the previous day. I rested my head against the tinted passenger window and let myself drift off knowing I was in good hands. Hands I actually wanted holding and caring for me.

Stark's phone rang and I peeled my eyes open, noticing we were through the mountains and on the coast. The big sea cliffs were craggy and dramatic, offering a much more spectacular view of the water that bordered the Point. There were no docks and shipping containers here. There was no city that seemed bleak and hopeless hovering on the edge of the waves. The water here was bright blue, stretching out endlessly, and crashing romantically into the rocks. It was hard to believe it was all the same body of water, that this clean water by proximity to its inhabitants turned so dirty and grimy the closer it got to the Point.

"What's up, Titus?" The call echoed through the cab as the Bluetooth connection sent the cop's voice through the truck.

"Goddard pled guilty to the charges. He didn't ask for another lawyer after you laid his first one out. I don't know what you said to him in there, but good job kid." I gasped when Titus complimented Stark for manipulating the legal system. I also blinked at the man sitting next to me when the deep voice continued, "The lawyer didn't say shit about pressing charges for assault, even though you fucked him up. His nose was drifting to one side of his face and he was holding his side like he had some busted ribs. I don't know if I should ask you for lessons in handling perps or put a detail on you to make sure you don't compromise anymore of my cases."

I must have made a noise because Stark's head cocked to the side and his eyebrows lifted. Wordlessly, he pulled the big truck off to the side of the road, the front wheels pointing toward a sheer drop off.

"My methods won't work for you, cop. You're one of the good guys." He was watching me closely because I was suddenly wide awake. He'd taken on Aaron for me. He'd hurt him, just like I'd dreamed of doing for so long. He'd not only refused to let me go without a fight, he had taken on my fight as his own. It was hands down the nicest and most unforgettable thing anyone had ever done for me. I struggled to get my seatbelt off while pulling my beanie off my head and crawling out of my hoodie. I needed to be as close to him as I could get and I didn't need any extra clothes getting in the way.

"You can be one of the good guys too, Stark. You already are when it's convenient for you." The cop sounded chiding and slightly put out. He wasn't wrong. My guy had all the makings of a hero, he just needed to decide if he wanted to save the world or not.

"I'm one of the bad guys when it's convenient too, King. I can go either way depending on the situation. You should toss a kidnapping and unlawful imprisonment charge against Goddard since he's being so agreeable." He let out an oomph of sound as I crawled into his lap, my back to the steering wheel as his hands settled on my hips.

"The DA had to agree to putting him in solitary for the duration of his sentence, but it was worth it to avoid a trial. He'll never get out." The cop sounded confident in his claim.

"Good. He doesn't deserve sunshine and fresh air. I gotta go, King. My hands are full at the moment." He leaned over and pressed the face of the display ending the call. His gaze locked on mine. "Even if they put him in solitary, there are still ways to get to him. Lockup is almost as brutal as the streets, and guys like Goddard don't stand a chance behind bars."

I put my hands on his cheeks, palms rubbing against the brush of his dark stubble. He was beautiful, conniving, and even if he didn't want to save the world, he had saved me. That was more than enough. It was more than I'd ever had.

"You went after Aaron." There was no hiding the relief and hint of awe that colored my tone.

"Of course I did. That's why I didn't get to you last night. He doesn't get any part of you ever again." His hands slid up to my ribs, taking my t-shirt with them.

I nodded slowly. "You're right, he doesn't, because you have all of me. You already had all of me even before I knew you kicked Aaron's ass." I leaned forward and rested my forehead against his, careful not to smash his glasses into his face. "I don't have much Snowden, but I want to give all of it to you."

He exhaled a breath and I parted my lips so I could taste it. "I've never wanted much Noe, just someone who understands me, someone who doesn't want me to be anything other than who I am. All I want is you."

His words, along with the rough press of his hands as he pulled my shirt the rest of the way off, made me shiver. His eyes burned with silver fire as they landed on the soft swell of my breasts underneath my plain cotton bra. I was never going to be a lace and satin kind of gal, but he didn't seem to mind. I would take every complicated, difficult inch of him, and I loved that he appreciated every delicate and hard part of me. I wasn't about to change him, and one of the big reasons I decided to stop running was because he didn't see anything about me he wanted to alter.

His rough fingertips danced over my spine as he tickled his way between my shoulder blades so he could unhook the clasp of my bra. I wiggled the straps down my arms and grabbed a fistful of his shirt. "Off." I pulled on it until he leaned forward enough so that we could wrestle the fabric off over his head. I sighed at the sight of all that coiled strength and power waiting for me, wanting me. His glasses tilted to one side and I reached up to set them back where they belonged. I didn't want him to miss any of what I was feeling shining out of my eyes and stamped all over my face as I leaned forward to kiss him. My chest pressed against his, my heart thumping against his in a fast, furious rhythm. His answered, racing to keep up.

My fingers touched his pulse and fluttered down the column of his neck. It jumped at the caress and he took over the kiss. His thumbs rubbed the underside of each breast and his tongue twisted around mine. I was grateful for the donated toothpaste and toothbrush at the church this morning because there wasn't a crevasse he didn't taste and touch. He followed the lower curve of my breasts with his fingers until my nipples were trapped between them. They instantly pulled into tight points, happy with the rough contact.

He pulled back and came at me from a different angle. His teeth tugged on my lower lip, matching the plucking motion of his fingers. I felt the pull between my legs, felt my body quicken and pulse in anticipation. Since I was sitting on top of him, I felt his body respond as well. His cock thickened and hardened behind his zipper and I rocked against the rigid length wantonly. I didn't care that we were parked precariously on the side of the road. I didn't care that both of us were sleep deprived and emotionally drained. I didn't care that it was going to be quick with clothes shoved out of the way so we could get to the good stuff. All I wanted was to be close to him, to watch him as I gave myself to him, as he took me.

I grappled with the button on his jeans, wrenching the denim open. I giggled, actually giggled, carefree and giddy, when he put a hand on my hip and lifted both of us up so that he could push the material out of the way along with his boxers. His cock rose up between us, wet at the tip, prominent vein throbbing along the underside. My fingers barely touched as I wrapped a hand around it and started to slide it slowly up and down. His eyelashes fluttered behind his glasses and his chest expanded as he sucked in a noisy breath. His hips shifted under me as I used my thumb to spread the moisture leaking out of the slit around the plump head. One of his hands cupped my chin as he positioned my face closer to his for a kiss. He bucked into my fist as I tightened my grip and squeezed the wide base.

I nipped at his lower lip and pulled back so I could crawl off of his lap. His hands tightened to hold me in place but I shook my head and told him, "I want to taste you."

He swore and lifted me like I weighed nothing so I was back on my side of the truck. Immediately, I got on my knees and put a hand on his thigh for balance as I lowered my face toward all his enticing male flesh. I wrapped my hand back around the thick shaft, his skin hot enough to burn. My naked nipples dragged across the leather seats and the friction made my entire body vibrate.

One of his hands threaded through the hair at the back of my head, holding on tight as my lips stretched to take him in. Snowden Stark was more than a mouthful. It took some work to swallow him down and to suck him off. My cheeks hollowed out as my tongue flicked along endless inches of hot, hard flesh. He scorched across my tongue and tapped the back of my throat. He tasted salty and earthy, all man. He guided my motions with a wide palm as my fist slid up to meet my lips. His ass arched up off the seat and he grunted as I traced that long, heavy line that ran up the underside of his steel shaft. I liked having him under my control, liked the way he felt filling my mouth. I wanted to take a bite out of him, so I used the edge of my teeth to tease the sensitive curve at the tip. I licked the slippery slit, and smiled when he barked my name in warning. For a second, I wished there wasn't so much of him, that I didn't need a hand to have all of him, because I could feel wetness gathering between my legs and that steady throb needed attention. I wanted to pull my fingers through that moisture and ease the ache, but if I did, I would fall on my face.

I moaned around his hardness and couldn't stop my hips from shimmying where they were propped up in the air. Stark muttered my name and a second later I felt his palm on the middle of my back. His fingers dipped into the little dimples at the base of my spine and then they slid under the waistband of my pants and stopped to cup my ass before disappearing into the soft valley between the twin globes. The unexpected caress had me sucking harder on his cock and forced my hand to tighten reflexively.

He chuckled and I felt the low rumble all the way through my core. "Does swallowing my cock make you wet, Noe? Are you getting off on the thought of sucking me dry?" One of his fingers circled that hidden spot that was usually off limits, and I almost choked as I gasped and pulled more of him into my mouth. Tears wet my eyes and I had to remind myself to breathe through my nose as his touch moved deeper between my legs to find my slick center. His fingers trailed through the wet folds and he let out a satisfied sigh. "I love that sucking me gets you hot. I love how wet and ready you are."

God, that mouth of his.

I had to let him go so I could pull in a breath. He made me lightheaded and dizzy.

His fingers fondled the waiting entrance to my body and chills raced down my spine. I looked up at him from under my lashes and noticed his glasses and the truck windows were slightly fogged over. He had a red flush above his scruff and his eyes raged just as furiously as the water below us.

My body fluttered around his fingers as I rocked into his touch. I was empty and he was the only thing that had ever filled up all those spaces. He was a weight that anchored me but never held me down.

I sighed in relief and his fingers started to thrust in and out of my body. I pushed back against him and lowered my head so I could swirl my tongue around the head of his cock like he was the sweetest treat I'd ever tasted.

His stiff length jumped in my hand and he grunted his pleasure as he added another finger. All of this was amazing and enough to make the big truck rock, but I needed more. I needed all of him filling up all of me.

I used my hold on his leg to push myself into a sitting position. He scowled when the move forced his hands out of my pants, but he got an evil glint in his eye as he brought his slick, glistening fingers to his mouth and licked them clean. I shimmied out of my loose-fitting pants and practically threw myself at him when I was naked. He caught me around the waist and spread my legs around his hips, hands on my thighs, as he guided me over his erection.

His lips landed on mine and I tasted my own pleasure. He sighed in satisfaction as our bodies lined up seamlessly. Mine open and hot with a burning need, his hard and heavy with anticipation. He pressed in slow and deep. I felt him drag along every nerve ending and across every sensitive place I had. I put my hands on either side of his neck and rubbed my nose along the curve of his cheek until I could nuzzle his ear. I bit down on the lobe and breathed out how good he made me feel.

I could swear in the short time we'd been together he'd molded my body to fit him and only him. I could feel him deep inside of me but I wanted him even deeper. Our chests rubbed together, my nipples dragging over all that taut muscle and his pounding heart, and like the waves crashing into the rock we were perched on, my orgasm pressed in, threatening to sweep me away.

His thumb traced my jaw and his eyes bored into mine as he told me, "When you run, I'm going to chase you, Noe. Always."

It might have sounded like a threat, but I heard it as a promise. We needed each other. We understood each other. We could find happiness together and I never thought that was possible, but I saw it there, hidden in the storm of his eyes, and I was sure it was reflected back at him in mine.

He kissed me again as his arms wrapped tightly around me. I laughed against his lips but it quickly turned into a gasp as his hips bucked upwards and he pulled me down tightly. My clit pressed against his pelvic bone and the rough sensation was enough to send me spiraling into delirious pleasure. I moaned his name and rocked into him, chasing my orgasm down and kissing every part of his face I could reach. His teeth bit into the curve of my neck where it met my shoulder. It wasn't a nice bite. It stung, and it was going to leave a mark, but it made my pussy spasm and had a rush of wetness covering the heavy cock he was pounding into me.

"Holy fuck, woman. You were made for me. I know it." He tossed his head back against the seat of the truck and held me still as my body milked long, hot pulses of satisfaction from him.

I fell forward, forehead hitting his sweaty throat as I told him, "I am the only one who knows how to fix that mechanical heart of yours." I put my palm on the tattoo, pleased that his skin was damp and warm all over. As long as I had him, I would never let him be cold again.

His reply was lost when a semi-truck came flying around the bend in the road, horn blaring to warn us that we had picked a less-than-perfect place to reconnect. He chuckled and pressed a soft kiss to my lips. "Let's get home."

I scrambled back into the passenger seat and fought to make myself decent as he pulled onto the road and took us toward the Point.

"Home sounds nice." It was the first time I'd ever thought that. Before him, the Point was simply where I survived, but now it was where I thrived.

He made everything better and I was determined to do the same for him. I wanted him to know he would always have a place with me.

CHAPTER 18

Stark

"**G**OT THE GIRL. SAVED the day. Punished the villains. Befriended the local law." I was trying to focus on what Nassir was saying to me, but I couldn't tear my eyes away from the debauchery and hedonism happening on the multiple monitors behind him. I thought I was fairly well versed in all the things that happened between consenting adults, but apparently, I was wrong. There were things happening on those screens I wouldn't have dreamed up when I was feeling my most inspired. "You must be feeling pretty proud of yourself."

I jerked my eyes away from a woman who was old enough to be my mother strapping a guy who was bigger than me, though several years older, face-down on some kind of table. She was buckling thick leather cuffs around his wrists and ankles. When he was secure, she pet him like he was an animal, soothing him before she rammed the biggest plug I had ever seen between his clenched ass cheeks. The guy bucked on the table and I winced in sympathy, baffled that Nassir seemed totally oblivious to it all.

When my gaze landed back on his, the golden gleam in his eyes was glowing with mirth and he was grinning at me. "The guy is a banker and the woman is a real estate developer. They're both married to other people who prefer missionary and lights out sex. They meet up once a month and do their thing. I give them a place to play and they both let me snap up property for a song. It's an arrangement that works well for all of us."

I shook my head and refused to look anywhere but at him. He'd called and asked me to come down to discuss a new service he was considering. He wouldn't give me any more details, and I would have blown him off since he was being evasive, but I wouldn't have Noe in my house and in my bed every night if it weren't for him. We both knew it, and Nassir wasn't a man who squandered his leverage when he had it.

"The outcome would have been much different without you, not that I'm telling you something that you don't already know. Cut to the chase and tell me why you summoned me down here in the middle of the night." Before Noe, time had no meaning, I didn't care that he woke me up and monopolized my time. Now it hurt to roll away from her warm body and head out into the night. I had someone I wanted to be around for, someone I wanted to keep safe. I needed to give the Devil his due so he couldn't pull on my leash when it suited him.

He laced his fingers together and put them under his chin. He watched me unblinkingly and I wished he were easier to read. I felt like he was toying with me and I had to fight the urge to squirm under his scrutiny.

"Booker ran down the plan you had to bring Goddard down before the girl came forward with her story. I was already impressed with how quickly you stripped him of his office and how thoroughly you decimated his reputation. You never exhibited that ruthless streak in any of the other endeavors you took on for me. Frankly, I didn't know you had it in you." I shouldn't feel the shot of pride that zipped through me when he said he was impressed, but I did. Nassir wasn't impressed by much. "I'd like to see more of it."

"Taking Goddard down mattered to me." Sometimes justice wasn't blind. Sometimes it could see crystal clear.

"What if I told you that your skill set, the way you get to men in power, is something I could use? There are places I can't reach, things I can't control, but if you do for me what you intended for Goddard, well," he rocked back in his chair. "I would be unstoppable. I could take control of the Hill as well as the Point. I could make significant changes to both."

I closed my eyes briefly and turned his words over in my head. "Are you asking me to be your digital assassin, Nassir?"

He chuckled softly and leaned forward so he could put his hands on his desk. "I am asking you to help me take the power from men who have done nothing to deserve it. I always knew there was more to you than your ability to hack into bank accounts and do background checks. You are an asset, Stark. Some men deserve to die and some men deserve to simply wish they were dead. I enjoy the idea of ruining lives without bloodshed. It is a very marketable skill. I see dollar signs when I close my eyes and imagine it."

I watched him carefully as I lifted my hand to my mouth and rubbed my thumb along my bottom lip. "Are you going to kill me if I turn you down?"

It was a fair question, but I was surprised at the way it made his eyes flicker in annoyance. "No. I still have use for you either way." And since I owed him, he would work me until I couldn't see straight. He was a businessman, after all.

I met his gaze but shifted uneasily in my seat. "Titus asked me to help him out at the station. Now that most of the bad apples have been shaken from the tree, he's pushing the department forward into this century. He needs my help with that. It's honest work, above board."

His dark head tilted to the side as he considered me silently. After a long moment he asked, "Does it matter what side you're on as long as you believe in what you're doing? There is no black or white in this scenario, Stark. We are all making the best of the gray that surrounds us."

I exhaled and put my hands on my knees as I leaned toward his desk. "Look, Nassir." I rolled my shoulders and looked back to the live action porno playing behind his head. "Poking around the Internet, looking at bank records, and digging into people's backgrounds is nothing. If I start messing with the big picture, start exposing your enemies and making life difficult for them, the people I've been trying to fool for years will come knocking. At least if I'm working with the police, they can't threaten me with jail. They can't scare me by threatening to hurt Noe. They won't have a reason to come after me."

Nassir got to his feet and unbuttoned his suit jacket. He crossed his hands behind his back and started to pace back and forth on the other side of the desk that separated us. He was looking at his feet instead of me when he quietly told me, "The feds don't need a reason to come for you, Stark. They think they own you, that you're their property, and if they decide they want you back, they will come for you no matter where you are or what you're doing. Wouldn't you rather have both me and the cop at your back? Why not cover all your bases?"

I was so stunned that he knew my story, I couldn't speak. I gaped at him wordlessly as he paused mid-step and turned on me. He put his hands on the center of his desk and leaned forward, his body coiled and tense under his perfectly tailored suit.

"I know what it's like to be ripped from your life by the supposed good guys. I know what it's like to be turned into a weapon, into a cold-blooded killer. I had my humanity stripped from me and I fought to get it back."

"How . . . what do you know?" I was still stunned and having a hard time making my words work.

"Race told me you disappeared one day. That your family was pulled apart. He also told me that the government showed an unnatural interest in you from the start. That they had an agenda where you were concerned. Been there, done that. I believed the promises I was told as well. One more mission. One more assignment. One more kill. I owed them. It was my duty. It was all for the greater good." He scoffed, and for a second, I saw everywhere he'd been and everything he'd done to become the man standing in front of me now. I never would have guessed that I had something in common with Nassir Gates, but there it was, the same things in our past that made us cold and emotionless until the right person came along and rattled all the rusty metal that caged us. "I won't let them take you out from under my nose, Stark. Neither will the cop. You have us at your back, whether you want us there or not. You are one of the few things King and I agree on."

I rubbed my hands over my short hair and shoved down the lump that had clogged my throat. "That sounds like you think of me as more than an asset."

He narrowed his eyes at me. "You are one of my people. I do what it takes to keep what is mine safe."

"You and the cop sound more alike than either of you realize." They had the same mission, only they went at it from drastically different angles.

"Work with me, Stark. If you do, I'll make sure you and your girl want for nothing. When I first landed in the Point, I went looking for papers. I needed a new identity. I needed to become the man who was going to make his mark here. Your girl is good; she's been helping rich kids and scared runaways become other people for a long time. I can use someone like her on the payroll. She won't have to hide in the shadows and slink through the dark. I'll make this work for all of us."

I doubted she would take him up on the offer. My little thief didn't answer to anyone and she wasn't for sale. I would appreciate having her under Nassir's protection and knowing she was safely tucked away in his pocket, but I had a feeling she would feel stifled there. The last thing I wanted was for her to push against someone who was so willing to push back. "Let me run it by Noe and see what she says."

I wasn't alone anymore. I wasn't sleepwalking. I was wide awake and present in every single moment. She had given me my purpose back. She had reminded me of my worth. She kept saying that she had taken her dignity back, but I told her she'd never lost it. She was the most dignified person I'd ever met. She made me believe I was special, not because I was always the smartest guy in the room, not because I was the biggest or the best, but because I was me. She didn't mind that I was quiet and often thinking. She didn't care that I wasn't smooth or sophisticated. She didn't cower away from my bad dreams or the fact my sluggish heart was struggling to keep up with her.

"One lesson I've learned and learned well is that there cannot be heroes without villains. You have to have one in order to appreciate the qualities in the other." Nassir's words rang oddly true.

"What about someone who hovers between the two? Someone who plays either role when it suits him? What's there to appreciate about someone like that?" I straddled the line daily, drifting either direction depending on the day and the circumstance.

"You appreciate his intelligence because that is a smart, smart man. Anyone who can play both sides is someone you don't want to underestimate."

I got to my feet and inclined my chin in his direction. "You let me have veto power. I get to choose when and where I work. If I decide the target isn't worth the time or effort, you let me opt out, no questions asked."

I thought he would refuse. He wasn't a guy who gave anyone else any of the power. Slowly, he nodded and moved to cross his arms over his chest. "Anything else?"

"I'm not going to be a ping pong ball between you and the cop. What I do for you stays here and what I do for him stays at the station, even if it's something that might hurt your business. I'm not going to betray either of you. I won't."

Nassir snorted, the sound weirdly elegant as he lifted his eyebrows at me. "You do remember Titus's very pregnant girlfriend is on my payroll? We might not like each other, and we definitely don't agree with how the other handles their business, but we are acutely aware of the fact that we need each other. I won't pit you against the cop, and I assure you, he won't use you to try and hang me."

Pushing my luck, I told him, "I need to have access to the target's computer. I need someone small, nimble, and quick on their feet. Someone who knows their way around electronics." Someone fearless and clever.

Almost as if he could read my mind, he pointed out, "You just described your girlfriend."

I grunted in agreement, not wanting to think about how easy it would be to talk her into doing something so risky and dangerous. She still lived wild, even though she had taken up permanent residence in my townhouse. It was going to be impossible to keep her away when I told her what I was doing. Her righteous streak was a mile wide and now that she had a taste of setting things right, she wanted more. She was a bona fide crusader. I wondered if I could talk her into a spandex body suit and a cape?

"If anything happened to her . . ." I trailed off because he didn't need me to finish that statement.

"You don't let a damn thing happen to her and she makes sure nothing happens to you. No one else has as much of a vested interest in watching your ass." That was true.

Grumbling under my breath, I stuck my hand out and watched as he gave it a firm shake. "Thanks for," letting me know I wasn't alone. That I wasn't crazy. That I wasn't the only one on this great, rotating rock that had been molded into something I never wanted to be. For making me feel slightly more normal and accepted. For getting involved when it didn't benefit him at all. For giving a shit. "Everything."

"Everything comes with a price, Stark. Don't forget that."

Like I could when he constantly reminded me. I gave him a gruff farewell and made my way out of the club. I ran into Chuck on my way out so we bumped knuckles and he congratulated me on a job well done. He was a man who had spent most of his life watching out for the girls of the Point, so he didn't bother to disguise his glee that I'd made a couple of abusers bleed. He told me he heard about the beat down I gave the lawyer and urged me to get in the circle. I told him I was a thinker not a fighter, and he laughed and told me I was both.

Wanting to get back to my bed and the woman in it, I didn't try and argue. I'd only ever used my fists to protect the things I cared about and I wanted to keep it that way. If I fought just because I could, just because I knew how and was good at it, I'd be no better than what the men who took me from my family and killed everything inside of me wanted me to be. I was ready to be more than that.

When I got back to my townhouse, I started stripping as soon as I hit the steps that led to the bedroom. I kicked off my boots, dropped my belt on the floor, and stripped my shirt off. I was leaving a trail to the bed that Noe was going to bitch about in the morning, but I didn't care. I wanted to feel her soft skin pressed into mine. I couldn't wait to be wrapped up in her sleepy warmth.

I tossed my glasses on the nightstand and my jeans landed on the floor with a thud as I pulled back the comforter and slid underneath. I was reaching for her at the same time she moved into me. Her dusky skin shone in the pale light coming from outside and her eyes roved over me, making sure I was in one piece.

"What did he want this time?" She wasn't a fan of Nassir's midnight business meetings and now that she was in my bed, neither was I.

"He offered me a job." I pushed my knee between her bare legs and pulled her closer until we were pressed tightly together. She had on one of those shirts that barely covered her tits and stopped halfway up her back and a pair of cotton underwear. I never knew that the combination of sexy and serviceable could be such a turn on, but then again, anything on her made my dick hard, even when she dressed like a boy.

"Man, you've got job offers pouring in from all over the place lately. What did you tell him?" Her voice hitched when I caught the side of her panties between my fingers and started to work them down over her slim hips. I'd fucked her in the shower before we went to bed and she'd sucked me off this morning before we'd gotten out of bed. We couldn't get enough of each other and I silently prayed that it never changed. I'd never been the beast people compared me to until she came along. She turned me into a hungry, uncontrollable animal. She made my mind go quiet and my body scream. She brought out my carnal side and I embraced that primal part of myself.

"I told him I was in as long as I got to call the shots. I'm too smart to say no to Nassir." I kissed her on the top of her nose and used my thumb to press my dick into her soft cleft. She was warm with sleep and silky in the way that only women were. I stroked my erection through her folds, making sure to catch her clit with the tip as her sleepy body started to respond. "He has some pretty clear ideas about how you fit into everything as well, but we can talk about that later. Were you dreaming of me?"

One of her hands had wrapped around my neck and her fingers were scratching lightly over the skin there. The other was resting on my ribs as her knee hiked farther up on my hip so I could rock more fully into her growing moisture.

"Maybe. Maybe I'm still dreaming." Her lips touched mine, her tongue darting out to trace the divot in my upper lip. "Sometimes I think you're too good to be true. It all has to be a dream."

When her breathing quickened, I grabbed the back of her thigh and pulled her leg even higher up. I grabbed the base of my cock and lined myself up with her entrance. I felt her body pull at mine, always eager, always ready, and it made me less than gentle as I pushed into her. I took her hard, settled in deep as she quivered along every hard inch. She shuddered against me, her hand slipping from my ribs to grab onto my ass. The muscle clenched reflexively as I bottomed out inside of her. I wanted her ruined for anyone who wasn't me. I wanted her to feel the loss of my cock when it wasn't buried deep inside of her.

I grunted and deepened the playful kiss she gave me. I thrust into her harder with each word I spoke. "I was caught in a nightmare before you, Noe. You woke me up."

She sighed against my lips, held me close. "Your mouth. I like it when it's filthy, but I love it when it's sweet."

That made me grin at her and I proceeded to move into her and over her as I told her she was the best I'd ever had. I told her she was sexier than anything I'd ever seen, that I could taste her on my tongue when I closed my eyes, that she made me hard when she smiled at me and when she pushed my buttons. I told her I liked her mind and her body. I told her I was entranced by her fire and her fight. I swore to her that I wouldn't leave her and promised her again that if she left, I would find her. I whispered that she was the reason I remembered what it felt like to love someone. She was the only person I liked every single piece of.

When she came, she did it crying and screaming my name at the same time. I had claw marks on my back and her legs wrapped around my waist. When I came, she told me I reminded her what home felt like and that I was the only person who made her feel safe. She told me I was the only person she liked every single part of.

This was intimacy, the connection we'd both been missing. We were good together when we fucked. We were good together when we fought. We were unbeatable when we put our minds together. But more than any of that, we were the best versions of ourselves when we were together . . . period.

Nassir had to fight for his humanity, I'd had to find mine. It was dressed like a boy living on the streets and running from a past that was almost as bleak as mine. She reminded me I was a man and not a machine. She made me bleed and beg. She made me promise and pray. She turned all the metal and iron inside me to soft, malleable things.

I was putty in her small hands, and I'd never been happier to be shaped into something new and vital.

I was never going to be the man my mother wanted me to be or the one my sister needed. I wasn't going to be who my father tried to mold me into or who the government trained me to be.

None of that mattered, because at the end of the day, I could and would be Noe Lee's hero. The man who kept her safe. The man she leaned on and turned to for help. I could be the man she trusted and relied on. I was the only man she let in, the only one she let catch her, and that was all I ever needed to be.

CHAPTER 19

Noe

FOR A GUY WHO obviously liked the finer things in life, Aaron sure had a crappy security system. It only took a minute to bypass the alarm and even less time than that to make sure the automatic call to the police when the system cut out was routed harmlessly to the burner phone in my pocket. Breaking into the townhouse that actually reminded me a lot of the one I was currently calling home with Stark was easy. Getting up the nerve to come here and confront my past was much harder.

I'd finally found my place. I woke up in the morning with a smile on my face and a rock-hard body between me and the rest of the world. Snowden Stark wasn't going to let anything bad happen to me, and he wasn't going to hold me down. I could run, because he was always going to be faster than I was. When Stark explained what Nassir wanted me to do for him, I agreed, shocking both my man and the man who made the offer. I told him I would forge identities and legal paperwork for his clients, as long as I also got to help his wife get the girls who were tired of the Point and hard living off the streets. It was much easier to start over somewhere new when you showed up to that place as a brand new person. Keelyn Gates and I made a good team and I finally felt like I was making an actual difference in the lives of the people who needed it most. If someone had offered me a way out back when I desperately needed it, maybe I would have that *more* that Stark told me I deserved. I had everything I wanted, but that didn't stop me from wanting to help other young women from reaching for the brass ring. They deserved *more* just as much as any of us.

The only thing that marred my newly acquired sense of serenity and security was the lingering unrest of knowing that Aaron lived a few miles away. Stark assured me we'd heard the last of my childhood tormentor, that he was very aware of what would happen to him if he dared breathe in my direction, but it wasn't enough. I adored my big, broody, badass genius for smashing Aaron's face in, for making the man hurt, but he needed to know I was done hiding from him, that he didn't scare me anymore. He was no longer my nightmare that I desperately longed to wake up from. Now, he was nothing more than a memory. One I planned on filing away and shutting the drawer on once I was done with him.

I was the one with the power now. I was the one who didn't wait for people to listen, I yelled so loud they had to hear me. I was the one who chopped down the beanstalk and took on the giants that fell from the sky. I was the one who had fallen in love with the Tin Man and watched him get used to his new heart. Stark didn't need the wizard to give him what he'd lost, he just needed someone who knew he already had all the pieces, they just needed to be tinkered with and maintained so they could work the way they were supposed to. Aaron had treated me like I was a possession, a piece of property, like I was his most coveted toy. Snowden Stark treated me like I was his equal, his perfect match. We balanced each other out, when he drifted too far into the dark, I pulled him back into the light. He told me every single day that I was difficult, but he did it with a smile. He liked the challenge I offered him and I never once felt like he was trying to own me. I stayed with him, in his house and in his bed, because that was the only place I wanted to be. He told me he would chase me and bring me back, but we both knew that was only because I would ultimately decide to let him catch me.

I was in charge of my life, my heart, and my body. None of those things would rest until I closed the door on my history with Aaron Cartwright . . . preferably hard enough to make him bleed.

I rented an SUV that wouldn't stand out in the perfectly manicured complex. It was shiny and clean. It cost enough that no one would think anything of it being parked in front of Aaron's building while I systematically cleaned him out. A nosy neighbor even stopped and asked if he was moving when I was loading his flat screen into the trunk of the car. I smiled at her and waved her off, telling her he'd bought some new stuff and was donating the old to charity. It was partly true. Everything I lifted from his swanky home, I was pawning. I wouldn't make as much as I had off Stark's, my man had better taste in electronics and an eye for quality . . . obviously, but whatever I made off Aaron's possessions I was giving to Key. I'd mentioned in passing that if some of the girls who ended up in her hands had real community programs in place, they might not end up on the streets or on a pole in the first place. Goddard had bastardized something that would have genuinely been an asset to the city. She liked the idea and was working on putting something in place. It only seemed fitting my asshole adoptive brother have a hand in funding it . . . even if he had no clue how generous he was going to be.

I cleaned him out. Everything that wasn't nailed down and I knew I could flip fast went into the rental. I took his watches, his juicer, his iPad, his passport, his Italian loafers. I grabbed his gaming system and I took a signed football jersey off the wall. I wasn't a Patriots fan, but I knew something with Brady's scrawl on it would sell in a heartbeat. The car was stuffed full and I swore I could hear the muffler scraping the ground as I pulled out of the driveway and drove out of the complex. I parked it in the spot in front of the motel I'd rented for the day and blew out a deep breath. My hands were shaking when I climbed out of the car, but a smile tugged at my mouth when the door to the room swung open and Stark filled up the space, arm above his head so he was leaning on the door jamb, just like he had when I first went to him for help.

He had on a pair of jeans that had a rip in the thigh and were thread bare around the zipper and pockets. The band of his black boxers peeked out of the top, drawing my eyes to the dark hair that arrowed down below his belly button. He didn't have a shirt on, so all that inked skin was pulled taut over stretched muscle and coiled strength. His black hair had started to grow out, making his light eyes pop even more behind the lenses of his glasses. He was gorgeous, grumpy, and ginormous. He was perfect, even though he'd been vehemently opposed to letting me face my demons alone.

He understood it was something I had to do, but he didn't want me alone with Aaron. The idea of anything happening to me or me getting injured made him irrational and argumentative. I didn't mind the fight because making up was fun. He never expected me to roll over . . . unless I was naked and he was taking me from the back. The compromise meant he came to the Valley with me and he had eyes on me the entire time I was executing my Fuck You grand finale. I had a pair of glasses on my face that were almost an exact replica of his, only mine had clear glass in the lenses and an optic camera in the arm that transmitted back to his laptop. He was seeing everything I saw, and if he didn't like the way things played out, he was getting involved. He trusted me to save myself, but just in case I couldn't, he was there. I loved that about him.

"All good?" His voice was gruff as his gaze slid over the packed SUV. One of Nassir's guys was coming to pick it up and drive it back to the Point. I'd always been alone, but I had to admit that having minions on call was a nice perk of working for my new employer.

I sighed and ran toward him. He caught me with no effort as I threw myself against his chest. I wrapped my arms around his neck and peppered his face with hard little pecks. I locked my ankles together at the base of his spine and gave him a full body hug. I could do this, but only because I had him to hold me up when I felt like I was going to fall.

"It will be." I pulled back and smirked at him, eyebrows quirking in amusement. "Did you see how fast I bypassed his security?"

He snorted and pressed his hips into mine. I felt the one part of him that had yet to soften and relax since the first time we'd been together. "I did. It was hot."

I tossed my head back and laughed as he set me back down on my feet. "Only you get hard over a security hack."

He raised an eyebrow at me and crossed his arms over his broad chest. "You were the one who shoved me in one of Nassir's private rooms and pulled my dick out when I told you about hacking into ICE's system and instigated the immigration raid on the Eastern Europeans." He'd managed to shut down the sex trafficking ring that had been plaguing Nassir for months. It was hot when he decided to wear a white hat . . . not that it wasn't sexy as hell when he wore the black one.

"Like you were complaining." He never did when it involved my mouth, my hands—really any part of my anatomy—and his cock. "I need to get back. Aaron usually gets home from work around now. I don't want to lose the element of surprise."

Stark swore and reached out to cup my face in his hands. "You don't have to do this. He's nothing."

I wrapped my fingers around his wrists and gave him a lopsided smile. "I do have to do this. Then he'll be nothing because I'll have everything." I stood up on my tiptoes and pressed a kiss to the hard line of his mouth. "I've got this."

He grumbled something against my lips but let me go, reluctance clear on his face and in his gaze. "I'm right here if you need me."

My heart flipped over and I swore it grew two sizes. It had to be big in order to handle all the things he made me feel. "I know you are. That's why I have to do this, so I can come back to you and leave him behind where he belongs. You are the only man I want taking up any of this valuable real estate." I tapped my temple above the glass frames.

He sighed, still too smart to pick a fight he knew he wouldn't win. "I'll be watching. If I don't like what I see, I'm coming after you."

I gave him a nod and turned so I could walk back to Aaron's townhouse. I could feel his eyes following me, worried and watching, but never weighing me down.

I slipped back into the townhouse and found the breaker so I could cut the power. I wanted him to come in through the front door, not the garage. There were tools and gardening gear in there that could be used as weapons in a pinch, and I didn't want him to be able to defend himself in any way. I wanted him completely at my mercy, the way I'd been at his for far too long.

I settled myself on his couch, a Taser identical to the one the dirty cop used on me clutched in my hand. I had the blinds shut and the sun was starting to go down, so it was dark in his home when I heard a car pull up in the driveway. I tensed, my flight or fight response going haywire and trying to make me flee. My heart was in my throat. My palms were clammy and damp. There was a roaring in my ears that was deafening, but my resolve was stronger than any of that.

I heard a deep voice swearing and a car door slam. That same voice was short and aggravated as it barked, "I don't know, Violet, but the fucking power seems to be out. Call the homeowner's association. With what I pay in HOA fees a month, this is unacceptable." He swore again and I heard keys scrape in the door. "It better not take an hour for someone to get out here. I have work to do."

A moment later, I was face to face with the person who had taken everything from me.

He hadn't changed much over the years. He still looked like a spoiled, rich kid, one who felt entitled to whatever he wanted. He was bigger than he was when I lived under his tyranny, but oddly less intimidating. I chalked that up to the fact his nose was taped up like he'd recently had plastic surgery and the twin yellow and green circles around his eyes a visual reminder of the man who always had my back. It had been weeks, but Stark's calling card was clear all over the man's face.

Stumbling in the dimness, I heard something fall as he tripped his way into the living room. He pulled up short when he caught sight of me, his eyebrows shooting up and his mouth falling open. It would have been a comical reaction if years of agony and suffering hadn't flashed through my mind as our eyes met. His briefcase hit the floor with a thud and I saw him swallow. His Adam's apple bobbed up and down as he reached up to pull on the knot of his tie.

His gaze darted away from mine and started to skate over the pilfered room. His eyebrows furrowed. "Did you steal all my stuff?" He was distracted by his empty home so he didn't see the weapon I was clutching.

I tapped the Taser against my open palm and stared at him unblinkingly. "Not exactly a fair trade, if you think about it, Aaron. You took my virginity, my innocence, my youth. I took your belongings."

He swore and raked his hands through his hair. "Does this have something to do with Goddard? I recused myself from the case. I'm not going anywhere near him."

He took a step closer to where I was sitting on the floor and I tensed. "No. This is about you and me. About what you did to me."

He snorted and rolled his eyes. "I didn't do anything. You were mine, everyone knew it except for you. My parents brought you home for me." Suddenly, he paused and cocked his head to the side. "Did you hear that Mom died? Are you suddenly popping back up because you think you're entitled to something? You aren't. You were never their daughter. She didn't leave you a dime."

He wanted the words to wound, but I was immune to them. He was right. I was never their daughter. If I had been, they wouldn't have let him touch me.

"No, Aaron, I'm here for you, just you." I got to my feet and braced myself as I aimed the Taser at him. The bars flew out faster than I could blink and hit him square in the chest. He fell to the ground, flopping like a fish on land.

His tongue lolled out to one side and his eyes rolled up into his head. I dropped the thing on the floor and stalked over to the man who took everything from me. I pulled the switchblade I'd started carrying out of one of my cargo pockets and lowered myself so that I was hovering over Aaron's twitching, supine form. I dragged the razor-sharp blade over his throat and bit back a smile of satisfaction as he choked and tried to wiggle away from me. The current that hit his body kept him from being able to control his muscles. He was trapped, stuck, unable to escape. I could see the fear working its way through his eyes as the blade kissed his skin.

"I'm not scared of you anymore, Aaron. You took everything, but I got it all back. I have more than I ever imagined I would, but I think it's time you know what it feels like to lose it all." The knife slipped under the knot of his tie and sliced through the silk like it was butter. I held the expensive fabric up in front of his panicked eyes with a smirk. "I think you should leave town. You should run away when it's dark, scared and alone. You won't know where you're going or how you're going to survive because you won't have any family or friends to help you. You'll be all alone, constantly looking over your shoulder because you'll never know if the person you're running from is looking for you."

I moved the tip of the knife to his cheek and let the point dig in just enough to draw a cherry red drop of blood. It beaded and trickled down his quivering face, chased by a tear he couldn't hold back. He was gasping, struggling to get his faculties back, but it was a losing battle.

"You can stay here, but if you do that, know I'll be watching you. Everything you do, every move you make, I'll be all over you, Aaron. It was so easy to get inside your house, so easy for my guy to get to you when you were at the police station. I can get inside your life without you even knowing I'm there." I smirked at him. I was channeling a bit of Stark's badassness and decades of my own pent-up need to put him in his place. "I'm going to ruin your practice. I'm going to destroy your career. I'm going to let everyone know what you did to me, what your family let happen, and when I'm done with you, I'm going to let the man who fucked up your face do so much worse than that. If you think he's scary when he uses his fists, just wait until you see what he can do with his mind. I'm going to make your life a living hell." I moved to the other cheek and gave it a matching mark.

I scrunched up my nose when I smelled urine and rose to my feet. I glared down at him, his body still quivering from aftershocks. "You're pathetic. You don't matter. What you did ruined me, but it also taught me how to survive. I'll fight you, Aaron. I'll be loud about it. I learned how to make people listen." I showed him the knife that was now decorated crimson. "So, what's it going to be? Are you going to stay or go?"

His mouth gaped as he tried to form words. I kicked him in the side and he groaned. "G-o. I'll go." It was garbled and broken.

I nodded and stepped away from him. "You'll go and you'll stay gone. You won't ever practice law again. You can feel what it's like to be ruined. I'll know if you reach out to someone to help you. I'll know if you weasel your way back into town. You're a ghost, Aaron. You vanish and you do it tonight with nothing." I wiped the blood from the knife off on my pants and gave him one last sneer. "I'm going to have all those convictions you won overturned. You're a shitty person but apparently a good lawyer. Of course, you put monsters back on the street. It made you feel less alone, less ugly. You couldn't bear to see animals like you in a cage. Fuck you, Aaron; I was never yours."

I stepped over him like he was nothing more than garbage in the gutter.

I was shaking from head to toe when I got outside and I didn't think my legs were going to hold me up any longer.

I put the knife back in my pocket and was pulling in noisy lungfuls of air when strong arms were suddenly around me. I didn't fight him when he picked me up and walked with me away from everything that had ever held me back and haunted me. The past was where it belonged, behind me, and all I could see in front of me were sharp, slate-colored eyes and man who came for me whenever I needed him.

"It's done." I whispered the words into the side of his neck as he carried me to his truck that was parked as bold as could be behind Aaron's BMW. He wasn't worried about being subtle. He wanted everyone to know he had my back.

He kissed the top of my head and slid the fake glasses off my face. "You're wrong, little thief, this is just the beginning."

As usual, he was right.

I'd rebuilt his heart, but he'd fixed all the parts of mine that stopped working. Now we're both running smoothly, comparable to the high-performance machines we were always supposed to be.

No more rust and wear, we were all polish and shine.

CHAPTER 20

Stark

I T WAS LATE.

I was tired and my eyes were heavy, but inside I was settled. I was as close to happy and satisfied as I'd ever been. I wasn't saving the world the way my mom always wanted me to, but there were moments when I was saving my little corner of it. Days when I could be a hero to someone who really needed one. I'd been at the police station with Titus for the last two days. He'd gotten a lead on a child pornography ring and wanted to know what I could do to help bring the organization down. It only took a couple hours to work on a program that would search all the major keywords and language patterns used by the perpetrators in the chat rooms, the ones spending money on their dirty perversions, across all social media platforms. Everyone was on Facebook, Tumblr, Twitter, Instagram, Pinterest, and Snapchat. Even pedophiles. The program did its thing and searched all those platforms and more. Within twenty-four hours, we had names and addresses of over fifty adults who were using the site. It only took a couple hours after picking up the offenders until Titus had the names of the people in charge of finding the kids and filming the filth. They couldn't wait to pass the buck and the responsibility.

I could have gone home hours ago, but I wanted to watch them do the perp walk. I wanted to see them dragged through the media circus out front. I wanted to hear what they had to say for themselves. As it turned out, it was a whole lot of nothing. No excuses. No remorse or regret. It was nothing more than business to them. They didn't see the faces of the children they'd destroyed, or the lives they'd stolen . . . just dollar signs. It was infuriating. The world and the Point would be better off when they were dumped in a deep dark hole, and I was proud of myself for having a part in putting them there. Titus was already in line for one hell of a promotion, but a bust of this scale, one that would bring national media attention, meant he was going to be the face of all the major changes happening in our city. The good guys were finally keeping up with the bad guys even though every single day was still coated in cloudy, murky gray. Titus King was the war-hardened, battle-scarred general who was leading them to victory. It all made for a fantastic byline and a lead story on the evening news.

I took my glasses off so I could rub my eyes. I was a few steps away from my front door and just a couple more minutes away from crawling into bed next to my girl. She'd stopped by the station a couple of times to see if she could help. Titus put her to work scanning the matching hits from the program, and she was the one who had tracked down their locations using their check-ins and photos on social media. We made a great team, no matter what side of the law we were working for, but I hadn't had enough alone time with her, hadn't been able to taste her or feel her the way I wanted.

When I didn't have enough of her, the chill that she chased away found its way back inside of me. Winter filled me up and frosted over all the things inside of me she'd worked so hard to thaw out. Without her, I was frozen, covered in frost and ice. With her, I was human, a man who ran hot and fast. She made my emotions wild and I loved that I couldn't control them or her. The way she made me feel was a problem I never wanted to solve because I'd had years of isolation, no check on my emotions.

I was reaching for the front door when a throat was cleared loudly behind me. It was testament to how tired I was and how good their training was that I hadn't heard their approach.

The men in black suits. Noe had started calling them K and J, just like in the movie, whenever I brought them up. It was fitting. They still wore the same severe suits they'd had on when they took me away from my sister all those years ago. They'd aged, but then again, so had I. It was clear the current state of the world wasn't easy on whatever no name branch of the government they worked. They looked as tired as I felt and possibly defeated.

"Gentleman." I kept my voice steady and calm. I wanted to throw the door open and hide behind it. I wanted to run away from them but knew they would chase me. I'd been expecting a visit. There was no covering up the fact I was up to my old tricks and no longer working with a broken mind. I was back, which meant they wanted me to return to the fold. They had no use for a grieving brother and disenchanted son. But when I was a man with an agenda, a genius with a thirst for revenge, they couldn't show up on my doorstep fast enough.

"You've been busy, Mr. Stark. All kinds of stories of your escapades floating around the Internet. We've been watching." That was said by the shorter of the two, the one who threatened to throw me in jail alongside my father if I didn't snap out of my grief over losing Savina.

I lifted an eyebrow. "Figured you would be."

The taller of the two watched me carefully. He put his hands on his hips, pushing back his jacket and showing the gun and badge clipped onto his belt. He was trying to remind me that they called the shots, but they were on my turf. This was my city, I was the one with the upper hand here. "We have a classified project we want you to come on board for. What do you know about EMPs?"

I snorted. "Electromagnetic pulses? I know that paranoid end-of-the-world-preppers and conspiracy theorists think that an EMP can bring about the collapse of our society. I know that, theoretically, a pulse can turn a developed country into a third-world nation. I know there isn't enough known about the long-term implications of weaponizing that kind of technology, but you've never cared about the implications much, have you?"

Both of them stiffened and exchanged a look. I wasn't the scared, malleable teenager they'd conned into being their puppet anymore. Their agenda wasn't mine, and I didn't feel like I owed them anything any longer.

"It's in your best interest to come with us, Mr. Stark. If you don't, we can make life very difficult for you. Don't forget you are still guilty of hacking into a secure government mainframe. That is a violation of the Computer Fraud and Abuse Act. We can throw you in prison." That was a threat that used to scare me, but not now.

I crossed my arms over my chest and leveled them both with a hard look. "Did you kill my mother? Did the government make the call to have her lab destroyed when she wouldn't give you what you wanted? I went looking for those answers and never found them. I'm much better at getting into the places you want to keep me out of now. You guys made sure I was trained to be the best. I can find the truth. I can drag that information out into the light, make sure everyone sees it. People are hungry for proof that our systems are flawed."

The taller one started to look uneasy as the shorter one puffed up his chest and warned, "We can make you disappear, Stark. No one would even know you're gone. Just like last time."

He was wrong. Last time, my sister missed me so much she died and this time, well, this time I had someone who wouldn't let me go without a fight. The door behind me flung open and suddenly a small, warm body was pressed into my side. I glanced down at Noe as she wrapped her arm around my waist. I took her weight and curled my fingers around her upper arm in a side hug.

"I'd notice if he was gone. The cop he's been working with would notice. The guy who has this entire town in his pocket would notice. His friends would notice." She narrowed her eyes at the men dressed in black suits and growled, "His father would notice if he stopped visiting, and I'm sure his sister's spirit would notice if he was no longer stopping by to put flowers on her grave. She sure as shit felt it when you pulled him out of her life. You can't have him. He's mine." Her fingers curled into the fabric of my shirt and she pressed even more fully into my side.

The short agent scoffed and pointed a finger at her. "We know who you are, Ms. Lee, formerly known as Alyssa Cartwright. You aren't much of an obstacle standing between us and what we want."

She looked up at me, dark eyes a shade lighter than the midnight sky overhead. Her lips were pursed in a sour look so I couldn't resist a chuckle as I bent down to touch them with my own. The suits had no idea who they were dealing with.

She had never been Alyssa Cartwright. That girl never got a

choice, never got a say. That wasn't who she was. She'd put that girl behind her. She never wanted to hear that name again, just like she never wanted to see Aaron again. Those two belonged in a deep, dark hole that would never see the light of day. She was Noe Lee and she was a force to be reckoned with. She wasn't afraid of the men who had taken me and broken me. She would do whatever it took to keep me right by her side. These idiots should be very, very worried.

She pulled away from me and pointed at the tall agent, body tense and fury making her spine stiff. She was stunning, all that fight and defiance that had first attracted me to her directed in my defense. "I know who you are too, Agent Franklin. You aren't married but you do have a long-term partner. No one in your agency knows you're gay, because you're right, that knowledge would more than likely slow your fast-track to the top. No one in your agency knows that you've been trying to adopt a child from Russia, but I do. I know all about it. If your superiors had that information, they would shut it down considering they don't want any of their agents to have any ties to Russia at the moment. It wouldn't look good if that got out; imagine how the media would twist that story. *Spy sells State secrets in exchange for a no-questions-asked adoption.*"

The man went pale, so white that he appeared to glow in the dark. He swayed on his feet and refused to look at his partner who was now blustering and walking toward Noe.

"Ms. Lee, I suggest you keep your mouth shut." He reached for her but before his hands landed, I was between the two of them, a hand on the center of his chest as I pushed him back.

"We know all about you too, Agent Grimes. We know about your gambling debt. We know about the first wife you beat and put in the hospital even though your buddies in the agency covered it up.

We know about the money you stole from the warlord you took out during your last tour in Afghanistan, money that was supposed to go to fund schools and infrastructure. Money that was supposed to be used to rebuild the villages we destroyed. Money you pocketed. We know about the second wife who mysteriously disappeared when you went diving in Australia. The DoD covered that up as well. I'm guessing you have dirt on someone higher up than you, maybe the asshole who ordered the hit on my mom." I gave him a shove that sent him stumbling back into his lanky partner. "While you've been watching me, it gave her," I hooked a thumb in Noe's direction. She bared her teeth in a feral smile that would make even the brassiest of balls draw up in fear. "All the time she needed to watch you. I'm not going anywhere, and if you think you can fuck with me again, we're pulling the curtain back. Not just on you, but on how this all started. I know your people were responsible for what happened to my mom. You stopped me from proving it before, you won't stop me now. I'll start a scandal before you step off this porch. No one is ever impressed by the wizard. They love Oz, but no one ever wants to see who's actually behind the curtain."

The agents exchanged a look. The tall one was worried. The short one was impotently furious. He looked like he wanted to lunge at me, but he knew I could kick his ass. We had the same kind of training, but I was three times his size and had years of built-up resentment. "This isn't over Stark. You owe your country."

I shook my head. "No, but my country owes me. It owes me all the years I spent motherless and angry. It owes me for turning my father into a traitor, a man who valued revenge more than family. It owes me for not keeping my sister safe like it promised. When my country can put my family back together and fix the promises it broke, then maybe we'll talk about who owes whom. Go away and don't come back. If you do, I'll dig and dig until both your graves are deep enough. There is a lot of dirt out there and the only person better with a shovel than me is her. You can shut me up, but there are people who will speak for me. Remember that if you're thinking of doing something stupid like taking both of us out of the game. There are new players in place and most of them are a lot scarier than you guys."

Noe peeked around my shoulder and snidely snapped, "They dress better, too. Did you get those suits at Walmart?" Considering she was dressed in one of her half shirts and a pair of sweats that were too big, it was particularly funny. She still dressed like she was going to be trolling alleyways and underpasses. I found it endearing. I liked that it kept curious eyes off her olive skin and tight little body.

"We're done. You're done. Go back to your bosses and tell them I'm not interested in war. I want to help people, not hurt them." I turned to the door and backed Noe toward the house. I didn't stop walking until she was inside and the door was shut firmly behind us. I wasn't tired anymore so I bent and put a shoulder to her middle and hiked her up in a fireman's carry. Her legs kicked in the air until I landed a hand on the swell of her ass. The smack was satisfying and so was the way her hands grabbed at my ass from her upside-down position.

"They'll be back." She sounded resigned but she wasn't wrong.

I nodded as I stopped by the side of the bed, tossing her on the mattress. She bounced with a squeal, eyes gleaming like polished jet as I tugged my t-shirt off over my head by the collar. "They will be. We stay one step ahead of them. We make it known it's a real bad idea for them to try and poke into our lives. We fight for what we have."

She hummed a soft agreement and yelped again when I caught

her ankles and dragged her to the edge of the bed. I kissed her hard
and bruising. I wanted her to remember my mouth there while it
was busy on other parts of her body. I stamped my intent on her.
I wasn't going anywhere and neither was she. I licked her bottom
lip then dropped to my knees between her dangling legs so I could
pull her baggy pants down. I kissed the sweet indent of her belly
button, licked my way to the apex of her thighs. She was sighing
into the darkness and wasn't shy at all when she threw her legs over
my shoulders. She never hid from me. It was all right there in front
of me, wet, willing, wanting. Her body always ready for whatever
I wanted to do to it, eager to respond to my touch.

She was already shiny and slippery, thighs tense and quivering
by my ears. I breathed out a damp breath against her plump folds
and growled in appreciation as one of her hands slid under her shirt
so she could play with her nipples. Her hips lifted impatiently off
the bed and I chuckled into her sweet skin. The vibration made her
moan and her head started to thrash as I slid a couple of fingers
inside of her. She pulsed around me, hot and silky. She moved with
my hand and gasped my name as I touched my mouth to her tight
clit. Her flavor burst on my tongue as she writhed in front of me. I
fucked her with my face and my fingers, building her up until her
body was as taut as a drawn bow in my hold. I rubbed the thumb
of my free hand along the back of her thigh and traced a line up to
the curve of her ass. We hadn't taken things that far . . . yet. I never
wanted to push her into anything she didn't seem comfortable with,
but the more time she spent at Nassir's club, the more curious and
creative she'd been. I was a man who was always looking to learn
something new, so I was here for whatever she decided she wanted
to experiment with.

She lifted up and wrapped her hands around my head, holding

my face to her body as she chased after her impending orgasm. I added another finger, curled them, and tapped that hot spot that made her convulse and quake. She gasped loudly and rolled her hips as my tongue relentlessly attacked her clit. I could feel her getting ready to come apart. Her small frame coiled tight and her fingers tugged my hair and ears. The diamond studs I wore were going to leave marks in the soft skin of her inner thighs again, but she didn't seem to care as her legs locked even tighter around my head. She was going to have those marks forever because I wasn't taking my earrings out and I wasn't giving up the way she tasted when she came on my tongue.

She moaned so loud I was sure the neighbors could hear her through our shared wall but I didn't care. While she was still coming, languid and heavy lidded, I pulled my fingers out of her soaked opening and stood. She groaned in protest until I grabbed her by her hips and flipped her over so that she was on her stomach.

"Face down, ass up, Noe Lee." I jerked my pants open and shoved them down so that my dick was free. Our size difference made taking her this way tricky unless I was standing behind her while she kneeled on the bed.

Obediently, she put a cheek to the sheets and lifted up her backside, wiggling her hips enticingly in front of my throbbing cock. I fisted the rigid shaft and leaned forward so I could drag the swollen head through her creamy wetness. I shuddered as her heat surrounded me, my dick kicking in approval. My fingers dug into the skin of her hips and I grunted in appreciation as her hand worked its way between her torso and the bed. Her clever little fingers hit her already sensitized and tender clit at the exact same time I thrust my length into her welcoming opening. Her body went liquid around me. I felt her pussy clench and a hot rush of pleasure surrounded me.

I pulled her back into my thrusts with a grunt of satisfaction. It was still a tight fit, still felt like she was custom made to take my cock. When I was inside of her, there was nothing else in the world that mattered. There was no space for anything other than me and her and the way we made each other feel.

Our skin slapped together creating an erotic soundtrack that mingled with our heavy breathing and her soft whimpers. I swore when I felt her fingers brush across my erection where it was spreading her open. Her fingers were slippery and soft against my heated skin. I felt her reaction to the contact when her inner walls shimmied around the heavy, thick skin working its way in and out of her. I bottomed out as she mumbled my name. She stopped touching herself so that she could brace her weight on her hands and push back against me. My girl was never one who laid there and got fucked. She was always an active participant. She always gave just as good as she got.

She was panting in time to my grunts as I rutted into her like an animal. There was no finesse to it, no plan or thought. I was operating on nothing more than feeling and sensation. It was the only time my mind went quiet and let my body and my heart take charge. It was the only time I felt normal.

I snaked an arm around her waist and pulled her up so that her back was plastered to my front. I palmed her breast, catching her puckered nipple in my fingers. I sank my teeth into her earlobe and brushed my nose along the gentle curve of her jaw. She lifted an arm behind her head and ran it over my hair. Her eyes were closed but her face was etched in twin lines of desire and need. She was perfect.

I replaced her fingers with mine between her legs and knew when her eyes popped open and her mouth went slack that she was close. Her fingers latched in my hair and she whispered my name as she was dragged into a second orgasm. Watching her response, knowing I was the one who put that pleasure on her face and made her body feel that good, sent me spiraling through my own. I nipped at the side of her throat and groaned long and loud into her sweaty skin. Now I was the one the neighbors could probably hear, and I hoped they enjoyed the show because I didn't ever plan on being quiet about how she made me feel.

I kissed her on the back of the head and let her limp body fall in front of mine on the bed. She looked annihilated and it made me want to pound my chest with pride, and sure enough my diamonds had left marks on her inner thighs. Marks that were now wet and glistening with the evidence of how thoroughly we'd destroyed one another. If anyone or anything thought they were ever going to take any of this away from me, they were going to find out how dangerous a brilliant man could be when he was inspired.

I hitched my jeans back up over my ass and meandered to the bathroom so I could clean up and get her a washcloth to do the same. She hadn't moved when I made it back to the bed, so I dragged the warm fabric over her skin, then got completely naked and pulled her on top of me.

It was silent in the dark as she nuzzled into the ink on my chest. That was the only mechanical heart I had left. My actual heart was all wrapped up in the woman I held in my arms. It beat only for her, functioned only when she was the one pulling the strings.

"You know I'll chase you too, Snowden. If anyone tries to take you, if you vanish on me, I'm coming after you. I meant what I said out there . . . you're mine." She kissed the skin her cheek was resting on and I threaded my fingers through her hair.

"I am yours, Noe. Everyone else wants bits and pieces of me.

You're the only one who wants it all. My heart, my mind, my body . . . my future. They're all yours. Everything I am belongs to you." She was the only one who knew how to handle all that I was and all that I would be.

She sighed into the night and snuggled closer. "You've got me too, Stark. You're the only man I've ever wanted to give myself to and the only one I've ever wanted to hold onto. No one is taking that away."

It was a good thing our love was forged in the fire of the Point, because if it could survive the place we called home, then it could survive anywhere.

The good guys were getting a leg up, but so were the bad guys who did good when it benefited them. However, they weren't alone. Standing next to them were even better women who had just as much at stake in saving this city. In a place that had been deemed hopeless and lost, love found its way into the darkest corners and scariest parts of the city.

There was light now.

There was a chance at something better.

There was hope and tenuous optimism.

And yes . . . there was love. Battered, dented, and a little rough around the edges, it had seen better days, but it was there.

Exactly like my heart.

EPILOGUE

A couple months later . . .

THE LAST TIME WE'D all been gathered in the hospital, it had been because Bax was clinging to life after getting run off the road by a garbage truck. His muscle car had been crushed in the accident and so had his leg and several of his vital organs.

This occasion was much happier, even if Nassir was noticeably absent. He and Titus might have an uneasy truce in the works, but there was no way the cop was going to let the devil anywhere near his newborn baby. Keelyn had dropped off a gorgeous bouquet, an expensive bottle of scotch, and a box of cigars a couple of hours ago. She was close with Reeve, the cop's girlfriend and new mother. She didn't make apologies or excuses for her husband, but she did tell Titus her husband sent his best. The big man grunted in response but he gave her hand a squeeze as she slipped out of the waiting room.

Reeve had given birth to a healthy baby boy they named Titan. It was the name of a warrior. A big name he was going to have to live up to. If you asked his uncle, the little guy was already destined for greatness. Reeve told everyone Bax was excited for the baby, but no one really believed her until it proved nearly impossible to get the small bundle out of the big bruiser's hands. Little Titan was already performing miracles. Bax didn't glare at his older brother or give Reeve a hard time at all while he was visiting. He was so smitten with his new nephew, he forgot old hurts and animosity. All of us were looking at fresh starts and new beginnings . . . well, all of us except for the two men who were faced off in the waiting room like opponents in the Colosseum.

No one else seemed to pick up on the tension radiating off of Race and Booker, but since I was the newest member of this motley group of misfits, I couldn't miss it. Plus, Booker spent a lot of time around my genius since they both dangled at the end of Nassir's string. The two of them were tight, even closer than he and Race had been back in the day. I think Stark felt indebted to Booker since he had a hand in saving my life and getting me away from Goddard, and I had to admit, I was pretty fond of the broody ex-con as well. He might not be as smart as Stark, but he seemed to know a whole hell of a lot about how the world worked. He had practical knowledge and it often kicked book smarts squarely in the nuts.

Race was watching Booker closely, his chiseled jaw locked and his golden eyebrows lowered over his amazing green eyes. He didn't look like a criminal. He looked like a model. He also looked seriously pissed off, but his anger didn't hold a candle to the scalding fury that blazed from the corner where Booker was propped up. Every line of his massive bulk was locked tight, making him look ready to fight. His expression was thunderous as he glared at his boss' business partner, and the scar on his face stood out white against his ruddy skin as his teeth noticeably ground together.

I put my hand on Stark's bicep to ask what that was all about, about to interrupt him in the middle of his congratulations to the cop. Titus was getting ready to forcibly drag his little brother away from his baby, which everyone thought was hilarious. Race's fiancée and Bax's girlfriend were standing off to the side gushing over babies and how amazing Reeve would be as a new mom. The pretty blonde, the one who was more put together and stylish than I would ever be, reached out and touched her equally polished man. Her eyes were wide and her voice was sad when she told him, "I wish I could have convinced Karsen to come home for this. She was so sad when she missed the baby shower. I feel like the more time she spends away at school, the less likely she is to come home for a visit."

I knew Karsen was her younger sister. I didn't know she'd been invited to the recent baby shower Keelyn had thrown.

Race looked at his woman with a heavy dose of sympathy and understanding. He pulled her into his arms and rested his chin on the top of her flawless hair. "She'll figure it out, Brysen. She's learning how big the world really is. She has options now."

A sound that was somewhere between a roar and a growl erupted from where Booker was lurking. Everyone in the waiting room, including those who weren't there to fawn over the Point's newest little King, started and turned to look at the infuriated man. He pushed off the wall and stalked toward the blond couple like he was going to run right over them. The woman cocked her head to the side in confusion but Race stiffened his spine and narrowed his eyes even farther.

"Options? Is that what you call what she has now, Hartman?

She gets to make up her own mind about where she wants to be and who she wants to be with? Has something changed?" The words were short and clipped, anger rolling off the man in waves that swept through the entire room. "Or are you still manipulating things so she does what you want, when you want, without her even knowing it?" He looked at Brysen with a sneer. "Your sister won't be back. Ask the asshole holding onto you why that is. Ask him about the options he left Karsen with." He shook his head as he pushed past them and shook off Bax's girlfriend's reaching hand. "Everyone thinks Gates is the dangerous one, the dirty one. If anyone was paying attention, they would see you play twice as rough as the devil, Hartman."

He stormed out of the room, leaving tense silence and unasked questions lingering in the air behind him.

Titus cleared his throat and mumbled he needed to get back to his family. Dovie looked at the couple with wide eyes as Stark pulled me into his side and dropped a quick kiss on my head. Anyone else would be wrapped up in the drama, curious about the outcome, worried about their friend. Not my guy. My quirky, disconnected genius mumbled something about the statistical chances of Titan ending up with Titus's unusual white spot in his hair and calculating the odds that any child we had together would get his hyper-intelligence. I was distracted by the idea of being pregnant, of carrying his baby, of having a family of my own, and I didn't process that he also mentioned twins ran in his family.

I was off in my own little daydream when Brysen's shrill voice brought me back to reality.

"What did you do, Race? What have you done?" She'd pulled out of his embrace and now she was the one squared off against him like she was ready to do battle.

Dovie put a hand on her friend's shoulder and offered softly, "Not the time or the place honey. Take this home."

The icy blonde nodded but shook off her man's hands when he reached for her. He whispered something in her ear that didn't soften her expression one bit. They swept out of the room in a cloud of tension that had Dovie offering up a shrug and an apology. "It's always something, I guess." She excused herself to find her man and the rest of her family while Stark started to lead me in the direction the others had gone.

"Where are we going?" I put a hand on the cut, defined plane of his stomach. We'd come to see the baby and hadn't gotten our turn yet.

He pushed the button for the elevator and looked down at me with a lifted eyebrow. His eyes were concerned behind his glasses. They were a new pair, tortoise shell instead of black but still designer and still hot as hell on him. His old pair had had an unfortunate accident while I was sitting on his face. Sometimes the man was too impatient, not that I could complain.

"I need to check on Booker. Something's been brewing and I knew it was going to boil over eventually. He usually keeps himself in check. That outburst was not good." He pulled me into the elevator and I slid my hand into his much bigger one as the car started to descend.

"You're worried about your friend." I squeezed his fingers. "Your heart is working just fine, Snowden Stark." I was proud of him and proud of me for being the one who fixed him.

"Thanks to you." He said it with all seriousness.

"Do you think Booker will be okay?" I'd never seen him so mad or so terrifying. That was the side of him that Nassir used to keep people in line. That was the side of him that had landed the big man behind bars.

Stark dipped his chin in a slight nod. "He's a man who is tired of waiting. Even the most patient men have their limits."

"What's he waiting for?" I was confused and intrigued by all of it.

"The same thing we're all waiting for. His shot at something better."

He pulled me out of the elevator and guided me to the parking lot where the sun was shining bright.

That's right . . . there was light.

The sun found its way through the clouds, fought its way through the fog and murky pollution. There was always a chance for something new to grow, for change and opportunity, as long as you never stopped trying to break through. All it took was the smallest hole, the littlest weakness for warmth and brightness to find their way inside.

Booker and Karsen's story,
RESPECT, coming in Summer of 2018

AUTHOR'S NOTE

WHEN I WAS IN college I had a roommate who had the same backstory story as Noe. She was given to an all-girls' orphanage in Seoul when she was four because her parents were poor and they already had a little girl. She was adopted by a well-off family from Denver and she really was accelerated and super smart. That's where the similarities end. Her family was great, loving, welcoming, and so proud of her. She had two older brothers who treated her like a princess and doted on her. I did think it was super weird that whenever we would all go out, people assumed she was on a date with one of her brothers since they obviously looked different. Once, I was at dinner with her and her father, and a waitress asked if she was his wife . . . so freaking creepy. (Which is clearly where the inspiration for all of Noe's tragic backstory came from.)

I always knew I wanted to base a character on this girl from my past. She was gorgeous and dynamic. She was a handful and a troublemaker . . . she was a real-life romance heroine. Men loved her. Women envied her. I spent my time loving and hating every single minute we lived together. I had some of the best times of my life with her, but she was also the catalyst for my entire world falling into chaos. At the end of the day, I couldn't keep up with her . . . but I still think about her and wonder where she ended up all these years later.

People ask me all the time if any of my characters are based on anyone in my own life and this is the one and only time I can say yes. Noe is absolutely based on someone who had a huge impact on my young adult life. It was so much fun pitting her against a man who was just as brilliant and just as difficult as she was. I'd like to think the real-life woman behind the character ended up with her perfect match as well. (Last I heard, she was in New York married to an engineer who moonlights as a semi-famous punk rock singer, and she has a daughter who was a child model . . . lol.)

We live in a world where one in six women is sexually assaulted or violated in some way. We also live in a world where one in five girls and one in twenty boys are victims of childhood sexual abuse—7.5 million reports related to child sexual exploitation have been made to The National Center for Missing and Exploited Children's CyberTipline since its inception. (missingkids.org)

Self-report studies show that twenty percent of adult females and five to ten percent of adult males recall a childhood sexual assault or sexual abuse incident.

None of that is fun to think about, but that is the harsh reality too many victims must face. The Point isn't real, but the atrocities that happen there are real . . . all over the world. When victims speak, it is important that we listen. Use your voice to help them be heard.

I'm no expert.

I'm no crusader or champion.

But I am here. I care, and I want anyone who needs to know that they have an advocate and supporter in me.

Here are some places that offer help if you or someone you know needs to reach out:

National Child Abuse Hotline: 1–800–422–4453

National Domestic Violence Hotline: 1–800–799–7233

National Sexual Assault Hotline: 1–800–656-HOPE (4673)

If you are looking for a place to start to help yourself or someone else, go here: www.thehotline.org.

ACKNOWLEDGEMENTS

IF YOU HAVE PURCHASED, read, reviewed, promoted, pimped, blogged about, sold, talked about, preached about, or whined about any of my books . . . thank you.

If you are part of my very special reader group The Crowd . . . thank you.

If you have helped me make this dream of mine a reality . . . thank you.

If you have helped make my words better and helped me share them with the world . . . thank you.

If you have held my hand and helped me through the tough times when it feels like everyone's against me . . . thank you.

If you help make the work part of writing the best job ever . . . thank you.

If you tolerate me being a horrible human and awful adult when I'm working . . . thank you.

I gotta give a major shout out to my girl gang for this one. Sometimes I have a character I think is just EVERYTHING. Hot, smart, difficult, interesting, and complex. But then I get caught up in wondering if I'm the ONLY one who thinks that way. I'm not wired like everyone else. I don't like the same ol' same ol'. I like to take risks and write different kinds of men and I wasn't so sure

Stark fit in in the Point and that I was expressing just how special he really was. My girls rode to the rescue. As always, I asked Mel, Rebecca Yarros, Denise Tung, and Heather Self all to give Stark a peek when he was about halfway done. It's hard to ask someone to read a book that isn't finished, but my girls showed up and gave me all the right words. They loved him and loved his story, and I honestly believe that has nothing to do with the fact they love me. The feedback was necessary and I needed them to assure me I hadn't gone too far off the deep end. I'm cool with dipping a toe in the water but I'm not looking to drown anytime soon. So, thanks ladies for being there when I needed you most. I'm a badass . . . but even badasses need a confidence boost every now and then.

I also have a pretty special girl gang of professionals who help me turn my words into an actual book. If you are looking for an editor I can't recommend Elaine York enough. I love getting to work with her. I adore her insights and her commitment to each project I send her way. She doesn't pull any punches and she's not scared to tell me that I'm not quite there yet. She makes me work for it, and as a result, my readers get the best book possible. She jumped into a long-standing series with no frame of reference to the existing storylines and characters and rolled with it. She's smart as hell and has a way of seeing nuances in a story I'll admit to never even thinking about. Unlike when I publish traditionally, I got to pick who I wanted to work with when it came to self-publishing. For me, Elaine was the only choice.

The same thing goes for Hang Le. She was my one and only choice to work with when it came to my covers. She's brilliant. I love her style and her flare. She takes what I want and makes it better than I could imagine. Pretty sure her beautiful covers do more to sell my books than anything I do.

If you want the pages and the guts of your book to be pretty, then you need to hit up my friend, Christine Borgford. She's one of the kindest, most supportive humans I've ever met, and not just because she's Canadian! She really loves books, romance, and the reading community. She wants our words to be as pretty as possible. Formatting is important. End of story. It makes your book look pulled together and professional. Let Christine play with your pages, you won't regret it.

My friend Beth Salminen handled all my copy edits and proofreading this go around. (I say my friend, which she is, but she's also Cora's roommate who just happens to be a word wizard so she doesn't have a choice because she has to like me . . . lol.) Beth is wicked smart and super funny. The only thing better than writing books is getting to work on them with people that care about making your words the best they can be. It's a bonus when that person also wants the writer to be the best she can be. Cora and I have been trying to talk Beth into editing full time . . . she's that good at it. (She already works in traditional publishing during the day but I'm trying to lure her away into the world of Indie.) If you are looking for a pretty blonde to cross your t's and dot all your i's you need to give Beth all your money.

I did something different this go around. Ever since the beginning I've been a solo show when it comes to creating stories. I've never used beta-readers or critique partners. I decided to give it a shot with this book. I wanted to put the best product out possible and decided letting a few pairs of impartial eyes peep my words before the rest of the world wouldn't be the worst idea I ever had. I want to thank Pam Lilley, Karla Tamayo, and Traci Pike for giving up their valuable time and precious moments to help me out. They don't get anything out of the deal other than my undying gratitude and unwavering thanks. There are some very special readers out there in Booklandia and I feel like I've been so lucky to have most of them in my court since the very beginning. If you notice fewer errors and less typos in this book it's all thanks to these lovely ladies.

You can also appease your inner stalker in all of these places:

www.facebook.com/groups/crownoverscrowd . . . My fan group on Facebook. I'm very active in there and it's often the best place to find all the happenings and participate in giveaways!

My website: *www.jaycrownover.com* . . . there is a link on the site to reach me through email. I would also suggest signing up for my newsletter while you're there! It's monthly, contains a free book that is in progress so you'll be the first to read it, and is full of mega giveaways and goodies. I'm also in all of these places:

www.facebook.com/jay.crownover

www.facebook.com/AuthorJayCrownover

Follow me @jaycrownover on Twitter

Follow me @jay.crownover on Instagram

Follow me on Snapchat @jay crownover

www.goodreads.com/Crownover

www.donaghyliterary.com/jay-crownover.html

www.avonromance.com/author/jay-crownover

CPSIA information can be obtained
at www.ICGtesting.com
Printed in the USA
LVOW10s1734050418
572436LV00012B/1374/P